GO DWARF YOURSELF

GO DWARF YOURSELF

DWARF BOUNTY HUNTER™ BOOK ONE

MARTHA CARR

MICHAEL ANDERLE

DISRUPTIVE IMAGINATION®

LMBPN Publishing
PMB 196, 2540 South Maryland Pkwy
Las Vegas, NV 89109

Version 1.03, January 2021
ebook ISBN: 978-1-64971-194-6
Paperback ISBN: 978-1-64971-195-3

THE GO DWARF YOURSELF TEAM

Thanks to our JIT Team:
Dorothy Lloyd
Diane L Smith
Jackey Hankard-Brodie
Misty Roa
Jeff Goode
Dave Hicks
Deb Mader
Paul Westman

If I've missed anyone, please let me know!

Editor
SkyHunter Editing Team

CHAPTER ONE

"If this doesn't work, I'll—" Johnny grunted with self-directed exasperation and the ghost of a smile twitched his lips beneath his thick, dark-red mustache. "Who am I kidding? Of course it'll work. *I* made it."

He inserted a tiny metal pick into the side of the device set on a black leather collar to activate the translator. Once he'd done the same to a second device on a brown leather collar, he lifted both from the worktable in his dining room-turned-workshop.

"All right, boys. Time for a test drive."

The dwarf's size-ten boots clomped across the wooden floor of his small, tidy cabin until he reached the living room. His two black-and-tan coonhounds sprawled on the rug in front of the empty fireplace he hadn't used since he'd bought the property. Both dogs raised their heads at his approach and their droopy ears perked up as they eyed the collars in each of their master's hands.

He glanced at the boar's head trophy mounted above the fireplace and the collection of old hunting rifles on the mantle—two of them from the end of the sixteenth century—and smirked. *This'll be the cherry on the swampy damn sundae.*

"Rex."

The coonhound closest to the fireplace sat and stared at him. His tail thumped once on the rug.

"You first, boy. Come here." He held a hand out toward the slightly larger hound and Rex trotted obediently toward him. The dwarf held the brown leather collar between his teeth while he fastened the black collar around the dog's neck, then raised his index finger. Rex sat immediately, and he took the other collar out of his mouth to call to the hound's brother. "Luther. Let's go."

Luther scrambled excitedly to his feet and practically leapt across the room toward his master. His tail wagged fervently while Johnny fastened the brown leather collar around his neck, but the dog sat as obediently as his brother when he raised his index finger again. Neither hound made a sound when he withdrew a small metal tube the size of a .44 Magnum shell from his pocket. *But they're about to make much more noise now.*

"See this?" Johnny held the tube between thumb and forefinger to show his hounds the last piece of his newest magical-tech invention. "We're about to take this to a whole new level. It only took me four years to realize we needed it, but you boys won't wanna go back. Watch."

He stuck the end of the tube against the side of his neck and pressed on the top end with his thumb. A sharp jolt seared through his neck and he grunted with a brief frown before he wiggled his nose under the intense but short-lived itch.

"Damn. That shit packs a punch and tastes like…is that onions?"

"Onions?" Luther's tail thumped wildly against the floor as he stared at his master. "He said onions, right? I want onions."

Rex didn't move. "We can't eat onions. He dropped one off the grill last summer, remember? I spent the rest of the day shittin' in the swamp."

"Ooh. The swamp. Let's go."

The dwarf chuckled and folded his muscular arms covered in

a thick layer of the same wiry red hair as his mustache and beard. "We'll head out in a little while, boys. And Rex is right. No onions for dogs. Although at this point, I reckon both of you have eaten twice your weight in shit you shouldn't have."

"Hey." Luther's higher-pitched voice filled his mind as the smaller hound cocked his head and let his tongue flop out of his mouth for a quick pant. "He heard you say onions."

"No, he didn't."

"Yeah, I did." Johnny nodded emphatically. "Look at this, huh? I can hear you and you can hear me. I'd call that a hell of a success."

"Cool." Luther straightened his back legs for a brief moment before a glance from his master forced him onto his haunches again. "So let's go. It's been a little while, right? Swamp time."

Rex licked his muzzle and uttered a low chuff as he stared at Johnny, waiting for his master to release him from his seat at the edge of the area rug in the living room. "Wanna eat?"

Luther's tail thumped wildly against the rug. "I could eat. Do we catch it? I could catch it too."

"Hey, chill out. There's an easier way to get what we want now." Rex's droopy eyebrows lifted as he tilted his head at his master. "Simply ask him over and over to let us out or feed us until he gives up."

Johnny smirked. "That's your smart idea?"

"Johnny." Luther uttered a low whine. "Johnny. Johnny. Let's get some food. Hey, Johnny. Come on. Food time. Swamp time."

The dwarf took two steps back and grinned at his hounds. "All right. Go on, git."

"Yes!" Luther kicked at the rug as he scrabbled onto his hind legs before he leapt and scrambled toward the dog door at the back of the house.

Rex stood hastily and trotted after his brother. "Yeah, we'll catch it. Do you want us to bring you something for fun?"

"Not if you eat it first," Johnny called as the dog door clicked shut again after his retreating hounds.

A loud, coonhound bay rose from behind the cabin, followed by the dogs' shouts that diminished as they raced across the yard at the edge of the swamp.

"It went this way."

"Get it! Faster!"

"Oh, man! I'm gonna rip its tail off!"

Nodding in satisfaction, the dwarf ran a hand through his thick, dark-auburn hair and turned toward his workshop. *That's how you get shit done. Screw man's best friend. I have dwarf's best huntin' dogs and two extra pairs of eyes. See if we don't triple the game we bring home after this.*

He entered the workshop and paused to regard the taxidermized alligator mounted on a well-oiled plank of oak right off the small kitchen. *Better than this 'gator. I wanna trade this one out for a fifteen-footer.*

At his worktable, he stopped and sniffed, smacked his lips against the slight aftertaste of onions, and set to work cleaning up after finishing the translating dog collars. That was part of his number-one rule. Keep it simple. And simple meant cleaning up after himself and everything in its place, no matter how happy he was with the way the collars turned out.

As he closed the jumbo-sized tackle box where he kept his magical tools, both hounds bayed wildly outside, followed by the clack and scrabble of the dog door when it whipped up and clapped down again. Their claws clicked across the floor toward the dining room.

"Johnny! Johnny, open the door." Luther raced past his master and skidded to a stop inches from the front door. "Open it."

Rex trotted after his brother and darted Johnny a glance. "Someone's here."

"No kiddin'." The dwarf placed the tackle box on the floor and shoved it under the worktable with the toe of his boot. He hiked his black Levi's up and headed after his hounds toward the door. "Is it anyone we know?"

"Black SUV," Rex said, stopped behind his brother, and shifted sideways when Luther's tail threatened to whack him in the face.

"It was blue," Luther added.

"Black."

"All right. Back away." Johnny trudged toward the front of the house as the hounds retreated, their tails wagging, and he stopped in front of the small square window beside the front door. He swept the plain gray curtain aside to peer outside. Sure enough, a black SUV rolled along the dirt road and stopped in front of the folding lawn chairs at the end of the drive.

"Black." Johnny frowned at the hounds. "Luther, what color are my boots?"

"Blue."

Rex stepped sideways again to avoid his brother's tail. "They're black."

"Huh." He snorted and returned his attention to the sliver of window behind the curtain in his hand.

The driver's door of the SUV opened and a nondescript man in an equally black and boring suit with a receding hairline stepped out of the car. He waved a hand in front of his face to clear the dust cloud he'd stirred up with his vehicle. Unfortunately, he wasn't nondescript enough for Johnny not to recognize him.

"What's this bastard doin' here?" He shook his head. "Same black sunglasses and everything."

"Let us out, Johnny." Luther uttered a sharp bark. "We'll go see what he wants."

"No one's gonna answer your questions when they can't hear you. That's only me." The dwarf frowned when the passenger door opened as well and a tall, slender woman emerged. His left

5

eye twitched, and he tugged the curtain into place over the window. "And he brought a friend. I don't care how long it's been. He knows I don't like him bringing friends."

"We like friends." Luther's tail wouldn't stop and he stepped toward the door and away again in excitement.

"Is it a dog friend?" Rex asked.

"No, she's a ten all around." He rubbed a hand over his mouth, chin, and beard, scowled, and moved toward the front door where he stood with folded arms. "Whatever he wants, he's shit outta luck."

"Johnny, open the door."

"Open it. We'll tell 'em to go home."

Johnny snapped his fingers and both hounds sat. "He'll discover it soon enough."

With that, he turned and headed into his workshop to finish cleaning.

"They're coming."

"They're here."

"Johnny, open the door."

The screen door creaked open, followed by three sharp, solid knocks on the front door. Both hounds barked once in reply.

"Leave it alone, boys. We're not entertaining guests."

The knock came again, followed by another sharp bark from each hound.

"Johnny Walker. I know you're in there. Open up. It's Tommy Nelson."

"Tommy." Luther backed away with a low whine. "Who's Tommy?"

The dwarf sneered. "Salesman."

"Johnny?" The man outside paused, then grasped the door handle. "If you don't open this door, I will."

The dwarf shook his head and swept the stray metal bolts and scrap pieces off the table and into his wide palm. "Go ahead. I didn't have dogs the last time."

"Want us to rip off his hand?" Rex asked with a low growl.

"Not yet."

"All right, Johnny. I'm coming in." Tommy cleared his throat. "This is your last chance if you wanna start this off by not being a dick."

He snorted. *Like that's even an option.*

"Fine." The agent muttered something under his breath and turned the door handle.

Rex and Luther each barked once but stayed where they were when the front door swung open.

Tommy Nelson removed his black sunglasses and paused when he saw the two fifty-five-pound coonhounds who greeted him. "Hey, pups."

Rex barked and the man jumped. "I'll knock him over if you want."

Luther whined, his tail wagging furiously as he panted and stared at the newcomer. "You think salesman tastes better than squirrel?"

Johnny shook his head and called from his workshop-dining room, "Whatever it is, Nelson, I'm not buying."

"Well, it's a good thing I'm not selling anything." Tommy inched through the front door, his gaze fixed on the dogs while he tried to stay calm and relatively friendly—or as friendly as a government liaison to monsters and magicals could ever be. "I'm the one who pays you, remember?"

"Not in a long time." The dwarf sniffed and dropped the handful of metal scrap into the tin pail beneath the worktable. "And not anymore."

Tommy glanced around the entry of the dwarf's house and skirted the animals. "I see you got yourself a few partners since the last time we talked."

"Yeah, and they're better company since the last time you were here too." Dusting his hands off, he finally stepped into the front hall from his workshop and hooked his thumbs

7

through the belt loops of his jeans. "Feel free to turn and head out again."

"I can't do that, Johnny. Not without laying everything out for you to see."

"Ooh! A lady!" Luther whined again as a tall, smoking-hot woman with long dark hair spilling over her shoulders stepped through the front door. "She smells good, Johnny."

The dwarf glanced briefly at the woman—who wore the same black suit as Agent Nelson but looked a hell of a lot better in it—and shook his head. "I'm not interested."

"You haven't even seen the—hey!" Tommy lurched away from Rex's snout nudging into his backside, turned, and pressed his back against the wall. "You have some friendly hounds here."

"Only if I want 'em to be."

The woman smirked and held her hand out toward Luther as his back half wiggled. "They're beautiful."

Johnny frowned at her. "They're dogs. Pick of the litter but still dogs."

Luther ignored the woman's outstretched hand and waited for her to shut the front door before he snuck around to sniff her legs and backside. "Whew. I knew she smelled good. Whad'ya think, Rex? Lunch an hour ago?"

Rex moved his nose up and down Tommy's pantleg and snorted. "He had the Rueben."

"Yeah? I'm gettin' shrimp."

The woman stepped tentatively away from the over-excited Luther and glanced around the inside of Johnny Walker's home. "You have some place here."

He ran his tongue along the inside of his cheek. "I'm not a fan of words that don't match facial expressions. Even when they're a compliment."

She looked quickly at him, studied him from head to toe, and smirked without another word.

Tommy stared at her and a small frown drew his eyebrows

down before he cleared his throat. "Hear me out, okay? Let me show you what we're lookin' at."

"I don't need to see it to tell you no, Nelson. You're wasting your time."

"What if I started by telling you the US Government's willing to double your normal fee for this one?"

Johnny shook his head. "You're still wasting your time. And mine."

"Come on, Johnny—"

"Fifteen years, Nelson. I'm outta the game. You know that and you know why. Things are simple here for me now. All I need is Sheila and two coonhounds and my guns."

"There's the crossbow too." Rex panted heavily and stalked after Tommy as the man inched down the hall. "Tell him about the crossbow."

"I like the grenades." Luther circled the tall woman two more times before he joined his brother in sniffing Agent Nelson disconcertingly thoroughly.

The dark-haired woman looked curious. "Sheila?"

Tommy darted her a glance with a barely perceptible shake of his head. "His Jeep."

She scrutinized the dwarf again and raised an eyebrow.

"And I don't need to explain myself," Johnny added. "The answer's no."

"Good leg." Luther nudged his wet nose against Tommy's pant leg. "It smells like it needs a good humping to go with it."

"Yeah, you test it and let me know," Rex replied.

Johnny smirked but when he caught the tall woman's gaze, he wiped the expression off his face completely.

"Well then, maybe you'll—" Tommy jerked his leg away from Luther at the first sign of the hound getting too close and sidled toward the dwarf again. "Maybe you'll be more interested in the nature of this case, Johnny. It has your name written all over it."

"Because you think I'll enjoy myself or because you can't find anyone else to take it?"

The man shrugged. "A little of both."

"So go somewhere else and find a bounty hunter who isn't retired and who gives a shit."

The woman clasped her hands behind her back and raised her chin. "I think you'll give a shit about this one, Mr. Walker."

"Naw, I don't do that mister crap. Only Johnny."

"Of course."

"You should take the job, Johnny." Rex sat beside the uncomfortably sidling Agent Nelson and his tongue lolled from his mouth as he waited for the man to step away from the wall. "You need to get out more."

"Hell, we get out more than you do." Luther sniffed Tommy's pants again and made one more half-assed attempt to climb the man's leg before the agent jerked his foot away again. "We're all the way out here in the Everglades and you have nothing to do when you're not hunting."

That's how I prefer it.

"We get laid more than you too," Luther added, panting now as he studied the government agent who refused to let his leg be objectified by either hound. "That's sad."

"Yeah, but the ladies he brings home aren't." Rex scrutinized Tommy intently and moved forward to give the woman a good once-over too. "Come on, lady. Quit turning so I can smell you. Oh, yeah. You were right. Definitely shrimp."

Johnny snorted and looked at Tommy Nelson. "If I take a look at your file, will it get you and the shrimp—uh…your friend off my property?"

"Nice one, Johnny." Luther panted and turned in a tight circle as an energetic chuckle filled the dwarf's mind.

The man retrieved the manila folder from under his arm and nodded. "Just take a look, yeah. That's all we ask."

Wrinkling his nose, the dwarf gave the tall woman another

cursory glance before he raised an eyebrow at Tommy. "You have five minutes, Nelson. Then I want you and your wannabe badass SUV off my property."

"You got it."

Johnny jerked his head toward the workshop. "The table's over here."

CHAPTER TWO

Rex and Luther circled their master's worktable slowly as Johnny, Agent Nelson, and the woman gathered around it. She pursed her lips and stared at the dwarf with a small, playful smile. "Are you gonna introduce us, Agent Nelson?"

"What?" Tommy slapped the manila folder on the table and glared at the dwarf. "Yeah, sure. Johnny, this is Agent Lisa Breyer with the Bounty Hunter Division."

"So you're doubling up with me, huh? Magical liaison and Bounty Hunter expert working together to bring Johnny Walker in. You're pulling out all the stops, Nelson."

"That was the plan," the man muttered and opened the manila folder slowly. He withdrew the top sheet of paper and spun it to face the dwarf. "This is a—"

"What are you?" Johnny jerked his chin at Lisa, his arms folded as he examined her warily. "Half-human, obviously. What's the other half? Light Elf?"

She smirked and darted Tommy a glance. "You have a good eye."

"Yeah, I know."

The other agent scowled at the heavy-hitting glances that

passed between them and cleared his throat. "Like I was saying, we have—"

"How old are you?" Johnny shrugged. "While we're on the subject."

Agent Nelson sighed heavily and rolled his eyes. "That's not the subject, Johnny."

"And I don't think that's an appropriate question," Lisa added.

"Why? You don't look older than twenty-five, maybe twenty-six." He tilted his head and regarded her speculatively. "I only wanna know if I'm close."

Lisa shook her head. "How old are you?"

"Eighty-five."

Her eyes widened. "Wow."

Tommy licked his lips in aggravation. "Yeah, yeah. We all wish we had the dwarf's perky youthfulness. Now can we get back to—"

"I bet you've gained considerable experience in eighty-five years." The smallest part of Lisa's bottom lip dimpled between her teeth.

Johnny smirked. "Somethin' like that, yeah."

"Jesus Christ," Tommy whispered and lowered his head to pinch the bridge of his nose. "Can we get back on track here?"

"I'm thirsty." The dwarf smacked a hand on the table and wagged his finger from one Federal agent to the other. "Do you want anything?"

Lisa raised her eyebrows. "What do you have?"

"A little of everything, but I'm not gonna waste the good stuff when y'all are gonna head out to wherever you came from in…" He glanced at his gold wristwatch. "Two minutes. So how about iced tea?"

She pursed her lips and failed to hide her smile. "Sure."

"I don't want anything, Johnny."

"Good. I didn't ask you." The dwarf turned and strode into the kitchen.

Tommy heaved a heavy sigh and turned to scowl at Agent Breyer. "You too, huh?"

"Me too what?" Her smile vanished when she met the man's gaze.

"Falling all over yourself 'cause Johnny Walker happens to be in the same room."

"I'm not falling all over anything, Nelson."

"Yeah, that's what they all say until they start falling all over him." Tommy pressed his knuckles onto the worktable. "I don't get it, honestly. This guy's as bristly as a damn cactus and scarred all over. Hell, he's a redhead. Forget the dwarf part. I haven't seen a single woman look at that asshole and not start drooling. What gives?"

Lisa smirked at the worktable and raised one shoulder in a shrug. "He has cookie-dough mojo."

"Cookie-dough. What the fuck does that mean?"

"You know he's not the best choice but there's simply something about him that makes you want to eat him all up."

"Jesus. Tell me you're joking."

"You asked, Nelson. I'm merely giving you a woman's perspective. And for the record, I don't drool."

In the kitchen, Johnny smirked as he poured the tea over two glasses of ice on the counter. *That's one of the better explanations I've heard. Most women can't even put it into words.*

"Hey, she said cookie dough." Luther trotted across the kitchen and his nails clacked on the floor as he sniffed the fridge dutifully. "You think he has some?"

"Yeah, can you get the fridge open?" Rex looked up to flash his master a glance before he licked the side of the fridge door. "For real. We should work on that."

"All right. Out." The dwarf pointed at the doorway out of the kitchen and toward the back door. "Go run it off, boys."

The hounds slid and skidded around the linoleum floors

before they barreled through the house. Luther knocked against the doorway and yipped. "I'm gonna eat the next one!"

"Not if I catch it first," Rex called as he leapt through the dog door.

Shaking his head with a tiny smile, Johnny returned to the glasses of iced tea, paused, and took the bottle of Johnny Walker Black Label off the counter. He uncorked it and counted to three as he topped his drink off. *I'm gonna need this to get through the next thirty seconds of Nelson whining that I wasted his time. What goes around comes around, bud.*

He swirled his glass, took a long sip, and shrugged before he brought Agent Breyer her uncut iced tea.

"Here you go." He set her glass down slightly in front of him, and the woman uttered an uncertain chuckle as she leaned across the table to take it.

"Thank you."

Johnny sipped his whiskey-tea and glanced at his watch again. "All right, Nelson. Your time's up and I'm still sayin' no. Good luck, though."

Tommy glared at him. "Just take a look."

"I said five minutes."

"And you spent the whole five minutes deflecting from—" The agent sniffed and glanced at Johnny's glass. "Are you drinking right now?"

"Huh." Johnny stared at the man as he took another sip, and when he lowered his glass again, his wiry mustache dripped with whiskey-flavored tea he didn't bother to wipe off. "And I somehow assumed your sense of smell would've disappeared with your hairline."

Lisa snorted.

Tommy gritted his teeth and jabbed a finger on the top paper of the file he still hadn't convinced the ex-bounty hunter to read. "You said you'd take a look. Don't think I'll simply walk out of here because you poured yourself a drink. We both know how well you hold your liquor."

"It's not a drink if it's a floater."

"Johnny—"

"Oh, for fuck's sake." He set his glass on the table and swiped his hand brusquely under his mustache to get rid of the cold on his upper lip. Then, he turned and snatched one of the rifles he'd mounted on the shelf of his workshop—the ones he used sometimes, not those purely for his collection—and the long tin box beside it. The box clunked on the table and the dwarf opened it. With a sniff, he pulled out his cleaning rod, cleaning patches, and solvent and refused to look at his unwelcome guests. "I don't like to say things more than once. And twice is already too many times, Nelson."

"You're gonna make me—" With a grunt of frustration, Tommy abandoned the briefing sheet and flipped through the rest of the papers in the file. One after the other, he slapped a series of enlarged photographs across the worktable and stabbed a finger at each one in turn. "If you don't want me to ease you into it, fine. I'll pull out the big guns."

Johnny chuckled and removed the bolt from his rifle. He glanced at the photographs and paused.

The scene was laid out in front of him in five parts from five different angles. The first two were blood spatter all over the walls of a middle-class living room. The third and fourth depicted a man and woman, both in their late thirties, sprawled across the light-colored carpet now soaked with their blood. The last was of a girl.

She lay on her side, her thin arm outstretched beneath her head. Long light-brown hair matted with blood covered most of her face, but he didn't need to see her features to know she was way too young to be photographed post-mortem like this.

"We found them like this two days ago," Tommy said in a low

voice. "Bruce and Denise Coulier. Their daughter Claire. She was twelve."

Johnny muttered a curse. *Yeah, he's pullin' the big guns out all right. A fucking child.*

"She has a fraternal twin," Lisa added. "Amanda. The assholes who did this took her and we need to find her."

Looking down again, Johnny inspected his rifle and selected one of the patches to rub the exterior of his weapon. "How old is she?"

The agents exchanged a knowing glance. Tommy nodded. "Twelve."

Fuck. He knew exactly what buttons to push with this one.

Johnny sniffed. "And you need me why?"

"It's a special case for the Bureau. We want the best of the best." Tommy withdrew another sheet of paper from the file, but the dwarf didn't give it a second glance. "Bruce Coulier was an investment banker. He did extremely well for himself and had personal ties to more than one US Senator, one of whom sits on the Bounty Hunter Department Committee."

"Huh." He laid the rifle down and popped the lid of the cleaning solvent open before he dipped the cleaning patch into it. He couldn't look at those pictures again, and all three of them knew it. "So what aren't you telling me, Nelson?"

"These are the facts."

"But not all of them."

"No." Tommy glanced at Agent Breyer, and she raised her eyebrows in consent. "Amanda Coulier has…special powers."

He looked sharply at the man. "You're gonna have to be a little more specific."

"She's a shifter. The whole family was and they did a damn good job of keeping that lineage secret."

"Until these bastards found out and decided they'd…what? Blackmail a senator and hold a shifter kid hanging over his head?"

"No." The agent rubbed his chin. "These bastards have no idea what she is. We got that information from the senator on the department committee. And they didn't kidnap her for blackmail."

"Then what do they want?" He stuck the soaked patch onto the end of the cleaning rod and pushed it through the barrel.

"A payday." Tommy glanced briefly at the gruesome murder-scene photos on the worktable, then looked cautiously at the dwarf. "The kidnappers are part of an aggressive gang on the East Coast specializing in drugs and human trafficking."

Johnny made a rough sound of disgust.

"This isn't the first time we've tried to close in on the Boneblade, as they like to call themselves. It seems to have stuck but either way, we haven't been able to touch them. None of our other contacts have had better luck, and we simply don't have time to approach this our way. We need the monster hunter."

Johnny removed the cleaning rod from the barrel of his rifle and set it gently on the table. "This is what you brought me."

Tommy nodded. "This is what we brought you. We need your help, Johnny, and this is the only option any of us could come up with. Trust me, a dwarf who's been in retirement for fifteen years for very good reasons wasn't anywhere close to our first choice."

"You're not making a very good case for yourself, Nelson." Despite how low and calm his voice remained as he reached toward the long metal box of his cleaning supplies, the kind of rage he'd spent fifteen years trying to smother flared inside him again. *It doesn't matter what he says. He knows I'll be on this case like a catfish on four fingers. The way I should've been for Dawn.*

"So what d'ya say, Johnny?" The man stuck his hands into the pockets of his black slacks. "Amanda needs you."

The lid of the tin box slammed into place with a sharp bang. "You need me to save your scrawny neck, Nelson. That's what this is about."

"This is about the girl—"

"And you came all this way to rip me out of my goddamn life knowing I can't say no."

"You know what?" Lisa tapped the back of her hand against Tommy's arm to stop him from saying anything else and smiled at the dwarf. "I think we should start over."

His red mustache bristled as he glared at her. "It's a little too late for that, Agent Breyer."

"You can call me Lisa."

"I can call you both a pain in my ass."

She nodded slowly and drummed her fingers on the worktable. "You've set things up nicely for yourself out here."

"Uh-huh."

"I wouldn't wanna leave either if I were you." She shrugged. "We need to get these assholes, Johnny. And this girl deserves another chance. She can't go home, at least not the way she's always known it, but she can be safe. Protected. You can give her the chance to rebuild after what's been taken from her. This is a one-shot deal. And when it's over, you can come back here into retirement. Deal?"

The dwarf's eyes narrowed. "I don't make deals, Lisa."

Tommy slammed his hands onto the table. "When are you gonna pull your head out of your ass?"

He glanced coolly at the man and smirked.

"What's so funny?"

With a sniff, he stepped around his worktable and headed into the hall toward the front door.

"What the hell are you doing?" The agent spun to watch him, fuming. After all this time, the damn dwarf and one of the best bounty hunters the Department had worked with in at least twenty-five years was as infuriating as he'd always been. "We're not done here."

Johnny opened the front door and emitted a piercing whistle. Three seconds later, the dog door in the back clapped open and shut behind Rex and Luther, and both hounds trotted obediently through the house toward their master.

Rex licked his chops now spattered with swamp water and what might have been blood. "We didn't do it."

"*I* did. Yeah." Luther's tongue lolled out of his mouth and pieces of shredded reeds peppered his soaked, short-haired coat. "What are we talking about?"

Tommy stared at the dripping dogs with wide eyes and took a step back toward the doorway of the workshop.

Johnny folded his arms, and his smirk widened into a slick smile that revealed his perfectly straight teeth as he stared at his former government liaison. "Boys, it's time to show Agent Nelson out."

The man gawked at him as Rex and Luther uttered low, matching growls. "Johnny…"

"Give him a good bite in the ass while you're at it."

Rex snapped at the man and darted toward him.

"Shit!" Tommy's shiny agent shoes squeaked across the hardwood floor as he barreled down the hall toward the dwarf and the open front door.

Luther responded with a sharp bark and raced after his brother and Agent Nelson. "Hey! Get back here!"

The screen door banged against the outside of the house as Tommy shoved it open and practically threw himself off the front porch. Both hounds raced after him and cleared the porch in a single leap.

"I bet he tastes better than squirrel."

"More fat on him too."

"Yeah, right on his fat ass. Get him!"

"Johnny!" Tommy roared. "Get these—oh, fuck!"

The man flung himself against the side of the SUV and narrowly avoided being tackled by Rex's flying jump toward him. The larger coonhound slid across the dirt drive when he landed and threw up thick plumes of dust. The agent fumbled with the handle of the driver's door, finally jerked it open, and scrambled into the front seat with a yelp of pain. As soon as he yanked the door shut again behind him, Luther leapt toward it and his huge front paws thumped on the window as he snarled in Agent Nelson's wide-eyed, terrified face.

Rex snorted, shook his head, and spat a shredded wad of black slacks and bright red boxer briefs into the dirt.

"You got him!" Luther shouted.

"No way is that better than squirrel." Rex pawed at his snout and snorted again. "Too salty."

With a short rasping chuckle, Johnny swept the front door closed and returned to his workshop. His hounds bayed outside, but whatever Agent Nelson's next protests were, they were too muffled by his car to be heard inside the cabin.

Johnny stopped in the doorway of his workshop, where Agent Lisa Breyer stood on the other side of the table in front of his cleaning box. His partially disassembled rifle admittedly looked damn nice in her hands. Her slow smile when she looked at him didn't hurt, either.

"That's not yours."

She ignored his gruff attempt to shake her and watched him with a raised eyebrow as he moved slowly toward the table. "You're taking the case, aren't you?"

The closest he could get to nodding was a half-assed shrug. *If she thinks she can weasel more out of me than that, she's in the wrong business.*

"Then I guess you and I are a team now, Johnny Walker."

He leaned away from her and frowned. "Uh-uh. You're barking up the wrong tree with that one, sweetheart."

"Why? Because I'm a woman?"

Johnny snorted. "Because I don't do teams."

"Hmm." Pursing her lips, she returned her attention to the rifle and her hands kicked into action. The trigger guard and firing mechanism slid out of the stock, followed by the stock, firing rod, and the assembly rod. "I'm on this case too, whether you like it or not. You can fight me all you want, and I know I can't force you to play nice."

In four seconds, she had his weapon pulled apart and raised her eyebrows without looking at him. Before he could respond, she slid all the components back into the right place in the right order.

"If you insist on not doing teams, Johnny, I'll simply end up tracking the Boneblade on my own. And you. I'll probably end up stepping on your toes and will slow you down. Or we can do this together. Who knows? I might even be more useful than you realize."

Lisa snatched the rod he'd removed earlier, slid it into place, and lifted his fully reassembled rifle in both hands. Her smirk returned as she stepped around the table and stopped in front of him to hand him the weapon. "Your call."

Johnny stared at her and narrowed his eyes. *She knows her way around a firearm. I gotta admit it's as sexy as hell.*

He sniffed. "If we do this, I'm layin' down some ground rules. Non-negotiable."

"I'd be disappointed if you didn't." She raised her eyebrows and waited for him to take his weapon. When he finally lifted it out of her grasp with one hand, her smile widened. "We leave in two hours for New York City. I'll get my bag out of the car. I look forward to meeting Sheila."

She stepped past him and headed toward the front of his house.

The dwarf ran his tongue along the inside of his cheek and strode across the workshop to return the rifle to its place on the shelf. His cleaning box followed and he shook his head. *Sheila stays the hell out of this.*

CHAPTER THREE

They caught the 3:45 pm flight out of Miami International to La Guardia, leaving Agent Nelson behind to ice his ass and use the good, long opportunity to reevaluate his choices.

As the first line of passengers moved through the cabin to board the plane, Lisa turned toward Johnny in the seat beside her and chuckled. "I have to admit, you pull considerable weight with the higher-ups."

He snorted. "Your higher-ups. Not mine."

"I didn't think they'd upgrade the tickets."

"I don't fly coach." Johnny kicked his legs out in front of him, clasped his hands behind his head in the roomy first-class seat, and closed his eyes. "They know that."

"They didn't know about the dogs though, did they?"

A slow smile lifted one corner of the dwarf's mouth. "They should have done their homework."

In the seat directly in front of him, Luther uttered a low whine. "I smell meat. They have meat in these flying metal boxes?"

Beside him, Rex opened his mouth wide for a long, squeaking canine yawn. He licked his muzzle and sniffed the headrest. "Bet there's a bunch of good stuff under these seats. We could take a look."

"Can we look, Johnny? I'm hungry."

"Sit back and enjoy the flight, boys." The dwarf shifted more comfortably against the back of his seat. "You'll have all kinds of things to sniff in NYC."

Lisa looked up from the newest *Businessworld* issue she'd opened on her lap and frowned at him. "Many people talk to their dogs like they can understand English too."

Johnny grinned. *I'm gonna let that one go.*

"We'll have a car waiting for us at La Guardia," Lisa added. "I'll get us to the hotel, and then we can start—"

"All right. Let me stop you right there." He removed his hands from behind his head and thumped both arms onto the armrests as he turned to look at her.

"Is there something wrong with that very simple plan?"

"Yeah. Remember those ground rules I mentioned?"

She nodded curtly and raised an eyebrow.

"The first one is that I always drive."

The woman raised an eyebrow at him before she turned away and tried to cover her smile. "That's not gonna happen, Johnny."

"It's non-negotiable. You agreed."

Lisa licked her lips and focused on the back of the seat in front of her—currently occupied by Rex the coonhound—and tilted her head. "Fine. You might as well lay out the others before we get to New York."

"Sure. I like music as much as the next guy, but if we listen to anything, it's heavy metal or nothin'. I don't do any of that other squabbling, squawking bullshit. It's simply not for me."

"Heavy metal. Okay…"

"And don't feed the dogs."

She looked at him quickly and frowned. "Why would I feed your dogs?"

Johnny shrugged. "Exactly. Don't even think about trying to

work out why you shouldn't. You don't wanna know what happens."

"Trust me, I'm not interested in going down that rabbit hole."

"Good." Folding his arms, he shimmied back against his seat again and closed his eyes.

"Is that it?"

"What?"

"Your only ground rules?"

"Those are the basics. Besides cleaning up after a mess and keeping things simple." He opened one eye to fix her with a stern glance before he closed it again. "That includes flights."

Lisa widened her eyes and returned to the magazine.

"Ooh, Johnny." Luther panted and stretched his head out over the side of his seat into the aisle. "Johnny, they have treats. We get some treats, right?"

"Yeah, what did you get us?" Rex added.

A blonde flight attendant with her hair pinned up in a neat bun and her uniform flawlessly pressed and ironed stopped in front of the dwarf. Despite the fact that his eyes were closed, she gave him a winning smile anyway. "I have your drink, Mr. Walker."

"Only Johnny." He opened his eyes and settled his gaze immediately on the glass of whiskey balanced on the tray in her hand. "Did that come from the right bottle?"

"Most certainly. Johnny Walker Black Label."

"Good. Thanks." He lifted the glass from the tray and took a long, slow sip.

The flight attendant's smile all but vanished when she looked at Lisa. "Do you want anything?"

The agent gave her a thin smile and shook her head.

The woman glanced at Johnny again, studied him quickly with hooded eyes, and bit her lower lip before she walked toward the front of the plane.

"I didn't know they still served that on flights these days."

He smacked his lips and swirled the blended Scotch whiskey around in the glass. Ice clinked. "They do on the right flights when the right person asks for it, I guess."

"Huh."

"Johnny, get us some of that meat," Luther said. "I know they have something up there."

He ignored the hound, took another sip, and rested his head against the headrest with a sigh.

"Would you like a pillow, Mr. Walker?" This time, a brunette flight attendant with bright red lipstick examined him openly with airline extras in each hand. "A blanket? Anything to make you more...comfortable?"

"Only Johnny." He flashed her a crooked smile and lifted his drink. "And I got everything I need right here, darlin'."

"Okay. Well if you need anything, my name's Darlene. Let me know."

"Yep."

The woman gave him a sideways glance with a coy smile and ignored Lisa altogether before she turned to check on the other first-class passengers.

The agent watched her and shook her head. "Are you sure that's not the reason you wanted to fly first class?"

"Naw." He sniffed and took another sip. "They do that in coach, too."

"Not for everyone." Closing her magazine, Lisa leaned toward him. "I need to get something out of my carry-on. Do you mind?"

"Why would I?"

She waited for him to get out of his seat or at least straighten and pull his feet back. When he didn't, she rolled her eyes and stepped over his outstretched legs with one boot propped on the other.

"Here, let me help you with that." A male flight attendant with curly brown hair stepped up behind her and flashed her a gleaming grin. "Do you need something from up here?"

"Yeah. Thanks." Lisa stepped back and nodded at the overhead bin.

"No problem." The man opened the compartment that held only her black roller carry-on and Johnny's small army duffel bag with a skull and crossbones embroidered on the side. "This one, right?"

"That's the one." She smiled as he removed her bag and handed it to her. Thinking he'd move on or at least turn and head to the front of the plane, she unzipped the front pocket of her bag quickly and pulled her tablet out. She tucked it under her arm and started to lift her bag into the bin.

"Oh, no. I got it." The flight attendant chuckled, took her luggage from her without waiting for a reply, and slung it into the compartment. "You shouldn't have to lift a finger."

"Uh-huh."

He closed the overhead bin and left his hand there, blocking her from returning to her seat while he studied her openly. "If there is anything you need during the flight, ask for Tom, all right? I'm your man."

"Oh." Lisa responded with a soft laugh. "I think I'll be fine. But thank you."

"You bet."

"Excuse me."

He finally stepped back to let her pass and smirked as he watched her step over her travel companion's outstretched legs to reach her seat.

The dwarf sipped his whiskey loudly and glared at the flight attendant over the rim of his glass. The man spared him a glance, looked up again to wink at Lisa, and wandered down the aisle toward coach. Johnny grumbled something under his breath.

"You don't have to do that," Lisa said.

"I don't know what you're talkin' about." He didn't look at her.

"Well, let me share one of my ground rules, then." She sat and turned her tablet on. "I can take care of myself when I want to."

"And when you don't want to?"

She shrugged and didn't look up from the screen. "That's what partners are for."

He scoffed and closed his eyes. "First, it's a team. Now, it's partners. Someone needs to make up her mind."

"While we're on this case, Johnny, it's both."

Rex yawned again and his claws scraping across the vinyl upholstery. "This is boring."

Luther hovered over the aisle-facing armrest and his head whipped one way, then the other as he watched one passenger after another board the plane. "I wanna play. Johnny, if we can't eat, at least let us—ooh. Ooh. Hi!"

A low whine escaped the smaller coonhound as a woman in a maroon tracksuit passed with her chihuahua's head poking out of her designer handbag. The tiny dog growled at Luther, and the coonhound whined again before he shrank into his seat.

"Jeez. That was rude."

Rex snorted, curled into a ball on the seat, and plopped his head on the armrest. "She didn't mean it. You know to not listen to chihuahuas, man. All bark and no bite."

"That little one outside the trailer park bit me last week."

With a chuckle, Johnny closed his eyes and set his drink on the armrest. *They'll be fine once we get where we're goin' and get to work.*

CHAPTER FOUR

"The city that never sleeps, huh?" Johnny shook his head and stepped around a pile of boxes at the top of the stairs leading into the subway. "I'm not gonna sleep here either."

"No one's asking you to." Beside him, Lisa turned her shoulders to slip between two men in business suits who powerwalked past her. "Should I be concerned that you're thinking about sleep right now?"

"There's nothing of concern about preferring peace and quiet over all this noise, especially since you mentioned a car, not this." He walked as close to the wall of the subway entrance as he could as they descended the stairs. "But you can feel however you want."

"I feel like we should check what's in that guy's pockets," Luther said. His voice rose loud and clear in Johnny's mind over all the noise that echoed even louder in the subway the farther they descended. "What is he wearing? A parachute?"

"Hey, thanks." Rex sniffed the hamburger wrapper that dropped out of a man's hands onto the step as the guy crammed his food into his mouth and jogged toward the street. "Aw, man, it's empty. Seriously? Do I look like I eat trash?"

"You do eat trash. I eat trash. Good stuff in trash."

As soon as the thin ropes connecting both hounds' collars to their master's hand grew taut, they both abandoned their sniffing and returned to Johnny's side to follow him down the stairs.

He reached the bottom landing of the subway station and stopped beside Lisa as she glanced at the time for the next approaching train. He slugged the two large, empty duffel bags off his shoulder and kicked them open with the toe of his boot. When he looked at the empty tracks, he caught sight of three orange-brown creatures with rat-like faces that scurried into the darkness of the tunnel on his right. No one else seemed to notice or if they did, they ignored it in typical New Yorker fashion.

He leaned closer to Lisa and nodded toward the dark end of the tunnel. "Do they come into the subway often?"

She glanced around impassively. "Who?"

"The Willens."

"Oh." She shrugged. "I don't know, to be honest. I don't spend much time looking for Willens down here. Given a choice, I prefer to not spend time in the subway at all if I can help it."

"It's not your lucky day, then."

She gave him a sidelong glance and shook her head. "I'll be fine."

A woman wearing three different colored tutus in alternating patterns and giant, bright yellow sunglasses shaped like flamingos stepped past them along the subway platform and adjusted the straps of her sagging, neon-orange backpack over her shoulders. The beagle puppy with his head and one paw protruding from the backpack uttered a sharp yip that echoed through the subway.

Rex responded with one of his quieter barks. "I know, buddy. You'll be okay."

Luther took four steps after the tutu lady and sat with two inches of slack still in his rope. "She stole him?"

"What? No." His brother sat and bent his head to scratch vigorously behind his ear with a rear paw. "She adopted him."

"Same thing, isn't it?"

Johnny looked at his hounds with a raised eyebrow. "That's how you honestly feel?"

"Did you steal us?" Luther asked.

Rex stopped scratching his ear and ducked his head lower to nip at the inside of his hind leg instead. "Not in a backpack."

Lisa eyed the hounds briefly. "Johnny, you heard what I said about dogs in the subway, right?"

He nudged one of the open duffel bags with his boot. "Why do you think I picked these up off that luggage stand?"

"And you're sure they'll be okay with it?"

"I don't care if they're okay with it. I didn't bring 'em with me to leave 'em in a damn hotel room. These hounds once tracked a 'gator through five miles of swamp. In the rain. If we get even a whiff of that girl or her kidnappers, Rex and Luther will track 'em down."

"Ah." Lisa clasped her hands behind her back and looked at the countdown on the screen again. "And here I thought you merely had an overly developed sentimental side."

Johnny chuckled. *Only where it counts. And not in a long time.*

He stepped away from the duffel bag and snapped his fingers. "All right, boys. Step in. Come on."

Luther whipped his head up to stare at his master, his tongue lolling from his open mouth. "You stepped in what?"

Rex looked up from licking himself. "Was it the puke on the sidewalk four blocks east? Smelled okay to me."

"The bags." Johnny gave a gentle tug on each of the ropes attached to his hounds. "Let's go."

"Huh. What's this for?"

"He's not gonna tell us." Rex stepped into the first bag. "It's New York. People do weird stuff in New York."

"Johnny, I don't get it."

"Luther," Johnny snapped and pointed again. "Now."

"Aw, fine. Jeez. It's not like—hey. Hey, there's some kinda cheese in here or something."

As Luther rooted around in the bag, Johnny bent quickly and pulled the zipper closed up to the hound's chest, nudging his head out of the way.

"Hey. What's that for?"

Rex stared with wide eyes and didn't move an inch as the dwarf zipped him up like his brother. "Not a funny joke, Johnny. I don't get it."

"No dogs in the subway unless they're in a bag." Johnny stepped between the duffel bags and took hold of the straps before he looked at Lisa. "My dogs are now in bags."

She responded with a genuine laugh and shook her head. "I honestly expected you to forgo the rules and simply walk them in anyway."

"Hey, rules are rules. And I don't break 'em unless I have to."

"As long as you don't break anything else." She examined the fifty-five-pound coonhound in each bag and raised her eyebrows. "This I've gotta see."

"Huh. You're one of those."

"One of what?"

Johnny sniffed and tightened his grasp around the duffel-bag straps. "A doubter."

Luther stretched his neck over the side of the bag and licked tentatively at the dwarf's hand. "Oh. The cheese was from your sandwich."

Lisa tried to wipe a small smile off her face as she leaned forward to peer at the glowing lights of the oncoming train. "I don't doubt your skills or your ability to do your job and close this case, Johnny, if that's what you're thinking."

"It's not." *And everyone underestimates a dwarf.*

"Whatever you say." She grinned and stepped back as the subway station filled with the rumble and whine of the next train's approach. This was soon followed by a gust of wind and a grating squeal of brakes on metal. "Ready?"

"Are you?"

The subway doors slid open with a hiss, and a crowd of pedestrians filtered out in a heavy stream, talking or staring at their phones. Most shouldered past each other to get to the stairs.

With a grunt, Johnny bent his legs to slip one strap over each of his shoulders and stood.

Luther uttered a startled yelp as his legs gave way in the duffel bag. "Holy shit."

"Woah, woah." Rex lowered his head as far as it would go over the side of the second bag. "Not cool."

"You're good, boys. We gotta catch this train."

Chuckling, Lisa stepped briskly toward the open subway doors. Strangers sidestepped the dwarf in the black leather jacket who carried more than a hundred pounds of coonhound over his shoulders. Most of them didn't even look up from their smartphones as they streamed past.

"I don't like this." Rex finished that with a low whine. "Dogs don't go in bags."

"The City says otherwise." With another grunt of effort, Johnny stepped into the subway and turned to face Lisa, who'd taken a seat and now watched him with an amused smirk.

Luther bucked around in his bag but stopped abruptly and licked his muzzle. "Uh-oh. Johnny, what if I have to take a shit?"

"Don't even think about it."

Lisa raised both hands and chuckled. "I didn't say anything."

"Good call." Johnny turned to put his back to the row of seats and caught a middle-aged man in plaster-covered jeans and a sweat-stained t-shirt across the train glaring at him. "What? Have you never seen a dog in a bag?"

The man shifted on the seat and peered into the takeout bag in his lap.

"Hey, Johnny." Luther didn't even notice the solid ground

beneath him again when the dwarf set both bags on the floor and left one empty seat between him and Lisa when he sat. "Hey. Ask him if he's gonna eat all those chips."

"Of course he's gonna eat them." Rex sat back on his hind legs and stared at the people filing into the train. "No one shares chips."

A soft chuckle came from a girl in her early twenties who boarded with two of her friends.

"Oh, my God. Look at that." She moved her purse to her other shoulder and leaned against the center pole to aim her camera-phone at the scowling dwarf and his zipped-up hounds. Her friends laughed and exchanged surprised looks before they pulled their phones out too.

"So this is what your cousin was talking about."

"People will do anything to get their dogs on the subway."

Johnny stared at the opposite side of the train as the doors closed with a hiss. *Tourists. Always taking pictures of the wrong thing.*

The girls' phones clicked in quick succession and they leaned together, whispering as they studied him openly and snapped away with their digital cameras.

"Hey." He leaned forward between his spread knees and pointed at the girl who didn't immediately stop taking pictures. "One more picture and your phone's mine."

"Whatever." She rolled her eyes and stuck her phone in her purse, but as they started moving and picked up speed, all three of them darted the dwarf constant glances over their shoulders and giggled.

Lisa crossed one ankle over her opposite knee and leaned back in her seat. "You're starting a fan club, I see."

Johnny sniffed disdainfully and thumped back against the seat. "They'll forget all about it when they see the Met and the Highline."

"And you don't like your picture taken?"

"I like to keep things simple."

"Right."

They got off the subway at the 81st Street station and set off toward the Museum of Natural History. Johnny pulled his sunglasses out of the inside pocket of his leather jacket and put them on. One duffel bag stuffed into the other and strapped sideways across his chest thumped against his back with every step. Rex and Luther fell obediently into line at his side, their noses pressed to the sidewalk as they zig-zagged enthusiastically to pick up the smells of the city.

Luther's tail wagged furiously. "It's like everything I never knew I wanted all in one place."

"What is that?" Rex asked

"It's a bratwurst stand," the dwarf said without thinking. "They sell brats."

"Rex. Rex! Bratwurst stand! Brats! Johnny, can we have one?"

"Two, Johnny."

He ignored his hounds and continued to move. He glanced briefly at the faces that passed them on the sidewalk. "I assume you know where we're headed."

"Washington Heights." Lisa put her sunglasses on. She'd traded in the black frameless ones for a pair of brown-tinted aviators, which went much better with the civilian jeans and maroon softshell jacket after she'd ditched the federal monkey suit.

"Upper West Side, yeah?"

"You got it." She turned to look at the dwarf who trudged down the sidewalk, each dog's rope slack so it scraped along the cement with every step. "How long has it been since you were here?"

"Not long enough."

She let that one go and took a deep breath of the cooling spring air as the sun started its descent and glinted off the millions of windows and the metal buildings rising all around them. "We'll ask around there first. One of our informants has a few connections with a smaller band of thugs in Washington Heights. He said these guys have mentioned Boneblade once or twice."

"Are they in the same business?"

"Only the general crime business." Lisa smiled at a man and his daughter holding hands as they passed.

The little girl's eyes widened when she saw the hounds and she pointed. "Daddy. Daddy, look. They're twins!"

"Uh-huh." He tugged her along and the little girl looked over her shoulder to wave at the dogs.

Rex paused briefly to look at her. "We could say hi."

"I like kids, Johnny."

"We're in the city, Johnny. Everyone loves dogs in the city."

Johnny clicked his tongue and both dogs trotted to catch up with him. "No drugs or trafficking, though?"

"Not at the same level as Boneblade." Lisa shoved her hands into her jacket pockets. "These are low-level wannabes in comparison but the information's good. We can't touch Boneblade but we can at least get to the guys who know where not to go if they wanna stay in business."

The dwarf nodded. "Right."

They approached the Museum of Natural History on their right as a stream of a dozen five-year-old kids rushed down the wide front steps, around the central statue, and toward the sidewalk, screaming and laughing. The boy leading the group wore a paper crown and clutched a fistful of balloon strings in his hand. Most of them read, *Happy Birthday!* and one even had the T-Rex skeleton printed on shiny cellophane.

"Hey, Mister. I like your dogs!" The child stopped short when he reached the sidewalk. "Are they friendly?"

"Mostly." Johnny frowned at the group of kids laughing and whacking each other with foam swords.

Four adults tried to corral them into some kind of organized group, and one of them reached toward the boy wearing the crown. "Come on, Ricky. We're heading to Grandma's after this."

"Dad, I wanted to pet the dogs."

"Well, you have to ask first, son." The man gave Johnny a wide-eyed look, but his features softened when he saw Lisa standing there with the dwarf and smiling. "Sorry. He knows to not run up to people. Especially people with dogs."

Ricky scuffed his sneaker against the sidewalk. "Sorry. Can I pet your dogs?"

Luther sat and gazed at the kid, his tail sweeping wildly across the concrete. "Come on, Johnny. Look at him. He likes me."

Rex walked in a slow circle at the end of his rope and sniffed the sidewalk. "They're kids."

Johnny exhaled a slow sigh. "Go ahead."

"Yes! Dad, he said I could."

"I heard that." The man looked at the dwarf and nodded. "He's begged us for a dog since he could talk."

"And you won't even say maybe." Ricky handed his balloons to his dad and stepped toward Luther with his hand outstretched. "What's his name?"

"Luther. And this one's Rex."

"Hey, Luther." The boy laughed when the hound licked his open hand enthusiastically.

"Yes!" Luther could barely keep his balance in excitement. "Oh, man. I knew I smelled cake. Rex, it's cake! Want some?"

Rex sat at Johnny's side and stared at the screaming, laughing children running around the front of the museum. "Now they're all coming."

Johnny scowled and rubbed his hand over his chin and mouth as Ricky's friends swarmed toward them. *The hounds will be fine but I can handle only one tiny human at a time.*

He opened his mouth to say thanks for petting his dog and now it was time to split, but Lisa beat him to it.

"Birthday party, right?" she said and gave Ricky's dad a sympathetic smile.

The man chuckled. "What gave it away?"

"It feels like it's way over the top now, but trust me. He'll remember this for a long time. Good memories can be hard to come by."

"Tell me about it."

The dwarf glanced at the federal agent playing compassionate stranger at a birthday party and frowned. *No way is she old enough to have kids. I call daddy issues on this one.*

"Hey, mister!" The gaggle of five-year-olds finally approached and the other three exhausted parents trailed closely behind them with watchful gazes. "Can we pet your dogs?"

"Go right ahead," Lisa said before the dwarf could reply. "This one's Rex and that one with the birthday boy is Luther."

Johnny tried to smile but rolled his eyes, although no one could see it behind his black sunglasses. "Don't make any quick movements or loud noises. Got it?"

Rex looked at him and panted. "We move fast and make loud noises all the time. What's wrong with you?"

He ignored the dog and scowled at the front steps of the Museum of Natural History.

The kids swarmed around the hounds, Lisa and Ricky's dad kept talking about birthday parties and young children, and the dwarf fought the urge to drop both ropes and keep moving down the sidewalk on his own until Rex and Luther followed him of their own volition.

Too many kids, man. Like this is normal.

The only thing that stopped him from taking a hike right then and there was Ricky's voice a few feet away.

"You're a good dog, Luther."

Luther's tail wagged fiercely as he lowered his head to sniff the kid's shoes. "You got any more cake, kid? That frosting was legit. What kind was it?"

"We had a chocolate cake with strawberry frosting for my birthday," the boy said. "You can probably taste it. It's my favorite. I wanted to save some but my dad said we had to let everyone have a piece."

"*I* didn't have a piece. Come on, kid. You gotta have leftovers somewhere. What about your pockets?" Luther shoved his snout against Ricky's pants pockets, and the boy laughed.

"I don't think dogs can eat chocolate anyway. It'll make you sick."

"Man, that smells good. Ooh, yeah. Yeah, right there." Luther leaned against the boy's thigh and his rear leg lifted and pumped at nothing but air as Ricky scratched him in what appeared to be the perfect place. "Hey, Johnny. Ask the big one if there's any cake left."

"We'll let you get back to whatever you were doing," the dwarf said gruffly and nodded at the kid's dad. Without waiting for a response, he whistled and tugged briefly on both slack ropes in his hands. "Rex. Luther. Come on."

"All right, kids," one of the chaperoning moms called. "Let's let the nice…man and his dogs get back to their day." She corralled the kids getting their final pets in with Rex and gave Lisa a grateful smile but didn't look at Johnny.

"Have a good one," the agent said. "And happy birthday, kid."

"Bye, Luther." Ricky grinned at the dog before he took his dad's hand and headed off with the rest of the group down the sidewalk in the opposite direction.

"See ya, kid." Luther uttered a sharp yip before he fell into line beside Johnny. "Bring cake next time, huh?"

The groups parted ways and the dwarf stared directly ahead down the sidewalk as they passed the museum.

"Are you okay?" Lisa asked although she didn't look at him.

"Peachy," he grumbled.

"Do kids make you nervous?"

41

"When a whole army of 'em run at my dogs? It makes me itchy, not nervous."

"Uh-huh." She shrugged and slid her hand in the pockets of her jacket again. "That was nice, Johnny. I bet it made the kid's day."

"Sure." He glanced at her through his dark sunglasses. "So who threw you a birthday party you never forgot?"

"What?" Lisa uttered a short laugh and shook her head. "That wasn't about me. Merely an observation."

"Yeah, you do a fair amount of that."

Her smile faded. "It's part of the job, Johnny. Are you trying to tell me I'm being too observant?"

He shrugged. "It had nothin' to do with the case."

"It's called being nice. Paying it forward."

"Sure. Next time someone asks to pet my dogs, I make the call."

"Okay. Sorry."

She stepped aside when Rex darted in front of her to sniff a smear of cheese on the sidewalk. "This place has everything, Johnny."

"Even kids," Luther added. "I liked that one."

Johnny glanced at his smaller hound and sniffed. *I bet he did. It sounded like the kid could hear him too. Is that a thing?*

CHAPTER FIVE

They reached Washington Heights on the Upper West Side as the sun sank behind the tall buildings. In another hour, it would be too dark to make out most faces in the doorways and darkened alleys but not yet.

"Chuck's Deli." Lisa nodded up the cramped street toward the deli that lay a little ahead on their right. "The guy who owns it runs the drug scene here for at least twenty square blocks."

"Another observation?"

"No, it was in the file." With her aviators now resting on top of her long dark hair and pulling it away from her face, she looked at the dwarf and raised an eyebrow. "Did you even read the rest of it?"

"No. That's why you're with me."

"Wow. Okay. I'll put that file in your room when we get to the hotel."

Johnny grimaced. "You can put it wherever you want."

They reached the deli and the brightly lit neon *Open* sign in the front window that was lost among all the other bright lights that spilled through panes and open doorways around them. "The owner's name is Pete O'Dagle. If we find him, we can at least find where the Boneblade draws its territory lines around here."

"Yep." Johnny glanced at Rex, who tugged once on the end of his rope to sniff a pile of black plastic bags out on the sidewalk.

"Lots of food in there, Johnny."

"Stay sharp, boys. Got it?"

"Like sharp cheese in there?" Luther trotted up the two narrow front steps toward the deli's front door. "You're gonna get us sandwiches, aren't you?"

He ignored the hounds' constant banter over food as Lisa opened the door. *They'll be on their game when we get down to business. They always are.*

A small bell dinged when they stepped inside. The man standing behind the glass case displaying cuts of meats and cheese wiped his hands on a rag and jerked his chin at the apparent new customers. "What do you want?"

"So much roast beef, Johnny." Rex raised his nose and sniffed the air.

The dwarf stepped aside with his dogs as Lisa approached the counter and he scanned the interior. It appeared to be empty except for the one man who ran the establishment.

"Johnny, do you want anything?" she asked.

"Yeah, Johnny. Get us something."

The dwarf shrugged. "Whatever you're having."

"All right." She nodded at the man behind the counter. "Get me two roast beef sandwiches. And I'm also looking for Pete."

The man raised his eyebrows and set to work making the sandwiches. "Pete's finished for the night. Come back tomorrow."

"Even if you want us to think he went home," Johnny said, "he's still here. Go tell him we wanna talk."

The man took a handful of meat from the display case and gave him and the hounds a scowling examination. "No one reads the damn sign anymore. No dogs allowed."

"The dogs stay with me." He pulled a chair noisily from

beneath one of the grungy, dented tables and sat. His boots thumped on the other chair beside him, and after a snap of his fingers and a raised index finger, both hounds sat beside him. "And we're stayin' here until Pete comes for a chat."

The man sucked something out of his teeth and flopped the meat onto two open hoagie rolls. "This ain't about the sandwiches."

"Nope." Lisa folded her arms and watched him swipe mayo and mustard across the bread with a huge spreading knife. "This is a different kinda business."

The only sounds in the deli now came from the hum of the fridge and the display case, the man adding lettuce and tomatoes to the sandwiches, and Rex and Luther panting heavily. Once he'd wrapped their orders and thumped them onto the top of the display case, the man fixed Liza with an expectant look. "Twenty-one eighty-four."

"For two sandwiches?" Johnny grumbled.

"If you want cheaper grub that tastes like shit, you shoulda gone to the Bronx."

The agent withdrew her wallet from the pocket of her jacket and handed the man her card. He rang it up and slapped her card on the display case. That done, he fixed Johnny and the dogs with a disapproving look. "Five minutes. If I see those dogs walkin' around, I'm tossin' all three of your asses outta here."

The dwarf dropped the ropes from his hands and folded his arms. Rex and Luther stayed where they were beside him. "That's not gonna happen."

Finally, the man turned, stepped into the back, and cast them all a final baleful glance before he disappeared.

Lisa took the sandwiches and joined him at the table. "Just so we're clear, I'm not buying all your meals for you."

"If I'd known we were stoppin' for supper, I would've suggested something different."

She raised her eyebrows. "Supper."

"You obviously haven't spent any time in the south."

Shaking her head, she slid one of the wrapped sandwiches across the table toward him and opened hers. "If you wanna get anything in this city, you have to pay for it one way or another. If we buy a few sandwiches, Pete's far more likely to come down and chat."

"He thinks we wanna talk drug business in Washington Heights."

"Let him think that." She shrugged. "This is the first good lead on someone who has the most direct contact with Boneblade, even if it's only by knowing when and where to stay away from them."

"Johnny." Luther's tail thumped once against the scuffed linoleum floors. "Johnny, open the sandwich."

Lisa bit into hers and nodded at the dwarf. "Are you gonna eat that?"

"I'll wait." He scanned the empty deli again and ignored the sound of the sauce dripping out of her hands and onto the paper wrapper beneath her sandwich.

She was halfway through when the guy manning the counter stepped out of the back room. He glared at the dogs seated obediently beside the dwarf. Both stared at the still wrapped sandwich on the table. The bell over the door dinged again, and a young couple in their twenties walked in to place their order. The woman stepped quickly away from the coonhounds but didn't say anything as she headed toward the counter.

In the next moment, the door on the far side opened and a huge bald man wearing black-and-red flannel pajama pants and a white undershirt beneath an apron stepped into the front room. The apron was covered with streaks and spatters of blood and grease, and he didn't bother to take it off as he entered his establishment. The man behind the counter met his gaze and nodded toward Lisa and Johnny.

The owner took the empty seat at the table, which groaned beneath his weight. "I heard you wanna talk business."

Lisa nodded at him and wrapped the rest of her sandwich. "Are you Pete?"

"Last time I checked. What do you want?"

Johnny glanced at the couple placing their order. The woman looked over her shoulder at them and turned quickly toward the display case. "Do you wanna have this chat right here in front of everyone?"

"Anyone stupid enough to repeat anything they hear in my deli shouldn't be steppin' foot inside." Pete folded his arms and glanced at the dogs. "They shouldn't bring mutts into my shop either."

The dwarf turned his head to look at the man. "Trust me, they won't tell anyone."

"Except for you," Rex said and licked his muzzle.

Luther shifted his front paws on the floor but remained seated. "Johnny, the sandwich."

"So start talkin'," Pete said. "I'm kinda in the middle of somethin'."

"We're looking for the Boneblade," Lisa said and lowered her voice. "I heard you might know where to find them."

The man turned toward her and narrowed his dark, beady eyes to glare at her. "Lady, I don't know who dropped you on your head when you was a baby, but you're fuckin' insane."

"You run at least twenty square blocks up here, right?" Johnny unwrapped the sandwich in front of him slowly.

"Twenty-five." Pete glanced from the undercover agent to the grizzled, red-bearded dwarf. "I thought you wanted to talk about that."

"We don't care about what you do in your territory," Lisa assured him. "We're merely looking for the edge of Boneblade's."

"Well, they sure as shit don't come around here."

Johnny snatched the sandwich and ripped it in half. Pieces of meat and cheese and globs of sauce plopped onto the paper. "They took someone, Pete. And we need to find her."

The man chuckled and rubbed the top of his bald head with a bloodstained hand. "That don't make you special. If you're askin' about those motherfuckers, you know what they do."

"They don't know what we do. It gives us a leg up, don't it?" Without looking away from the proprietor, he dropped both halves of the sandwich on the ground, one in front of each of his hounds.

"Yes!" Luther wolfed his half in one mouthful, snapped his jaws twice, and swallowed the whole thing before he licked the floor. "Got any more? Rex, how about you give me—"

A low growl issued from Rex's throat as he snacked on his sandwich half. "Mine."

"Jeez. Fine." Luther looked at his master again with puppy-dog eyes. "I can at least lick the paper, yeah?"

Johnny ignored him.

Pete scowled at the dogs eating his sandwich and glanced at his employee behind the display case. The man who'd made dinner for two coonhounds glared at the dwarf and shook his head slowly.

"It won't come back to you, Pete," Lisa said. "We're not trying to make things hard for anyone but the Boneblade."

"And yourselves." The man shook his head. "They don't like people asking questions."

Johnny scowled. "Too fucking bad. We're asking."

"They don't like people givin' out information about 'em, either. If anyone finds out I told you—"

Johnny snapped his fingers and both hounds looked at him expectantly. "If you don't tell us, you'll have more than pig blood on your apron, I can promise you that."

Lisa cast him a sharp glance but covered it in a split second.

Rex sniffed the air and fixed his eyes on Pete. "He already does."

"Pig blood. Cow blood. Human blood." Luther uttered a low growl. "Not his, Johnny."

Pete shook his head. "I ain't scared of a couple of pups and two green assholes who think they can walk in here and start askin' the kinda questions that'll get them killed."

Johnny's hand moved to his hip faster than anyone could follow. The click and glint of his dual action automatic blade followed as it opened, and a second later, the blade had buried itself in the top of the table's edge directly in front of the man.

The bald man stared at it but didn't even flinch.

The click of a pistol hammer being drawn back came from behind the counter as the man there aimed his weapon at the dwarf. "Don't even fuckin' think about it."

The couple who'd just bought their sandwiches darted out of the deli. The door slammed open and shut behind them and the bell dinged, and no one else moved.

"Well, that's one way to make a point," Lisa said flatly. "Everyone needs to calm down."

"I'm calm." Johnny leaned toward Pete and jerked his chin up. "As long as you and your bodyguard stay calm too, we'll all walk away from this with what we want."

"I want you the fuck outta my place," the proprietor grumbled. He raised his hand toward the handle of Johnny's knife but stopped when Luther snarled and uttered a low growl. He glanced at the hound suddenly beside him and leaned away. "Man, this is why the sign says no fuckin' dogs. Get 'em outta here."

"Give us a territory line, Pete." He inclined his head and fixed him with a hard stare. "That's all."

"Do you want me to take care of 'em?" the man behind the counter asked. "The fucker fed my sandwich to his dogs. I'm happy to do it."

Pete glanced at his employee and shook his head. "They'll be dead before they find who they're looking for."

"We'll take our chances," Lisa said. "All you have to do is point us in the right direction and everything you're doing here keeps running the way you want it to." She reached into her pocket and pulled her badge out to flash it quickly at the man. "Otherwise, I might have to call a few friends. Shake things up in here, you know?"

"Shit." Pete scowled at her. "I knew you was too straight to be runnin' anything. Cam, put the fuckin' gun down."

Behind the counter, Cam pushed the gun's hammer up and returned it to its place under the counter. "Fuckin' Feds."

Lisa ignored the comment and raised her eyebrows at the proprietor. "So where do we find them?"

The man scowled at Luther, who snarled in response but didn't move. "We don't go south past Hell's Kitchen for a start. That's where my deals end, at least. I can't tell you much more than that 'cause I'm smart enough to stay the hell away."

"Do they make it clear to not cross that line, or are you merely throwin' out a guess?" Johnny asked.

"You don't wanna guess with this shit, man. Now get the hell out." Pete's chair scraped noisily across the floor when he stood. "If I see those dogs in here again—"

"You won't," the dwarf assured him with a grim smile. "Unless you're jerkin' us around."

Shaking his head, Pete stormed across the deli toward the door in the back. "We're closin' early, Cam."

"Yeah, no shit."

Johnny stood and jerked his knife out of the table before he slid it onto his belt. He picked up both ropes attached to his hounds' collars and turned toward the door.

"Good sandwich." Lisa picked up the rest of hers and slid it into the pocket of her jacket. "Have a nice night."

Cam didn't say anything and instead, glared at them as they exited the deli and stepped onto the street. Once the agent and the dwarf with his snarling fucking dogs disappeared from view, the clerk stepped around the end of the counter and headed to the front door to turn the *Open* sign off and lock up. He didn't need to turn to know his boss stood behind him in the center of the deli. "Are you gonna make the call?"

"We're both dead if I don't." With a grunt, Pete pulled his cell phone out. "Next time some dipshits ask for me, you'd better make sure they're legit. That asshole in the back's probably passed out by now. It's gonna be real hard to wake him again."

"Did he tell you what you wanna know?"

The man pressed the call button and lifted the phone to his ear. "Not yet."

CHAPTER SIX

"You have some kinda finesse," Lisa said as she drew the uneaten half of her sandwich back out of her pocket. "Is pulling a switch-blade out your regular go-to method these days?"

Johnny stared directly ahead as they walked down the side-walk toward mid-town. Car horns blared around them, and the drilling buzz of construction across the street cut through despite the darkening sky. "It's a dual-action hunting knife."

"Right." She stopped beside an overflowing trashcan and almost threw the rest of her sandwich in it before Luther uttered a low whine.

"Hey, that's perfectly good food."

"Johnny, we could eat it."

She glanced at the hounds. "I'm not gonna feed your dogs, but do they want it?"

He sighed dramatically and snatched the sandwich from her hand. In silence, he unwrapped it, tossed the paper onto the over-flowing bin, and divided the rest of Lisa's meal in half and fed it to his hounds. The food vanished in seconds.

"You're the best." Luther sniffed the trashcan. "What about the chicken in there, huh?"

"Johnny, I like her." Rex panted, his tail wagging as he stared at Lisa. "You like her too, right? Good one. You should get her to—"

Johnny snapped his fingers, and both dogs quit talking in his head to fall into step beside him. "It wasn't my first time squeezin' information out of some low-level asshole. And the knife got him to talk."

"Are you sure it was the knife? 'Cause I remember having to flash my badge."

"That was the unnecessary part." He glanced at a middle-aged woman and her daughter yelling at each other about curfews on the front stoop of their apartment. "If that guy talks—"

"Who's he gonna talk to, Johnny? The guy's too scared of Boneblade to tell them there was a federal agent in his shop asking questions. With good reason, too."

"He might not say you were a Fed but he wasn't nearly scared enough to keep his mouth shut. If you'd let me keep goin' my way, he would've been."

"And put 'more than pig blood' on his apron?" Lisa shoved her hands into her jacket pockets and shook her head. "What was that?"

"A warning. If this tip goes bad, you can at least bring your friends into that deli. I'd bet my truck he was doing an interrogation when we interrupted him."

"Because a guy who owns and runs a deli and probably makes the butcher's cuts himself in the back had blood on his apron? Come on."

"Because a guy who runs a low-level drug enterprise in Washington Heights didn't only have pig blood on his apron."

Lisa frowned at him. "How do you know that?"

Johnny shrugged. "It's merely an observation."

"What?" Luther looked at his master. "You're gonna take the credit for that one?"

Rex snorted. "Typical."

The dwarf ignored them. *She'll keep trying to crack me if I say my hounds told me.* "So, what? Another twenty blocks to go?"

"Something like that. Do you think you can keep your knife on your belt for that long?"

He scowled "We'll see what happens."

They made it twelve blocks before Rex and Luther both barked sharply.

"Hey, you smell that?"

"Yeah. Same smell in the deli. On that dented square on the floor."

Johnny stopped on the dark street corner. "Hold on."

Lisa had almost stepped onto the crosswalk in the street before she realized he wasn't beside her anymore. "What?"

"Somethin's off."

She fixed him with an irritated look. "Johnny, you gotta give me more than that."

"Hold on a sec." He looked at his hounds, both of whom had turned at the ends of their ropes. Their tails pointed straight out behind them as they faced the alley they'd passed. "In the alley."

"We still have almost ten blocks to go until—"

Rex interrupted with a long coonhound bay, his head tilted toward the sky. Luther growled.

"When my hounds pick a scent up, Agent Breyer, I don't let that go."

"You still won't call me Lisa, huh?"

Johnny bent to quickly untie the ropes from his dogs' collars and they rushed toward the alley. "Come on."

"Are you serious?"

"As a heart attack."

She sighed and hurried after him. "Do you mind explaining to me how your dogs picked up a scent we want to track when we haven't even found Boneblade yet?"

"Pete was lying. He's had more interaction with them than he wants anyone to think."

They turned into the alley that branched at the end between the rows of buildings around them. Lisa unzipped her jacket so she'd have better access to the service pistol strapped in her shoulder holster. "How do you know that?"

"Look, if you don't understand how hound dogs work, I'm not about to explain it to you."

Rex and Luther trotted down the alley, their noses to the ground as they followed the scent. "Stronger now."

"Real strong, Johnny. Damn, these guys stink."

"What are we lookin' at, boys?"

"Right. Like they're gonna tell you—" Lisa's shoe kicked a discarded soda can and it clattered down the alley.

"Magicals," Rex said. "Like that witch in Goodland. But dirty."

Then we're on the right track.

Luther bayed this time and the howl echoed through the narrow alley.

It cut off abruptly when a sneering man in a tan bomber jacket rounded the corner on their left. A bolt of yellow light sprang from his fingertips and cracked against the wall on Johnny's right, inches from the dwarf's head.

"Would you look at this, fellas?" The wizard chuckled. "These idiots did our job for us."

Six other magicals turned the corner to join him. The last one was twice the size of the biggest thug among them and his slicked-back hair and eyebrows were coated in a thick layer of glittering frost.

Great. They brought a Crystal too.

"You should be more careful where you throw spells," Lisa said as she moved her hand slowly to the open zipper of her jacket.

"And you should be more careful where you go sniffin' around in shit that don't concern you." The wizard sneered and summoned a bright, swirling ball of the same yellow magic. "'Cause now, you're fucked."

"I don't know what you've heard—"

"And you don't need to." A man with long brown hair tied back in a ponytail and a well-groomed goatee examined her derisively and sniggered. "We heard you're askin' too many questions about Boneblade. If people do that, sweetheart, they don't stick around long enough to find the answers."

Johnny glanced at her with a somewhat smug expression. "Told you."

"Yeah, I get it. Leave 'em breathing, huh?"

He shrugged. "As long as they cooperate."

Rex and Luther lowered their heads and snarled at the thugs.

"So you're Boneblade," Lisa said and inched her hand slowly into her open jacket to draw her firearm.

"The first and the last you're gonna see." The wizard launched his spell at her and she ducked before the yellow light careened into the wall of the alley.

She thrust her hand toward him and released a roaring fireball that caught him in the shoulder. He shouted and clapped a hand over the charred bomber jacket, and the rest of the Boneblade members charged.

Johnny yanked his knife from his belt and flicked it open. "Let 'em have it, boys."

"I never tasted wizard before." Luther snarled and darted toward the oncoming thugs.

"Rip his throat out!" Rex howled and launched after his brother.

The goateed man with the ponytail shucked his jacket and shirt before he shifted in mid-run into a shaggy brown wolf to meet the hounds in the center of the alley.

The Crystal trundled forward with a dark chuckle and blasted a stream of tinkling ice shards at Johnny. The dwarf ducked the attack and brought his knife up to slice at the ribcage of another wizard who laughed wildly as he swung a heavy club toward him. The laugh cut short abruptly and the wizard stumbled sideways with a cry of pain and a shallow incision through his shirt and flesh.

A witch with bright green hair launched two red orbs of light toward Johnny. He snatched the lid of a trashcan by the handle and held in front of his face before the red orbs exploded with crackling light and pelted the metal. As soon as it failed, he lowered the lid and tossed it at her like a frisbee. She didn't have time to cast another spell before the spinning edge of the projectile caught her in the throat. With a gurgled protest, she choked and dropped to her knees, gasping for breath.

"Do you wanna play explosives? Fine." The dwarf reached into the inside pocket of his leather jacket and retrieved a round black disk two inches thick. He punched the button on the top and lobbed it down the alley. A Boneblade Wood Elf who raised his gun toward him jerked his head to the side to avoid the spinning disk, then sniggered and aimed.

He shrugged at his would-be assailant and smirked seconds before the device he'd built himself detonated behind the elf. It launched the Boneblade member forward onto his face, and the gun lurched from his hand to clatter across the alley. Johnny ducked beneath the Crystal's next icy attack, switched his blade from his right hand to his left, and picked the Wood Elf's gun up. "That was fun, right?"

Lisa grunted as she grappled with another wizard's firearm and disarmed him. She cracked the butt of his weapon across his head and leveled his weapon at him before he'd even landed. "Don't move."

The magical with the charred shoulder summoned another spell aimed at her, and she squeezed a shot off with the gang member's weapon that struck him in the thigh. His spell snuffed out as he screamed and fell, clutching his leg. "The fireball wasn't enough? Come on."

With a roar, the Crystal stormed toward them, leaving a trail of frozen footsteps in his wake. A gusting, freezing wind kicked up in the alley, blocking Lisa's view with the instantly material-izing blizzard.

Another gunshot filled the alley. The large attacker roared and fell and the concrete trembled beneath him.

The blizzard faded, and Johnny looked at the wizard's gun in distaste. "I guess that'll do."

"Thanks." Lisa smoothed her hair away from her face and looked at the Boneblade thugs sprawled on the alley paving, groaning and clutching their non-lethal wounds. "I should call this in."

On their left, Rex and Luther had cornered the shifter against the wall and snarled at him, snapping their jaws as the wolf bris-tled and growled.

"Good work, boys." The dwarf strode toward them.

"If we take these assholes in," Lisa said as she threw the weapon that didn't belong to her across the alley behind her, "we can get far more information about who's running the show."

"I'm not gonna stop you." Johnny glanced at the witch, who was still choking and holding her half-crushed throat. A dark-red light bloomed beneath her palms and he aimed the wizard's gun at her. "Whatever you're tryin' to do, don't."

"Johnny." Rex snapped at the shifter. "What do we do with this one?"

"I can take him," Luther added. "He's slow."

"Keep him there for a sec." He stepped toward the witch. "Can you talk?"

She sneered at him. "Boneblade's gonna rip you apart!"

"That's a yes. We're looking for a kid—"

The woman responded with a dry, raspy chuckle. "Good luck."

"Now, see, that's not the kinda answer I'm lookin' for—"

A quick scuffle, snarl, and yelp came from the hounds and the shifter.

"Johnny! Hey, let him go!" Luther leapt toward the shifter who now had his brother pinned to the ground. He snarled and snapped at the brown wolf who stood with his forepaw crushing Rex's throat. "Get off!"

The wolf snapped at Luther, and Johnny forgot all about interrogating the witch.

The dwarf squeezed a shot off and struck the shifter in the hip. The wolf yelped but didn't release his pressure on the hound's neck.

"Off!" He leveled the gun at the wolf's face. "You touched my dog. Now, you're dead."

The shifter snarled at him and pressed even harder. Rex bucked and squirmed under the pressure, and Luther darted forward to clamp his jaws around the wolf's bleeding hip. The beast howled, and Johnny took the opening.

He dropped the gun, switched his knife into his right hand, and swept the blade into the wolf's chest a little below the neck as he barreled into the shifter's shaggy hide. Both wolf and dwarf thumped against the wall of the alley.

Rex scrambled to his feet with a whimper and turned to snarl at his assailant. "Fuck you, asshole!"

"You get him, Johnny?" Luther looked from his brother to their master. "You get him?"

The shifter melted into his naked human form as Johnny jerked his blade from the man's chest. Staring at his assailant with wide eyes, the man coughed bubbles of blood that dribbled into his neat goatee and stopped moving.

"Johnny—" Lisa started.

"Hey!" The shot and burned wizard tried to get to his feet. "You'll fucking pay for that, you—"

Johnny spun and threw his knife into the man's neck. As the other maimed Boneblade members protested and tried to rise for another fight, the dwarf picked up the other wizard's stolen gun and fired three more rounds. The Crystal and two other magicals fell with bullet holes in their heads, and he hurled the gun down the alley. "I can't believe this still has decent aim."

The Wood Elf and the witch scrambled to their feet and bolted away in the direction from which they'd come. She tripped over the Crystal's outstretched hand, uttered a croaked shout of surprise, and lurched against the alley wall before they vanished around the corner.

Johnny sniffed and knelt beside Rex. "How you doin' buddy?"

"Like I got stepped on by a wolf." The dog licked his muzzle and let his master examine him. "Thanks."

"We're a team. Luther?"

"I'm good. They're getting away, Johnny."

"Not fast enough." He petted Rex's head and stood to look at Lisa. "Shall we?"

"Shall we what?" She looked at the Boneblade bodies that littered the alley and shook her head. "Five bodies wasn't enough? I said I was gonna call it in."

"And then that fucker tried to choke my dog."

"And now we don't have anyone to question. What are you doing?"

"Lighten up, huh?" He nodded down the alley to where the two living gang members had disappeared. "I'm a Level Six and I have a license to take out the trash however I want."

"That doesn't explain why you let them go."

"Huh." He approached the dead wizard with his knife still in this throat and stepped on the guy's chest to pull the blade out and wipe it on the side of his jeans. "I assumed you would have realized we need someone to trail."

Narrowing her eyes, Lisa glanced at the hounds as they turned to face the end of the alley, then shrugged. "Lead the way."

"You heard her, boys. Let's go huntin'."

CHAPTER SEVEN

Rex and Luther remained on the escaped Boneblade members' scent across Manhattan to a mid-town West Side social club. From across the street on the other side of the back parking lot, the two watched the witch and the Wood Elf barrel through the back door of the Nightlights social club and disappear inside.

"We'll go in quietly, boys. Understand?"

"Got it."

Rex's nose zig-zagged across the ground. "Still got the scent, Johnny."

Lisa folded her arms and scanned the back of the building. "You want to follow them in there."

"It's not like they have anyone guarding the back door." He looked challengingly at her and adjusted the long loops of coiled rope over his arm. "You handled yourself fine in that alley. You'll be fine in there too."

He pushed into a jog across the street toward the parking lot that could only fit a maximum of ten cars. His hounds trotted quickly at his side.

Lisa glanced up and down the street and hurried after them. "I was better than fine, Johnny. I know how to handle myself."

"Yeah, that's what I said." He paused at the back door to let her catch up, grasped the handle, and found it unlocked. "They made this too damn easy."

He held the door open for his dogs, gestured for her to step inside first, then followed and let the door bang shut behind him. No one heard it over the constant drone of conversation, laughter, and clinking glasses in the front of the club. The hallway was dark there, and the wounded Boneblade members hadn't lingered to see if they were followed.

"Johnny, up here." Rex panted and stopped at the bottom of a narrow stairwell on the left.

"Ooh, yeah. That's blood." Luther sniffed at the second step. "The elf's."

"Head on up." He strode after them and made no effort to hide the clomp of his boots on the stairs beneath the noise of the crowded club.

Lisa glanced at the front of the establishment, then headed grudgingly up the stairwell. "So you randomly choose the stairs, huh?"

"Hounds don't do random, darlin'. Not even in the city." He turned and pointed at a smear of blood barely visible on the dark wall. "Plus, I reckon you'd call that evidence, yeah?"

Her eyes widened at the blood smear and she didn't say anything else.

They reached the second floor, and Rex and Luther continued down the hall with their noses to the floor. It wasn't that hard to find the room where the wounded members had taken refuge. The doorknob was covered in blood too. Johnny gestured toward the door and stepped back to let the agent take the honors if she wanted.

She drew her service weapon and stepped forward to jerk the door open. Before she could even identify herself in the dimly lit room, the witch jumped from behind the open door and another red orb materialized in her hand. Lisa raised her elbow and swung it into the witch's throat. The other woman staggered, dragged a gasped breath, and her eyes rolled back in her head.

Johnny and the dogs thrust in after the agent, and the Wood Elf seated in a desk chair while he tried to wrap a tourniquet around his leg scrambled to stand.

"Don't move." The dwarf whipped his blade out again and pointed it at their quarry, who snarled despite how pale he'd grown.

The elf lunged forward, and Rex leapt at him and thrust him against the rolling chair and to the floor. "Get it off me!"

The hound snapped at him and pressed a paw on the magical's throat. A string of saliva dripped onto his captive's forehead. "Not so fun, is it?"

Luther skidded to a stop behind the elf and snarled at his head. "Wood Elf. That tastes like squirrel, I bet."

Johnny stepped around Rex and placed his boot on the captive's chest as Lisa closed the door and locked it. Both hounds backed away with low growls. The dwarf's glinting blade-tip pressed against their prisoner's neck, and the dwarf leaned forward with a grimace of distaste. "It looks like someone will be demoted, asshole."

"Fuck you."

"Sorry. I'm not into Wood Elves. But you have bigger problems on your hands right now, so don't feel bad."

The Boneblade member sneered and tried to shake the puddle of dog drool off his forehead. "You're dead."

"No, your buddies in that alley are dead. Whoever sent you thought you could eliminate me, Agent Breyer over here, and two coonhounds. But you failed. And now, the Feds know where you and the chokey witch hang out. There are probably many more of you who frequent the establishment too. Do you think your boss is gonna be happy about that?"

The Wood Elf grimaced beneath the blade pressed against his throat and it drew a small bead of blood. "What do you want?"

"Start talking about the girl."

The prisoner started to chuckle but stopped when his Adam's apple bobbed against the knifepoint. "Which one?"

"Amanda Coulier." Lisa moved toward the desk where the elf had been seated and the three computer monitors on it. "Your gang killed her family and took her two days ago."

"You mean the one with the twin? I knew we should have taken 'em both." The man sniggered.

"Keep laughing and it'll be the last time you think anything is funny." Johnny leaned over his knee and his boot remained planted on the magical's chest. "Where's the girl?"

"The little bitch is waiting for auction, asshole."

"What auction?"

"Fuck you."

The dwarf sighed. "I thought we covered this." He drove the handle of his blade into the elf's temple, and the magical's eyes rolled in his head.

Lisa scowled at the groaning, mostly unconscious Wood Elf. "What are you doing?"

"Getting a better angle." He slid his knife onto his belt and hauled the Boneblade member up by the front of his shirt. Almost carelessly, he dropped him forward again to thump face-first onto the floor. "If he tries anything, boys, feel free to take the softest pieces."

"Nice." Luther licked his muzzle. "Wait, what parts are those?"

"Any parts when he's flopping around on the floor like that, huh?" Rex's low chuckle filled Johnny's mind. "You can bite his ass this time. I've had enough after the last guy."

The dwarf pulled the coils of rope off his shoulder and got to work securing the Wood Elf. When he had finished, he dragged the magical to the other side of the room and propped him halfway up against the wall. "Like a trussed pig. It's a good look on you, dipshit."

The prisoner's eyelids fluttered and he uttered a small moan.

"Look alive, son." He smacked the elf's cheek and squatted in front of him. "We're only getting started."

Lisa glanced at the witch, who lay in a crumpled heap. The woman was still breathing, at least, but that was the only sign she was still alive.

"What..." The Wood Elf groaned, realized he'd been bound, and struggled against the ropes. "Fuck. My head."

"That's nothin'. If you can talk, you can think." Johnny slapped him again. "What auction?"

The elf's head rocked back against the wall. "Quit hittin' me."

"Quit being a fucking moron. What auction?"

"Okay, okay. Jesus." The magical blinked heavily and licked the split corner of his mouth and the blood that trickled toward his chin. "All the merchandise gets put up for auction. The girl you want will go to the highest bidder."

"Where do we find whoever that is?"

"You don't. Not yet. It's all done on the dark web. The bidding's already started." He grunted. "Come on. I can't feel my hands."

"Good." The dwarf stood, snapped his fingers, and pointed at the prisoner. "Keep an eye on him, boys."

"Yeah, I'll watch him all night." Luther trotted toward the elf and growled as he stood over the trussed magical.

"Move. I dare you." When the prisoner looked at Rex, the hound snapped in his face.

The elf lurched away and slid too far to the side to right himself before he fell sideways against the wall. "Shit."

Johnny stalked toward the computers on the table. "Dark web."

"So I heard." With a small smile, Lisa conceded his effectiveness. "And I didn't even have to flash my badge."

"So now we're on the same page." He studied the monitors on the table, which displayed an order page for cases of liquor, a guest list for the club, and someone's last Google search for how to cut out an ingrown hair. "We need to find this auction."

"I'm very sure I can get us in." She raised her eyebrows when the dwarf stared at her in disbelief. "So if you don't mind…"

"Yeah." Johnny stepped aside and pulled the rolling chair in front of the desk.

She sat and began to click through the computer.

"Do you spend much time on the dark web?"

"Enough to know how to get in and find my way around, for the most part." She looked at him with a smirk. "Don't tell me you didn't know that's where most magicals do their business when they don't want anyone else to see."

"Most humans too."

"True." Lisa's fingers flew across the keyboard, and he turned away to let her do her thing so he could do his. Right now, that was mean-mugging the Wood Elf, who lay on his side with his eyes closed and tried not to move while the coonhounds loomed over him.

"What are you gonna do with him after this?" Rex asked.

"Yeah, we could chase something. I like chasing. I like catching even more."

"We'll let him decide that one for us," Johnny muttered.

Lisa darted him a brief frown before she returned to the keyboard. "What?"

"Nothin'."

CHAPTER EIGHT

"Okay. Here we go." Lisa clicked and typed for another twenty seconds, then leaned back in the chair and lowered her hands into her lap. "Oh, man. There she is."

Johnny scowled at the monitor and the picture of a wide-eyed girl with matted brown hair and a bruise across her cheek. *Even when they took that, she wouldn't let them see she was scared. Tough kid.*

The description the Boneblade had put up of Amanda was even worse:

Twelve-year-old girl fresh from home. Feisty and spirited. Unbroken. Clean. Orphan. Likes to bite.

"Did you read the description?" he asked.

"Assholes." She shook her head. "But they left out a major detail."

He cracked his knuckles. "They wouldn't leave it out if they knew." *Putting a shifter on the auction would bring in a much higher price. They have no idea.* "We need to get in on that bid."

"I didn't get approval to use funds to bid on a person, Johnny."

He shrugged. "I'll put the money up. That's not a problem."

"This is in the tens of thousands already." Lisa gestured at the bidding screen. "Are you sure?"

"Whatever we have to do to rescue her. I'm good for it, trust me. Get us in and place a bid."

"Yeah. You got it." Her face scrunched in surprise, she focused on the computer and created a fake account for them. "Here we go. How much higher do you wanna go?"

"It's at twenty-four thousand now. Put us down for thirty."

She typed obediently and the highest bid updated on the site.

Johnny snorted. "Bulldog? That's your preferred dark-web handle?"

"It's the first thing that came to mind. Did you want me to put your name down instead?"

He smirked at her and returned his attention to the screen. "That was a big jump. All these other sick bastards were movin' up a thousand at a time. We'll get this in the bag for sure—"

The highest bid updated again to thirty-five thousand dollars.

"Great." She grimaced. "It looks like this Lemonhead idiot has a ton riding on this."

"Okay. Bulldog's better than Lemonhead, I'll give you that." He gritted his teeth. "Take it up to fifty thousand."

Lisa turned slowly to look at him from the chair. "Fifty."

"That's what I said. Do it."

She typed their bid in and their Bulldog handle remained at the top of the bid list for three seconds before it changed again. "Jesus. And Lemonhead kicked it up to seventy-five."

Rubbing a hand over his mouth and wiry red beard, Johnny turned away from the computer desk. "This asshole's gonna pay, all right. Much more than seventy-five thousand when we're done with him."

He marched to the Wood Elf, caught the magical by the front of his shirt, and hauled him up before he pounded his head against the wall. The prisoner groaned. "Who the fuck is Lemonhead?"

The elf merely glared at him.

"Start talkin', asshole. My hounds are always hungry."

"You might as well kill me now, then," the prisoner muttered. "If I tell you shit about Lemonhead, I'm already dead anyway. And you won't find anyone else who'll tell you, either. This guy doesn't fuck around. He doesn't stop with only one moron who opened his trap. He takes out everyone you know and you never see him comin'."

"You didn't see me comin' either. He's leading the bid on the girl and I need to find him."

Luther snarled. "I want a turn, Johnny. See if he doesn't spill it after I take a few chunks out of him."

Rex snapped at the side of the Wood Elf's face. "No one hurts a pup. No one. We'll make him remember."

"Naw." He thumped the Boneblade member against the wall again and shoved him to the floor. "This bastard was sent to eliminate us in an alley. He doesn't know shit about Lemonhead. Whatever he gives us is useless anyway."

"You wanna try bidding again?" Lisa asked.

"Nope." The dwarf straightened and snapped his fingers. The hounds snarled at the bound magical one last time before they returned obediently to their master's side. "There are a few places I wanna try first. We might be able to find better information."

"Where are those?"

"I'll tell you when we get there." Johnny walked around the back of the computer table and grasped a chunk of cables. With a quick jerk, he ripped them apart and let them dangle over the side of the table. A few sparks sputtered. "No one's keeping tabs on the kid from here."

Lisa stood and glared at the Wood Elf before she followed her partner and his hounds out of the room.

"Hey," the prisoner called and struggled against the ropes. "Hey, you can't leave me here like this."

"Watch me." He gave him the middle finger as Lisa opened the door. Neither of them bothered to close it again before they made their way down the stairs.

"They're gonna send someone else after us when he gets out of your ropes." Lisa peered down the hall leading to the front of the club before she turned toward the back door.

"Let 'em." Johnny opened the door into the dark night and held it open for her. "They had a tip from Pete but no one knows where we're goin' now."

"Except for you, right?"

He smirked and nodded down the sidewalk. "Come on."

The colorful lights of Manhattan's Lower East Side spilled across the streets and lit everything almost as bright as daytime. He checked his watch before he scanned the rows of buildings ahead. "Eleven-thirty. Things are only startin' to kick up."

"Things are always kicked up here. Hey, watch it!" Lisa leaned toward the dwarf as a bicyclist raced past too close to the sidewalk. "See?"

"I was talking about one place in particular, though." He pointed ahead. "A friend of mine owns the bar there on the corner. Or at least he used to. It's been a long time since I've stepped foot in the place."

"You have friends in New York?"

"I have friends in a lotta places." He shrugged. "Hopefully, some of 'em stuck around longer than I did."

When they reached the corner, Johnny smirked. "That's a good sign."

"What? A rundown front door?"

"A rundown screen door, sure." He opened it with a creak and held it aside so Lisa could open the bar's front door. "Ernie's half-assed attempt to decorate. Here's to hoping nothin' else has changed too much."

The dogs trotted up the two steps after Lisa, and the screen door slapped shut behind the dwarf.

The inside of the Low Place was barely lit by dusty, bare

yellow bulbs hanging from the ceiling. Despite the grungy feel and the name that didn't particularly strike excitement in passersby, the bar was packed with magicals. Most of them had seen better days—the general crowd was fairly advanced in age and haggard-looking. They muttered in low conversation across tables or didn't bother to talk at all as the patrons focused on their booze instead of their company.

A gnome in a paperboy cap thunked his peg leg onto the wooden floor and pointed at Rex and Luther walking beside the dwarf without leashes. "Hey. You can't bring dogs in here."

Rex stopped and stared at the gnome. "Want me to bite him for you, Johnny?"

"He's not worth the time." Johnny kept walking toward the bar without so much as looking at the heckler.

Luther wagged his tail and began to sniff the sticky floor beneath the occupied bar stools. "He looks too stringy, Rex. Smells like licorice."

"Yeah…" Rex growled at the gnome who growled in response before the hound rejoined his brother.

"Hey, Ernie," the gnome shouted. "Tell this asshole he can't bring his dogs in here."

"Man, who thinks it's okay to—" The old elf slinging drinks behind the bar looked up with wrinkled, hooded eyelids and caught sight of Johnny. His scowl morphed into a tired-looking, crooked smile, and he handed an overflowing drink to a gnarled wizard at the bar before he thumped a hand on the sticky wood. "Well, I'll be damned. I thought you went off to die under a rock somewhere, Johnny."

"It's good to see you too, Ernie."

"The dogs," the gnome shouted.

"Mind your own business, Jerry." Ernie waved the prickly magical off. "The dogs are mindin' theirs. Grab a seat, Johnny. Who's your friend?"

Before the dwarf could say they weren't exactly friends, Lisa extended a hand toward the old elf and smiled. "Lisa."

"Take a seat." Wiping his hands on a wet bar rag, the proprietor turned without shaking her hand and took a bottle of Johnny Walker Black from the shelf behind the bar. He poured four fingers for his old friend and set the glass on the bar as Johnny and Lisa took the last two empty bar stools at the end. "What are you having?"

"Gin and tonic, please."

"Got a preference?"

"Wells is fine. Extra lime, though."

"Sure thing." With a smirk, Ernie turned again to retrieve another glass from the almost empty stack behind the bar.

She leaned toward Johnny with a curious smile. "He didn't even ask you."

"He doesn't have to. I only drink this right here, and anyone who knows me knows that." The dwarf took a long sip of his whiskey and nodded. "It tastes good in any city."

"Okay." She chuckled and adjusted her seat on the stool.

"Here you go." The proprietor set her overflowing gin and tonic on the bar, glanced around the rest of his establishment to make sure no one was doing anything they shouldn't, and wiped his hands on the rag again.

"How much do I owe you?" Lisa asked.

"Naw. It's on the house." The man wiped the sticky bar absently. "Only the first one, though. I can't let old friends drink for free forever. I'da been outta business ten years ago, otherwise."

Johnny snapped his fingers and lowered a fist toward his hounds. "Take a load off for a while, huh?"

Rex and Luther lowered themselves to the floor and rested their heads on their front paws. "I smell nuts up there."

"Peanuts, Johnny?"

"Ooh, never mind." Luther stretched his head out under the dwarf's bar stool to lick the crumbs on the floor. "Found some."

"So where have you been, Johnny?" Ernie asked. "I haven't heard a damn thing about you in...shit. Twenty years."

"You know I retired." He sipped his drink again.

"I asked where, not what you were doin'." His friend smirked. "I guess I should ask why you're here instead."

"He's taking a break from retirement," Lisa said. When both the dwarf and the old elf stared at her with matching frowns, she shrugged and lifted her drink to her lips. Her eyes widened. "Wow. That's...strong."

Ernie pointed at her with a crooked finger and looked at Johnny. "Are you sure she's with you?"

"For now, yeah." The dwarf settled both forearms on the edge of the bar. "She's not wrong, though. I couldn't turn this case down, and I thought I'd come to ask you a few questions."

"Exactly like back in the day." The elf opened the mini-fridge beneath him, pulled a beer out, and popped the lid off before he took a long drink. "So. What do you wanna know?"

"Anything you have about a demented bastard rollin' around the dark web callin' himself Lemonhead."

His old friend raised his eyebrows in surprise and looked thoughtful before he took another swig. "It's not much."

"Anything you can tell us would be really helpful," Lisa said.

Ernie studied her curiously. "Uh-huh. No one knows who Lemonhead is, Johnny. He maintains a strict policy of not showin' his face but he controls most of the East Coast human trafficking and drug trade."

Johnny sniffed. "It sounds a lot like Boneblade."

"Yeah, it does. But he's even higher up than that and unaffiliated." The proprietor shrugged. "This guy's had the highest bounty on his head for...shit. At least fifteen years. Every bounty hunter in this bar would love to take his ass in. Hell, every bounty hunter in the States. The price on Lemonhead could set you up in retirement twice over again if you caught him, but good luck with that."

"He's that hard to find, huh?"

"No." Ernie glanced at Lisa and took another long pull of his beer. "Everyone I know has already tried. The bastard doesn't show his face but he doesn't keep it a secret how to find him. Which I honestly don't get, but these crime lords out here do shit I'll never understand. The stories would make even you shiver, Johnny."

The dwarf snorted. "I doubt it."

"But they come back to tell the stories?" Lisa asked.

"Only the ones who don't end up dead." Ernie nodded toward Jerry the gnome and the huge half-Kilomea with a scar running down the side of his face seated at the table with him. "The rest of 'em come back crippled and pissed."

"Well, there's one bounty hunter who hasn't tried." Johnny lifted his drink. "Do you feel like helping a dwarf on this one?"

Ernie exhaled a breath through pursed lips and shook his head. "You're determined, huh?"

"I'm on a job, Ernie. You know how that works."

"Yeah, yeah. Johnny Walker doesn't give a shit about horror stories." The elf snorted and shook his head before he lifted his beer to his lips again.

"I'm tracking a kid," he added. "Her whole family was murdered, and this asshole's shellin' out some serious cash to buy her."

Ernie choked on his drink and thunked the bottle onto the bar. A few of the patrons turned to look at him but he didn't pay them any attention as he wiped his dripping chin with the back of a gnarled hand. "Shit, Johnny."

"Do you have anything else?"

"Yeah." The elf swallowed and cleared his throat. "Yeah, I have something for you. There's a Monsters Ball tomorrow night at Falcon Towers in the Financial District. It kicks off at eight-thirty. I'd bet you this girl you're looking for will be there too. Those assholes don't throw parties like this unless they're gettin' down to some seriously nasty business."

Johnny nodded. "How about a way to get in?"

"Sorry. I don't deal in the how, Johnny. Only the what, when, where, and who."

"Yeah, okay. What about someone who does deal in the how?"

Ernie pressed his wrinkled lips together and shook his head slowly. "Your best bet is to raid that place tomorrow if you can."

"That's not good enough." He knocked back the rest of his drink and slammed the glass on the counter. "It's good to see you, Ernie."

"You too."

The dwarf slid off the barstool and whistled for his hounds. "Let's go."

Lisa took a long drink of her gin and tonic that was still only half-empty when she finished and slid off her stool too. "Thanks, Ernie."

"Uh-huh." The old elf jerked his chin at her. "You're learning from the best, lady. Pay attention."

"Oh, I'm not—"

"Lisa," Johnny called as he beat Jerry the gnome's attempt at mean-mugging him again and flipped the peg-legged bounty hunter the middle finger. "Time's up."

With a sigh, she hurried after him and caught the gnome glaring at her now too. "Do you have a problem?"

Jerry thumped his wooden leg onto the floor again. "Yeah, I'm lookin' at it."

"Enjoy your drink." Shaking her head, she crossed the bar and barely managed to catch the screen door as it swung into her face. "Johnny."

The dwarf marched down the sidewalk with his hounds trotting at his side.

"What's wrong? We got a good lead for tomorrow night."

"That's too far away," he grumbled. "Someone's gotta have more information."

"Like who?" She pulled her phone out of her pocket and scrolled through the pictures she'd taken of the file on Amanda Courier's case. "The only real lead we had was finding the Boneblade through Pete. Which we did—"

"The Boneblade is a fucking Least Killifish now."

Lisa stepped around the large group of young people who stood outside the next bar they passed. The venue pumped out what she thought was heavy metal with all the screaming instead of actual words. Everyone in the group wore dark, heavy makeup and black clothes with silver studs, and two of them sported mohawks. She waved the cloud of cigarette smoke out of her face and ignored the goth group's laughter. "A what?"

"It's a tiny fish in the Everglades." Johnny shoved his hands into his jacket pockets. "Lemonhead's the Redfish we're after now and Ernie can't be the only magical in this damn city who knows anything about the guy."

"He said no one knows who Lemonhead is."

"I know what he said. I'm not saying he's wrong but he's wrong. I'll find something."

"Hey, Johnny." Luther pressed his nose to the sidewalk, his tail wagging furiously. "There were four other dogs here, like, an hour ago. We should find 'em. Friends in the city, remember?"

"I need a bush." Rex uttered a low whine. "Johnny, where's all the grass? I need grass or at least somethin' soft to shit on. Come on."

The dwarf stopped and looked at the dog. "Go ahead."

"For real? On the sidewalk?"

He glanced around and snatched up a plastic bag from the gutter. "Hurry, Rex."

"Okay, okay." Rex sniffed in a tight circle and hunkered to do his business.

"What?" Luther stepped away from him and lifted his head to

both look and sniff up and down the street. "No one wants to see that."

"I can't hold it."

When Lisa realized what the hound was doing, she looked away quickly and folded her arms. "Our best lead to follow now is to get into that Monsters Ball tomorrow. Whatever that is."

Johnny fixed her with a surprised look and ignored Rex's relieved sighs filling his mind. "You're with the Bounty Hunter Department and you don't know."

"I'm not a bounty hunter, Johnny. I'm only the middleman."

Shaking his head, he stooped to pick the dog's mess up with the plastic bag and tied the handles together in a tight knot before he continued down the sidewalk. "The Monsters Balls don't come around very often, but when they do, you can be damn sure every high-level criminal and dark magical with their hands in the same fucking pie is gonna be there."

"Including Lemonhead."

"Yeah, but we won't only be up against him if we crash the crime party."

Lisa cast him a sidelong glance and smirked. "Don't tell me you're worried about that part."

"Going to a Monsters Ball doesn't fall under keeping things simple. Anything could happen."

"Well then, we'll take care of it. Roll in, grab Amanda, and roll out. And you can take the trash out however the hell you want."

With a grunt, he tossed the smelly plastic bag into a pile of already stinking trash at the mouth of an alley and wiped his hands on his jeans. "Yeah. I guess that'll hafta do."

CHAPTER NINE

The next morning, Lisa knocked on Johnny's hotel room door and it opened immediately. "Hey. I thought you might wanna get breakfast."

"I already did." At her confused frown, he stepped aside and gestured into his room. "Come on in."

She stepped inside and turned to frown at him as he shut the door. "The restaurant's only been open for fifteen minutes."

"Room service kicks in early, though."

"You ordered room service?"

"Why not?"

Lisa shook her head. "And you paid for it, right?"

"I put it on the room."

"Johnny, I said I wasn't gonna pay for all your meals."

He stopped and stared at her. "Are you fronting the hotel bill too?"

"No, that's on the Bureau."

"Then so is breakfast." He shrugged and gestured toward the tray on the desk. "Help yourself."

With a sigh, she moved toward the desk and found Rex and Luther lying between the bed and the window and going to town on what was left of their T-bone steaks, which was essentially only the T-bones. "These dogs get better treatment than most people I know."

"They work harder and with better results, too. Look, we have orange juice, coffee, toast, eggs, and bacon. That's a given. And an extra plate and silverware. So go ahead."

Lisa tried not to smile when she turned and to where the dwarf sat on the edge of his bed and munched a handful of bacon. "You planned this, didn't you?"

"I decided it was possible you'd knock on my door, ready to head out. Don't make a big deal out of it." He stretched for the coffee mug on the bedside table and took a long sip.

"All right. Well, thanks for breakfast, then."

"Thank the Bureau."

When they'd gone through everything on the breakfast tray, Lisa refilled her coffee mug and leaned back in the hotel room's single armchair. "So, we have eleven hours until the Monsters Ball and I thought—"

The dwarf rolled his eyes. "Here we go."

"I'm serious." She blew on her coffee and took a tentative sip. "In all the times I've been to New York City, I've never gotten to see it, you know? It's always going from one place to another for whatever assignment and holing up in hotel rooms like this. We should get out. See the city."

"You go do whatever you want. I'm good here." He swung his legs onto the bed with a grunt, leaned back against the neatly stacked pillows, and folded his hands behind his head.

"Come on, Johnny. It'll be fun." Lisa grinned. "I can finally do the whole *Sex In the City* thing. Take the kinda tour you take when you're in Manhattan for fun. And you know your way around. I have the perfect guide."

He closed his eyes with a heavy sigh. "I don't know what the hell you said but it's not happening."

"Johnny." Luther's head popped up over the edge of the bed

and his tongue flopped out onto the top of the neatly made bedspread. "We want out too. A tour, Johnny."

"Yeah." The sound of Rex crunching on the T-bone filled the hotel room. "We got a few things in mind. You can't keep us in this room forever."

"Please, Johnny?" With a soft laugh, Lisa set her coffee mug on the desk and leaned forward. "You won't regret it."

"Whenever someone says that it usually means the exact opposite."

"Oh, come on. You can't come out of retirement simply to stay in a hotel room all day."

"Watch me."

Luther jumped up and slapped his front paws on the bedspread. "See? She's got the right idea. I need air. Rex is farting in my face over here."

His brother crunched the bone again. "Then move your face."

With a heavy sigh, the dwarf pushed off the pillows and waved her forward. "There's only one way to settle this."

Her eyes widened above a hesitant smile. "And that is?"

"Rochambeau."

"Gesundheit."

He gave her a deadpan stare. "That wasn't a sneeze."

"Well, I don't know what you're talking about."

"You're a Yankee through and through, aren't ya?"

She laughed. "What?"

"Get up on the bed. Come on. I won't bitecha."

"Not until you tell me what ro shampoo is."

"Rochambeau." He waved her onto the bed again a little more forcefully. "Does rock-paper-scissors ring a bell?"

"Oh." Smoothing her hair away from her face, Lisa stood and approached the bed slowly. "That's how we'll decide our day?"

"Like I said, darlin'. There's only one way to settle it."

"I can't believe I'm doing this." She climbed tentatively onto the bed and stopped well away from the center.

With a snort, Johnny crossed his legs beneath him and held his hands out, one fist above his opposite palm. "You do know how to play, don't you?"

"I know how to play."

"Ro-cham-beau." He held her gaze the whole time and went with paper.

Lisa glanced at their hands and grinned. "Scissors beat paper, Johnny."

"Shit."

"I'm ready to go." She slid off the bed and gestured expansively. "We can't desecrate the rules of Roachy…whatever. Rock-paper-scissors."

"Hey, Johnny." Luther uttered a sharp yip. "Johnny, do one with us. Come on."

"Yeah, okay." The dwarf hopped off the bed and brushed past a completely confused Lisa to make his way between the bed and window toward the hounds.

"What are you doing?"

"I don't want the boys to feel left out." The dwarf hunkered down and both dogs walked toward him before they sat on their haunches. "Ready?"

Rex and Luther both barked softly. "You're on, Johnny."

"We're so gonna win. Not because you let us, either."

He smirked. "You know how it goes. Three counts and you lay out those paws."

Lisa chuckled with confusion and shook her head. "What is happening right now?"

"Ro-cham-beaux." Johnny bounced both fists three times, and his hounds did the same with a forepaw.

"Ha! We win!"

"Paper beats rock, Johnny. Yes!"

Both hounds slapped their paws on the tops of his fists, panting in excitement.

"All right." The dwarf pushed to his feet. "You win fair and square. Where do you wanna go?"

She folded her arms. "Central Park's a good place to—"

"Hold on." He held a finger up for her to be silent. "Just a sec."

"You're asking the dogs?"

"They won."

"Wow. He's asking the dogs."

Luther stood, his tail thumping against the side of the mattress. "Central Park. That's a good one."

"Lots of dogs in Central Park," Rex added. "Ooh, hey. And that statue of a dog. The Balto guy you told us about once."

"Balto!" Luther punctuated that with another sharp yip.

Johnny sniggered and ran a hand through his hair before he turned to face Lisa with a shrug. "I guess it's Central Park."

"Uh-huh." She frowned at the dogs as they followed the dwarf toward the door but couldn't hold back a smile. "That's what the dogs told you?"

"Would you believe me if I said yes?"

"Honestly, I have no idea."

"Come on, lady. Keep up!" Luther spun in a tight circle as Johnny retrieved his leather jacket from the hook near the door. "You don't wanna miss it."

"Balto! We get to see Balto!" Rex uttered a low whine as his master opened the door, but both dogs stayed there until the dwarf snapped his fingers for them to join him in the hall.

Lisa closed the door behind her and followed them toward the elevator.

"Johnny, this'll be great. You'll love it." Rex stopped to sniff a suspicious stain on the wall.

"Wait." Lisa hurried to catch up with them. "Can you truly hear your dogs?"

Rex sneezed and bashed his head against the wall before he shook it off and trotted to catch up.

Johnny smirked. "Gesundheit."

CHAPTER TEN

They had to go through Times Square first to get to Central Park, and Johnny was the only one who wasn't practically jumping up and down about it.

"Wow." Lisa gazed wide-eyed at the blazing billboards and brilliant colors. "Look at all the lights."

"They are kinda hard to miss, yeah."

She laughed. "Are you committed to not enjoying yourself?"

"Only when I came to New York for another reason."

"I thought we went over this."

He sniffed. "I'm here, ain't I?"

"You are. Okay, well...try to loosen up a little while we're out, okay? There's nothing we can do until tonight. And then it's all business."

"Yeah. Loosen up." The dwarf rolled his shoulders. "I'll work on it."

"Johnny. Johnny!" Luther barked. "Look at the naked guy!"

"Why would I wanna do that?"

"Do what?" Lisa looked down and clapped a hand over her mouth. "Oh, my God. I thought the Naked Cowboy was only...I don't know. Only on YouTube or something."

Johnny shoved his hands in his pockets and kept walking. Rex and Luther tagged along at the end of the thin leashes he'd purchased at a Walgreens. "He looks real to me."

"He even has the guitar in front of his crotch and everything." She barked a laugh. "I can't believe he's still here."

They passed the middle-aged man standing in nothing but cowboy boots, tighty-whities, and a huge cowboy hat with his guitar strap slung over his shoulder. The Naked Cowboy jerked his chin at Johnny and pointed with a grin. "Hey. I haven't seen you in a while."

"Yeah, you too." The dwarf kept walking.

"Wait, you know him?"

"Everyone knows him." He pulled his sunglasses out of his jacket pocket and slid them on. "You haven't been out much here, huh?"

"Well, I didn't make it up simply to screw with you." Lisa turned over her shoulder for another glance at the Naked Cowboy and shook her head. "This is great."

They pushed through the crowds of people milling around under all the flashing lights and scrolling signs.

"Johnny, they have all the food here." Luther stopped to sniff a hot dog stand upwind on their right. "Come on. How 'bout hot dogs today?"

Rex snorted. "I'm not sure I wanna eat anything with the word dog in it."

"Hot dogs aren't made from dogs."

"Aren't they? Honestly?"

Luther walked faster toward the stand but stopped every time the leash got even remotely taut. "Come on, Johnny."

"Central Park. That was the deal."

Lisa gave him a confused glance. "Yeah, I know."

He stared directly ahead. *Talking to my hounds is gonna get real old real fast if she thinks everything's aimed at her.*

"I've never had a hotdog from a street stand before," she added. "What about—ah!"

A man dressed head to toe in a Batman costume—complete with mask, utility belt, and cape—leapt out from behind the hotdog stand and spread his cape behind him. "I...am...*Batman,*" he all but growled.

She burst out laughing. "I can see that."

The man swirled his cape around him as he turned and leapt in front of another group of pedestrians. "I'm watching you!"

Two women in the group shrieked and hurried away from him.

"Yo, Batman!" the hotdog vendor shouted. "Take that shit somewhere else, huh? I'm tryin' to make a livin' here!"

Batman zig-zagged across the sidewalk to crouch behind a trashcan to wait for his next unsuspecting victims.

"Never mind the hotdog," Lisa muttered. "But I love this city."

"We'll find somewhere better." Johnny slid his hands in his pockets and the slack leashes trailed from the sides of his jacket.

"Oh, yeah? Where?"

"You'll see."

"Central Park first, Johnny." Luther couldn't decide whether to keep his nose to the cement or to raise it and catch every other scent on the air.

Rex raised his head and howled. "Balto!"

A woman wearing at least five different hats one on top of the other and pulling two roller suitcases behind her dropped one of the handles to point at Luther. "You have a dancin' dog there, mister. Ha! Look at him go. Buckin' bronco, dog!"

She fell into a fit of cackling laughter and turned to continue to point at Luther sniffing the ground, then the sky, then the ground again.

"She thinks you're a horse." Rex abandoned his focus on his brother when a man crammed a huge sandwich into his mouth as he walked past and left a trail of dripping cheese sauce behind him. "This is the best."

"I'm not a horse."

"I know that."

"I'm a—pigeon! Hey!"

Johnny whistled sharply, and both hounds whipped their heads up to look at him. "If either of you goes off chasing anything, we're gonna have us a long chat we all know you won't like."

"Yeah, yeah."

"Those birds are asking for it."

Lisa smiled at the dogs. "How did you train them to stay so close to you like that?"

"They know who's boss." He shrugged. "And I let 'em run around in the swamp until they're too tired to think about not listening."

Rex's laughter filled his master's head. "Dumb answer, but okay."

"It's 'cause we like you, Johnny. And you feed us."

"Except for right now. One trash can, Johnny. I'll knock it over and you give me twenty seconds."

The dwarf stopped to let a string of men and women dressed in brightly dyed, gossamer fabric with flower crowns on their heads and their faces painted like butterflies dance across that section of Times Square. The last of them pounded on a tambourine as she lifted it skyward and lowered it in rhythm.

"I'll take Batman over this."

"You gotta hand it to 'em, though," Lisa said. "They got creative with the costumes."

"I guess."

The woman with the tambourine paused in front of Johnny and batted her eyelashes at him before she darted after the rest of her troupe.

"And there it is." Lisa shook her head as they kept moving.

"I don't know what you're talking about," he grumbled.

A group of middle-aged women with designer handbags and stiletto heels walked past with to-go coffees in their hands. Two of them slowed to turn and watch the dwarf and flashed him appraising smiles.

"That. You didn't see the cougars checking you out?"

"You can't call 'em cougars if I'm almost twice their age."

She frowned and considered that. "No, I guess not."

"I don't get it." Rex sniffed the women's eclectic mixture of perfume and sneezed. "Those females wouldn't look twice at you if they were in the Everglades."

Johnny smirked. *I'm not gonna find women like that in the Everglades.*

"Yeah, but check out the poodle," Luther said. "Man, she's lookin' twice at me. Hot dog."

"Don't even try it with the city types, Luther. We're country hounds. Doesn't work."

"The way she's waggin' her tail says otherwise, brother."

"Trust me. I saw a documentary by that historian. That, uh... that Walt Disney guy. *Lady and the Tramp.*" Rex snorted as his brother barked at the poodle. "That was the one exception, man. Not gonna work for you."

"You don't know." Luther turned reluctantly away from the poodle when his leash drew taut and hurried to walk at Johnny's side again. "Man, I didn't even have a chance."

"That's what I'm sayin'."

The dwarf felt like he could breathe a little easier when they left Times Square and crossed the last few blocks before they finally entered Central Park. *At least I can pretend there's fresh air here.*

"Now this is what I'm talkin' about," Rex said. "Look at all those trees."

"Trees. Let's go mark some trees. Come on, Johnny. Let us off."

"Sorry, boys." He gazed at the tall trees and down again when two kids ran screaming from one of their parents chasing after them with giant, exaggerated steps. "Rules are rules. Hounds gotta be leashed."

"And not kids? What gives?"

"Yeah, they're ten times messier."

Lisa smiled as they strolled down the walkway. The city sounds had faded into a distant background roar and they could hear the birds and the laughter of people enjoying themselves. Cyclists passed on the bike paths, and two elderly men sat side by side on a park bench, reading their newspapers without looking at each other.

"Johnny." She caught his upper arm in excitement and pulled away again quickly when he looked at her hand. "Sorry. I only... You can hear that, right? The music?"

"Yeah. So?"

"So that's the carousel."

He exhaled a long sigh and stared directly ahead.

"It's right on the other side of that dog statue. Look." She pointed beyond the statue at the carousel already packed with kids and adults. "Come on, Johnny. Ride on the carousel with me."

"No."

"It's beautiful out here. Come on. It's spring in Central Park! How can you say no to that?"

"Damn easily, actually."

"You're not even trying."

"You said 'try to loosen up' not 'try to ride a carousel in Central Park.'"

She pursed her lips. "Maybe you'll change your mind when we get there."

They approached the huge statue of the dog that looked more like a wolf than anything else. Rex thrust his head skyward and howled. "Balto!"

"Come on, Johnny." Luther panted and glanced from the dwarf to the statue. "We gotta pay our respects."

He snorted. "Statue first. It's on the way."

The bronze statue erected on a mound of rock glinted in the sunlight that spilled through the trees.

"Yes. Johnny, we gotta get closer."

"To pay our respects."

Johnny took his hounds to the edge of the rock and stared at the statue. "Sled dog, huh?"

"He's a hero, Johnny." Luther sniffed at the base of the rock.

"Saved a lotta human pups, too. And grown ones. You remember the stories better than we do." Rex knocked against his brother's shoulder as they passed each other, their noses to the grass.

"I read something about Balto once," Lisa said. "He helped to save an entire town in Nome, Alaska in the early nineteen-hundreds. Maybe 1920."

"1925," Rex corrected. "A damn hero. Johnny told us all about him."

"I think that was when antibiotics were first—what?" Lisa glanced at the sound of water hitting rock and found both hounds with their legs lifted over the bottom of the statue's rocky base. She wrinkled her nose. "Oh…"

"All right." Trying not to laugh, Johnny whistled and tugged lightly on the leashes. "You've paid your respects. Let's go."

"Yeah. Thanks, Johnny."

Rex howled again. "That was epic."

The music from the carousel grew louder as they approached, along with the shrieking laughter of the kids riding the damn thing incessantly.

"Okay, let's try this again." Lisa's wide eyes glistened eagerly as she grinned at the carousel and the trees in full spring bloom all around them. "Only one ride."

Johnny shook his head. "No."

MARTHA CARR & MICHAEL ANDERLE

"Please. This has been on my list for—" She froze and swallowed awkwardly.

He paused with a slow smirk and turned to look at her. "You have a list?"

A light blush rose on her cheeks. "Only a small one. Things I wanna do in New York. That kinda thing."

"Uh-huh." His smile widened as he nodded at her. "Let's see it."

"What? No. You don't wanna see this."

"Are you embarrassed by your wish list, Agent Breyer?"

She flashed him a scathing glance. "No. It's only…personal."

"All right, I don't have to see it. List 'em for me."

"Johnny…"

"Maybe there's something on there we can go do that won't make me miss the swamp more than I already do."

She glared at him, glanced at the trees, and sighed. "Fine."

"Let's hear it."

Lisa pulled her phone out of her pocket and scrolled through her notes until she found her list. "Okay. Carousel at Central Park."

"We covered that one. Next."

"Go to the Plaza Hotel for tea."

He snorted. "Tea. Nope."

"Ride a gondola in Central Park."

"The only boat I step into is my flat-bottom airboat. Next."

She avoided his gaze as the blush deepened in her cheeks. "Go to the top of 30 Rock."

"Good grief."

"Are you gonna say no to everything?"

Johnny glanced at her phone. "Is there anything else on the list?"

"No." She glared at him.

"Then yes." He stepped away from a four-year-old girl who

babbled excitedly to her mom about riding the carousel and hauled the woman toward it. "Moving on. Are you hungry?"

"Well…not now."

"Come on." He nodded down the path and kept moving to put more distance between him and the carousel. "This will make you forget all about that list."

Lisa shoved her phone into her pocket and walked slowly after him with a final longing look at the carousel. "I seriously doubt it."

CHAPTER ELEVEN

"Okay, wait." Lisa pulled her hair away from her face that glistened with sweat and tied it in a loose ponytail. "Where are we now?"

"West Village." Johnny sniffed and turned the corner onto Bleeker Street.

"We're almost there, right?"

"Yeah. It's right here." He studied her quickly and gave her a brief smile. "Are you feeling winded, Agent Breyer?"

"If I'd known you wanted to take us all the way here from Central Park, I'd have gotten us a taxi."

He chuckled. "I like walking. Plus, there's nothing like a good long walk through Manhattan to work up an appetite."

"Yes. Food!" Rex panted heavily and licked his muzzle. "That's what we're doin', right, Johnny?"

"Thank the canine gods." Luther sniffed the sidewalk and left a string of drool puddles in his wake. "I thought I'd have to start eating shoes if we waited any longer."

"Everyone's gonna love this," the dwarf said. "There's only one thing I gotta do every time I make it out here, no exceptions."

"Walk for an hour and a half without giving your partner a little heads' up?"

Again with the partner business? Let it go, Johnny. "I gotta get a slice of New York pizza. And John's is the real deal."

"It doesn't have anything to do with the fact that you guys have the same name, does it?" Lisa shrugged out of her jacket and tossed it over her arm.

"John and Johnny are not the same name." The dwarf nodded at the long string of people standing on the sidewalk in front of them. "And no. He could've named the place Tim's Pizza and that line would still stretch this far out the door every day."

"Wow. That's...some line." She grimaced and adjusted her aviator sunglasses.

"It moves quickly. And we still have time to kill, right?" They reached the end of the line and stopped. Johnny looked at his federal tagalong and raised his eyebrows. "Try to loosen up, huh?"

She gaped at him, her mouth open in exasperation. Then, she laughed. "Yeah, Johnny. I can loosen up."

"Perfect."

Over half an hour later, they finally stepped up to the window to order their pizza.

"Yeah, give me a Hawaiian with extra pineapple," Johnny said, "and three waters. Are you good with Hawaiian?"

Lisa shrugged. "Sure."

"You got it." The man shouted their order to the kitchen behind him, the dwarf paid the man in cash, and they stepped aside to wait for their food.

"John makes every single one of them back there by hand," he said. "It's the best damn pizza you can get in this city."

"It had better be with this kinda line."

"If it wasn't, it wouldn't have the line."

"Chris?" the guy behind the food counter shouted.

A man in skinny jeans and a baseball cap stepped forward to

take his pizza box and a handful of napkins before he turned to head to a seat outside. He stopped when he saw Johnny and gave the dwarf a hasty study before he shook a finger at him. "Hey. I know you."

"Probably not."

"Yeah. Yeah, I do. Aren't you that guy from that show?"

"Yep." He nodded toward the tables and turned away from the man. "Go eat your pizza."

"I knew it." The stranger walked away, maneuvered around the other patrons with his giant pizza box, and darted Johnny another look over his shoulder.

"What show?" Lisa asked.

He shook his head. "It doesn't matter. It was a long time ago."

"Oh, come on. Tell me."

"No."

She folded her arms. "I showed you my list."

"You read me your list. Look it up if you're so interested."

"Maybe I will."

The guy at the window called Johnny's name shortly after that, and they took their food and moved away to find a place to sit and eat outside.

When they settled and Johnny opened the box, Lisa stared at the slices inside. "This is huge."

Rex snorted. "That's what she said. Right, Johnny?"

Luther responded with a high-energy laugh. "Literally. Come on, Johnny. Show your hounds some love."

He cracked a bottle of water and leaned over to pour some into his cupped hand for Rex first, then Luther. "That's New York pizza for you. It's still hard to not eat all of it."

"And you're gonna eat the rest? I can't have more than one slice?"

The hounds lapped the last of the water and he shook his hand and took two pepperoni and extra-pineapple slices. "No. Dogs who want pineapple on their pizza get extra."

"Johnny, you're the best."

"Seriously, I could kiss you."

"He could kiss you for me."

As soon as the slices touched the ground, Rex and Luther were all over them. They licked the pools of grease and loose pineapple piled on too high to stick to the melted cheese.

"Of course they do." Lisa shook her head and stared at the massive slices inside the box. "There's no way this isn't gonna fall apart when I pick it up."

The dwarf leaned forward and rested his forearms on his thighs. He smirked as he watched her try to lift the crust with one hand and support the greasy, floppy end of her pizza with the other. She managed a small bite but couldn't get the rest of the slice to do what she wanted.

"Yeah. Maybe I need a fork."

He chuckled. "And you've never eaten New York pizza."

"It would seem not."

Folding his slice in half, Johnny held the fold with both hands and took a massive bite. "It keeps all the good stuff right where you want it."

"Fold the pizza." Lisa laughed with embarrassment. "So simple."

"See? Now you're gettin' it. Keep it simple." He took another massive bite and wiped the grease from his beard and mustache with an already crumpled napkin. "If I missed anything about New York, it's this."

"Johnny, if I'd ever been to New York," Luther muttered through the snuffling of his perfectly content pizza-eating, "I'd miss this too."

"I already miss it," Rex added.

Lisa took his advice and folded her slice in half for another bite. "Yeah, it's good. I'm still not sure if it's worth waiting in line that long, though."

He lowered his pizza and scowled at her. "That's crossing a line."

She laughed. "Sore point. I get it. My bad."

"Uh-huh."

They ate their pizza and watched the other New Yorkers eating their slices from John's Pizzeria on Bleeker. It seemed most of the pedestrians had boxes in their hands or at least a slice taken from their friends' boxes. A construction crew at the end of the street had stopped to take their lunch too, and Lisa thought she even saw a John's Pizzeria box on the open tailgate of a truck.

"Oh, no." She wiped the grease that dribbled down her chin and nodded at a woman who walked toward them down the sidewalk. "Is that woman walking her cat?"

"It's not the weirdest thing." Johnny opened a bottle of water for himself and handed her the third.

"Thanks. What's the weirdest thing?"

"On a leash? I've seen ferrets. An iguana. Hell, people sometimes."

Her eyes widened and she guzzled the water. "Only in New York, right?"

"Probably not. You merely see everything in one place here."

"It almost sounds like you know New York as much as a New Yorker does."

"Something like that." He shoveled another huge bite of pizza into his mouth and flicked a stray piece of pineapple onto the ground for the dogs. *Something we're not gettin' into right now. Or ever.*

Lisa studied him as she twisted the lid onto her bottled water. "Where did you live before Florida?"

Johnny grunted. "Too many places to count."

"Okay, well give me one."

"That cabin in the Everglades is the only place I'm interested in calling home. We'll leave it at that."

"Okay." She tilted her head and took another bite. "What if you could live in any place in the world? Where would you go?"

"That cabin in the Everglades."

She laughed and fought to keep the pizza from spraying out of her mouth. "I mean if money weren't an option."

"It's not. I was right where I wanted to be before you and Nelson arrived and turned the whole thing upside down."

Swallowing quickly, she snatched another napkin and wiped the grease trailing down the side of her wrist. "Well, when we get that Lemonhead asshole tonight and bring Amanda back with us, you can return to the swamp and...whatever you do down there."

Luther licked his chops and raised his head to sniff the box between the dwarf and the federal agent. "We won't be eatin' a feast like this, that's for sure. Got any extras, Johnny?"

"Yeah, me too." Rex licked up the last few pieces of pineapple from the ground. "I could keep goin' forever."

Johnny grabbed two more slices from the box and dropped them in front of the dogs. Neither hound said another word as they attacked the food in the way only good hounds who knew the value of Hawaiian pizza could.

He dusted his hands off and sniffed. "Damn straight."

CHAPTER TWELVE

On their way to the hotel, Johnny was quieter than usual. To anyone who knew it, this was significant.

"Is there anything else I have to see before we get our heads in the game for tonight?" Lisa asked and gulped the last of her bottled water.

"Nope." He belched loudly and thumped his fist against his chest. "I could go for a nap, though."

"You can sleep before going after a target?" She tossed her water bottle into the trash and shook her head. "In the middle of the day?"

"Technically, it's late afternoon. Lack of sleep is the number-one..." He slowed six feet in front of the open doorway to a smoke shop and clenched his teeth.

The memory he'd spent the last fifteen years trying to remove from the forefront of his mind flared again in vivid detail—as vivid as the first time the pictures had been laid out in front of him. Dawn's small, helpless body sprawled across the doorway. She had blood in her hair exactly like the picture of Amanda Coulier's twin sister. And that fucking giraffe in the corner of the frame appeared in at least two photos with the same dent in the metal side of the doorway.

No.

"Number-one what?" Lisa twisted to look over her shoulder, found that he'd fallen behind, and spun with a frustrated gesture. "Johnny? You can't start with something like that and simply drop it halfway through." The dwarf's fists clenched so tightly around the ends of the hounds' leashes, all his knuckles popped at the same time.

"What's wrong?"

"That fucking giraffe."

She laughed uncertainly. "The what?"

"I've seen that before." Johnny glanced at the marquee over the shop. *They didn't bother to catch the fucking storefront in the crime scene photos.*

"This giraffe?" Rex poked his head through the doorway to sniff the three-foot-tall bronze statue of a giraffe bending its neck toward the ground. "Want me to shake it, Johnny?"

"Yeah, we'll play fetch," Luther added.

He snapped his fingers and both dogs sat. With a low growl, the dwarf reached for each of their collars and unhooked the leashes, which he let fall onto the sidewalk without a second thought. "Stay close, boys."

"Johnny?"

"You can stay out here or you can follow me, but if you do come with me, you do everything I say and save the questions for later." He didn't wait for her to reply before he strode into the establishment and headed directly to the counter.

"Welcome to Vape Your Day." The clerk was a man in his mid-twenties with giant rings in his ears and piercings all over his sharp-featured face. "Woah, man. Sorry. No dogs allowed—"

Johnny thumped a hand on the glass top of the display case. "Who's the owner of this place?"

"Hey, man." The clerk raised his hands. "I only work here—"

"And you have a fucking boss! Give me a name!"

"Yeah, yeah. Sure. Brad."

"Brad what?"

"Brad...D-Denton, man. What gives?"

He nodded toward the door at the back of the shop. "Does he live upstairs?"

"Yeah, man. It's his store."

The dwarf stormed through the rows of hand-blown glass pieces and smoking paraphernalia and his dogs trotted at his heels.

"Hey, you can't go back there!"

He jerked so hard on the doorknob that the screws stripped and the knob came off in his hand. The door pounded against the wall and almost knocked over a whole shelf of hookahs, and he tossed the brass knob onto the floor. "Watch me."

Lisa hurried through the shop after him.

"Hey, lady!" The clerk pointed at the stairwell behind the door where Johnny and the hounds had disappeared. "He can't do that. Tell him he can't—"

"FBI business." She flashed him her badge without sparing him so much as a glance. "Stay where you are."

"Shit." He shrank away from the counter and stared at the ceiling. "I knew I should've called in sick today."

Johnny's boots clomped heavily up the dark stairwell to the second story and the hallway that stretched across the apartment level above the row of shops below. He glanced at the three doors at the top of the stairs, judged which one was directly above the smoke shop, and headed toward it.

"Johnny. Will you at least tell me what's—"

"I said no questions." The dwarf pounded furiously on the door. "Denton! Open up!"

A rustle of movement came from inside the apartment but no one answered.

"This is not the day to fuck with me, asshole. Open the door!"

Rex uttered a low growl. "Definitely someone in there, Johnny."

"Someone scared," Luther added.

"Fine. We'll do this my way start to finish." Johnny reached into the front pocket of his jeans and pulled out a handful of large black beads. He chose two, replaced the rest in his pocket, and crushed the tops of the two he'd retained to activate their timers. The sticky substance now coating the underside of each made them an easy addition to the doorknob of this asshole's apartment. Johnny stepped back and hooked his thumbs through his belt loops. "You might wanna cover your ears."

"What?" Lisa's eyes widened and she stepped toward him. "Johnny, this is—"

"I have a license!"

The tiny, precise explosives he'd spent the last fifteen years perfecting to flush out fish and smaller critters in the Everglades detonated with a deafening crack, followed by the ping of broken metal and the thunk of the doorknob on the floor. She clamped both hands over her ears and doubled over with a grimace.

He stormed toward the door and thrust it open with one swift kick of his heavy boot. After a sharp whistle, he drew his knife from his belt to flick it open. Rex and Luther snarled and leapt through the cloud of dust and plaster beside him.

"What the fuck, man?" A guy wearing a red tracksuit jumped from the brown swiveling armchair with tattered upholstery and reached for a firearm on the table beside him.

Rex leapt at the man and caught him squarely in the chest with his front paws before he brought him down.

"Vinny!" A second man—this one with slicked-back hair and wearing nothing but a pair of black-and-white basketball shorts —managed to retrieve the automatic rifle beside him on the long folding banquet table and lifted it in an arc to aim it at Rex. "Fucking dogs—ah!"

Luther clamped his jaws around the second man's ankle and

jerked fiercely as he shook his head and snarled around a mouth full of asshole leg.

Johnny stormed toward the man who tried to kick the hound off his ankle, his knife raised in his hand.

"FBI! Don't move!" Lisa stormed into the apartment with her service pistol leveled at the second man's chest. She kicked the door shut behind her but without a doorknob, it slammed against the doorframe and bounced open again. With an aggravated sigh, she ignored it and moved farther into the apartment.

The dwarf whistled sharply and cut through the scuffling struggle of Vinny trying to remove himself from beneath Rex and the second man's shouts of disbelief and pain as Luther played tug of war with his ankle. "Luther. Release."

The hound obeyed immediately and backed away two steps to snarl at his target with his hackles raised. "I could've ripped it off, Johnny."

"Drop your weapon," Lisa ordered.

The man with the rifle widened his eyes at her, gauged the aim of her weapon against how quickly he could lift his own, and dropped the rifle onto the table.

Johnny pointed his blade tip at the second man. "If you reach for that again, Luther won't hold back on the other leg."

"Fuck." The man glanced at his ankle and the thin trickle of blood that trailed toward his bare foot.

"Get this fucking dog off me, man. I fucking hate—"

Rex snapped in Vinny's face, and the man fell silent.

"Good work, Rex." The dwarf emitted another sharp whistle in a lower tone. "Step down."

"I had him, Johnny." Rex responded with a low growl and finally removed all fifty-five pounds of coonhound from Vinny's chest.

As soon as the dog released him, the man sat quickly and reached for the automatic pistol on the table.

Johnny threw his knife and buried it in the chipped wooden

floor between Vinny's legs, less than an inch from his crotch. "Don't fucking move."

"Jesus." The man raised both his hands and stared at the knife. "What the hell do you want, asshole?"

"Answers." He strode toward Vinny, caught a fistful of his red tracksuit, and jerked his blade out of the floor with the other hand. With no apparent strain, he hauled the guy to his feet and shoved him into the chair. The knifepoint pressed into the prisoner's ribcage as Johnny leered at him. "Is that other piece of shit with a new hole in his leg Brad?"

"What?" The man in basketball shorts looked from the enraged dwarf to the federal agent with her weapon leveled at his chest. "No, man. Brad ain't here—"

"Shut your fucking mouth, Jay—"

"You shut yours." Johnny pressed his knife harder against Vinny's side and gave the front of the man's tracksuit a quick shake. "I'm looking for Brad Denton and you morons are gonna tell me where he is. Now."

"He's not—ah! Hey, back up with that knife, will ya?" Vinny glanced at the dwarf's knife-hand. "Do you know how hard it is to think with something like that stickin' in your ribs?"

"Yeah, actually. I do." He shoved his face closer to the man's until their noses almost touched. "If you move in any way I don't like, my hound will be on top of you again, this time with his teeth around your throat."

"Fuck, man. I get it." The prisoner nodded. "Fine."

Johnny shoved the man against the swiveling armchair, released him, and stepped back. "Someone had better start talking. Brad Denton."

"Man, he ain't been here for months," Jay said, his hands still raised as he watched Lisa and her gun warily.

"This is his apartment and his smoke shop downstairs," Johnny countered. "Where is he?"

"Shit, man." Vinny tried to calm his breathing and rubbed the sore place where his ribs had almost been skewered. "He moved, all right? He still owns the business but he don't live here no more."

"Then where does he live?"

"Fuck if I know, man."

Johnny glared at the man, then pointed his knife at Jay. "Are you as stupid as your friend?"

"Hey, I only work here." The two men exchanged a quick look and the dwarf didn't miss their gazes flickering to the long banquet table between them.

"If they so much as twitch, boys, rip 'em apart."

Rex and Luther responded with twin growls and each of them focused intently on the closest idiot.

"Oh, come on, man." Vinny raised his hands and grimaced at Rex. "Why you gotta bring dogs into it?"

"They're smarter than you, for one." Johnny stepped toward the table to scan the piles of square, two-inch Ziplock baggies. Two piles of them held a yellow-white powder. The other three were filled with a muddy brown powder. He didn't particularly care about the illegal drugs stashed inside to soon be distributed across Manhattan and maybe beyond. The only thing he could focus on was the red stamp in the shape of a boar across each and every little baggie.

Fuck. It's like I'm living that nightmare all over again.

"Who's stamp is this?" he asked. "Who's the fucking guy putting this stamp on all his shit?"

When neither of the thugs answered, he whirled away from the table.

"I asked you a goddamn question!"

"We ain't sayin' shit!" Vinny spat on the floor and scowled. "Fuck you."

"Do you think whoever you're working for can hurt you more than I can?" He turned to the table and pressed the tip of his knife against one of the baggies to slice through the mark of the boar he hadn't seen in fifteen years. He'd been so sure the mark would lead to his daughter's murderer, but that lead had gone cold within the first six months. *Now I'm right fucking back where I started.* "Whoever you answer to isn't here, dipshits. *I* am. Start talking."

"Nothin' you can do is worse than what happens to snitches," Jay said. "You're shit outta luck."

"Speak for yourself." Johnny swung his knife behind him toward Lisa, then pointed at the baggies again. "Are you gettin' all this?"

"Oh, yeah." She nodded and stared at Jay, her weapon still raised. "I'm making tons of mental notes too."

"This can be as easy as opening your fucking mouths," the dwarf said, "or it can be the worst thing you've ever—"

The floor creaked in the hallway down the right-hand side of the apartment. He scanned the room and found the one thing he'd failed to see when he'd stormed in there fueled by fury and his reemerging need for vengeance. A cigarette on an ashtray on the far side of the room still filtered smoke into the air and a bag of Cheetos lay spilled on the floor.

He pointed his knife at each of the thugs in turn. "Do either of you smoke?"

CHAPTER THIRTEEN

Vinny and Jay glanced at each other seconds before an electric-green ball of energy burst from the hallway on the right side of the apartment.

Johnny ducked the attack and whirled to face the wizard who stormed down the corridor and summoned another attack spell between his hands. "Shit."

The two thugs sprang into action at the same time, leapt toward the banquet table, and scrabbled for their weapons. Rex and Luther jumped after them and snapped at their heels. Vinny's pistol thumped against Rex's chest and knocked him back. Luther closed his jaws around Jay's other ankle and bit viciously. The man screamed and tried to kick the dog off before he attempted to aim the rifle.

Johnny threw his knife at him and it struck home in the center of Jay's palm.

"My fucking hand!" The rifle clattered to the floor and the wizard in the hallway released another burst of crackling green magic at Lisa this time.

She turned to dodge the spell and it cracked against her outstretched hands instead of her chest as she swung her pistol toward the wizard. Her service weapon flew from her hand and skidded across the kitchen floor on the left side of the apartment. Shouting in surprise and pain, she launched a fireball at her attacker. Her spell grazed his cheek as he dodged sideways and seared the side of his face. He screamed and summoned a blazing ball of white light that flashed brighter and brighter between his hands.

Johnny shielded his eyes from the glare that blinded everyone in the apartment but the wizard. He yanked his sunglasses out and slid them on quickly. The magical light was dampened instantly, and he spun toward Lisa and lunged at her. He dragged her to the floor before the wizard's spell erupted and launched a stream of searing white energy toward where she'd stood seconds before.

The spell impacted against the far wall of the apartment and left a huge, smoldering hole.

He looked at the agent and nodded. "Are you good?"

She grimaced. "Sure."

The wizard staggered against the far wall. His one-off spell had drained him for at least the next thirty seconds before he could summon anything else.

The dwarf rolled off Lisa, crouched, and retrieved another explosive black disk from his belt. He lobbed it at the wall between Vinnie and Jay. The disk exploded and pelted both men with a brief electrical charge as the wall behind them crumbled. The thugs sagged. He didn't miss a beat and darted around the table toward the gun held loosely in Vinnie's hand as the man tried to collect his wits.

"Catch!" He tossed the pistol toward Lisa and she snatched it from the air with perfect timing before she aimed it at the still-recovering wizard. Johnny snapped his fingers and pointed at Vinnie. Rex charged again and latched onto the man's arm as his master slid under the buffet table. The whole thing tilted sideways when he stood again over Jay, spilling semi-organized piles of drugs all over the floor.

He kicked the man in the ribs before he could pick himself up after the explosion and snatched the automatic rifle.

Luther clamped his jaws around a mouthful of Jay's basketball shorts and boxer briefs and shook his head vigorously. The man screamed and tried to crawl away with the blade still lodged in his hand.

Rex yelped when Vinnie began to punch him over and over in an effort to free himself.

Johnny turned with the rifle and fired a shot over the table that struck Vinnie in the chest and knocked him away from the hound. He stepped closer to Jay and turned the rifle on the wizard who had once again begun to fire magical attacks at Lisa. "Now's your chance to—"

A firm hand wound around the dwarf's ankle and pulled him down. With a grunt, he kicked Jay's grip off his leg and swung the rifle like a bat into the man's head. The weapon was already so slick with blood that it flew from his hand and crashed against the wall. The thug's head thumped onto the floor and he didn't make a sound when Luther got a better grip on his backside, this time including flesh.

The dwarf yanked his knife out of Jay's palm and pushed to his feet. He barreled across the apartment toward the hallway and ducked his head and shoulders in a charge as Lisa squeezed off a non-lethal shot that struck the wizard in the thigh. Her adversary screamed and would have fallen if Johnny hadn't collided with him first. Both wizard and dwarf careened down the hall.

After a brief scuffle, he got behind the man, wrapped his legs around his torso to pin his arms at his sides, and squeezed. One muscular, forearm pulled against the wizard's throat, and the knife in Johnny's other hand pressed against his adversary's ribs.

"I know you wasted that heavy-hitter spell, asshole," he jeered in the wizard's ear. "And now you're outta moves so don't even think about it."

Lisa stepped into the hallway with Vinnie's pistol held steady in both hands. All three of them were breathing heavily. Johnny hooked his ankles around the wizard's torso and increased the pressure to make his point.

The man wheezed and finally stopped fighting to simply stare down the barrel of the gun in Lisa's hands.

"You seem to be the smartest one of the group," the dwarf snapped. "You managed to hide before those two morons even knew I was here. And now you're the most alive fucker out of all three of you. So you're gonna answer me, ya hear?"

The wizard grunted.

"Where's Brad Denton?"

"I don't…know," the wizard croaked.

"Is he still heading this fucked-up operation you're running out of the apartment he owns?"

"No."

"Then who's his boss?"

The wizard tried to chuckle and couldn't quite manage it with a dwarven forearm crushing his throat. "Do you think low-level scum like us know every single mobster calling the shots from above?"

Johnny pressed the knife harder against the wizard's ribs, and the man sucked in a hissed breath. "You tell me."

"I don't know, okay?"

"What do you know about Lemonhead?" Lisa asked.

He looked sharply at her and she shrugged. "Answers, wizard."

"I heard he's scared," the man snapped.

The dwarf frowned. "Of what?"

"New…monster in town. Tearing things apart and even threatening Lemonhead, whoever he is."

"So who's the new monster?" Lisa asked.

"No…clue…"

Johnny pulled back on his arm around the man's throat and the wizard choked. "Wanna try again?"

For as much as he couldn't move, the man managed an impressive nod. When the dwarf eased his hold, his captive gasped and coughed. "It's merely a rumor, okay? But people are talking about this new guy heading to the Monsters Ball tonight. Every major player on the east coast will be there. They're puttin' up an auction—"

"Yeah, I don't wanna hear shit I already know." Johnny lightened the pressure of his knife against the wizard's ribs slightly. "Tell me about the mark of the boar."

"It's on the fucking baggies, man—" He croaked again when Johnny gave his throat another warning squeeze.

"Who does it belong to?"

"I don't...I don't *know*. I swear."

With a grunt, he rolled them both over until he straddled the wizard's back. The thug wheezed under his weight and he grasped a fistful of the guy's hair to shove his cheek against the carpeted hallway. "Do you have anything else you wanna say to me?"

"Uh...sorry?"

Johnny froze in confusion for a moment, then shrugged. "Good enough."

He pushed to his feet and pointed at the magical with his knife. His adversary gasped for breath and rubbed his throat as he struggled somewhat shakily to sit. "Now get the fuck outta here."

The wizard sat and glanced at Lisa with wide eyes before he tried to stand. His injured leg gave out twice before he finally managed to control it and hobbled down the hall. She stepped aside and Vinnie's pistol followed the man across the destroyed living room until he threw the front door open and stumbled into the hall.

With a sigh, she lowered the weapon, ejected the magazine,

and tossed both pieces into the corner of the living room. "Wanna tell me what that was about?"

"Finding information. I thought that was obvious." Johnny closed his knife and slipped it onto his belt before he strode out of the apartment hallway.

"Not when it starts with you shouting, 'That fucking giraffe.'"

"But it ended with new intel we didn't already have. So what's the problem?"

"Johnny—"

"How you doin', boys?"

"Like a million bucks, Johnny."

"Like a million Cheetos." Both dogs rooted around through what was left of the spilled Cheetos bag, the contents of which they'd quickly demolished. Rex looked up and licked his muzzle as his brother stuffed his face into the empty bag. "Can we raid the kitchen?"

"All right, that's enough." Johnny snapped his fingers and both hounds turned to face him and immediately sat.

"Hey. What gives?" Luther shook his head vigorously to dislodge the bag from the end of his snout. The bag fluttered to the floor. "Oh. Hey, Johnny. There you are."

"Time to go." The dwarf nodded toward the front door and the hounds immediately fell in on either side.

"Well, hold on a second." Lisa grimaced when he disappeared through the broken front door and she jogged toward the kitchen to retrieve her firearm. She checked the magazine, shoved it into place, and returned the weapon to her shoulder holster before she hurried through the door after them. "Seriously, Johnny. I'm glad you squeezed the info out about this new monster, whoever the hell he is."

"Bigger than Lemonhead. It's the perfect size to go after."

"Right. And I'm...well, I'm not sure how I feel about you letting that wizard go. I'm still mulling that one over."

He stopped at the end of the hall and turned to frown at her as he reached the door of the main staircase. "You're worrying about the wrong guy."

"Not worried. Merely...unsure."

Johnny jerked the door open and strode down the stairs. The hounds squeezed through the heavy door before it shut, and Lisa shoved it open again with both hands.

"Thanks for the backup, by the way."

She shrugged. "Well, yeah. That's what partners are for."

"Okay."

"You know what else partners do?"

Johnny rolled his eyes when he reached the bottom of the stairs and turned to push the door leading out to the alley behind the building. "I have no idea. I never had one."

"Partners share what's going on." The heavy door clacked shut behind her as she hurried down the alley to catch up with him.

"If you say I need to start sharing my feelings, Agent Breyer, I can't promise it won't be the feeling of my fist hitting something you might not like."

She exhaled a heavy sigh, finally caught up to him, and cast a glance at Luther trotting between them. "Look. No offense, but your feelings are the last thing on my priority list right now."

"None taken. That's how I prefer it." He turned onto the next street to head toward their hotel in Tribeca and ignored the other pedestrians. Most of them stared at the sight of a dwarf with a gray dusting of plaster and pieces of wall in his auburn hair and beard and smears of blood on his hand.

"But I do think you owe me an explanation for why you barged into that apartment because of a damn giraffe statue. I don't see the connection."

"I didn't expect you to." *She wasn't there fifteen years ago. And she didn't spend fifteen years trying to come to terms with how useless she was when it mattered. I did.*

"Johnny. Come on."

He spun toward her and pointed at her with a blood-smeared

finger. "No. If you bring it up again, I'll finish this job on my own. And I promise you won't be able to find me in this city."

Lisa folded her arms. "I could but that's beside the point."

His lips twitched into a tight, humorless grimace of a smile. "Sure."

Taking a deep breath, she hurried to catch up with him again. "So now what? Are we looking for Lemonhead at this Monsters Ball tonight or the new monster who's threatening the guy everyone else is afraid of?"

"Both."

"That's not keeping it simple."

"It's fucking simple to me." *Eliminate Lemonhead at the ball, bring Amanda home, and find out who the fuck this bastard is putting his mark of the boar on everything again. Dawn's killer is still out there and I'm gonna take everything from the fucker who took my daughter from me.*

CHAPTER FOURTEEN

Johnny scrolled through the old contacts on his phone to refresh his memory as they approached the Greenwich Hotel in Tribeca. *There's gotta be someone who'd know about this boar mark. Or at least someone who can point me in the right direction.*

"So I guess we're done touring Manhattan," Lisa muttered as she looked at the huge sign on the front of the hotel.

"You are." He glanced away from his phone and nodded toward the hotel. "I'm dropping you off."

"You what?"

"I gotta take care of a few things."

"No. Absolutely not. You can't simply lock me in my hotel room and finish whatever crusade you started above that smoke shop." She pointed at him and raised an eyebrow. "If you say, 'Watch me,' I will knock you out right here on this sidewalk."

Despite the rage burning through him at the knowledge that Dawn's killer was out there and almost challenging him to eliminate him, the dwarf smirked. "Fair enough."

"Good. If you're heading out somewhere else, I'm coming with you."

"No, you're not. This isn't part of the case so you're excused from dealing with it. I'll be back before it's time to head to the Monsters Ball." He looked at his phone and continued to scroll through his contacts as he strode down the sidewalk.

"Yeah. We both will." She hurried after him again, scowling at the hotel. "I'm not staying behind."

"I'm not having this conversation—" His phone buzzed in his hand and he frowned at the number for The Low Place. "This one, on the other hand…"

"Who is it?"

He ignored her and accepted the call. "Ernie."

"Hey, Johnny. Listen, I heard a few things about that girl you're looking for."

He paused. *Not Dawn. Of course it isn't.* "Yeah, lemme have it."

"Word's spreadin' about the Boneblade makin' moves to get ready for that ball tonight. They're moving the girl. I wish I could tell you from where, but one of my guys mentioned Brooklyn. Someone else heard they might be comin' from The Bronx too, so it's a tossup. But if you wanna strike before you try to blast into the Monsters Ball—"

"Now would be the time. Thanks, Ernie."

"Yeah."

"Hey, Ernie. Maybe you can help me with somethin' else."

"I can try."

For a brief moment, Johnny considered asking the old elf about the mark of the boar. *It isn't a conversation to have over the phone and certainly not something I can make a top priority right now. Amanda can't afford it.*

"Never mind. I'll come down to the bar later and run a few things by you."

"That works for me. Good luck, Johnny."

"Luck doesn't have a damn thing to do with it, but thanks." He ended the call with the sound of Ernie's low chuckle the last sound he heard. With a small smile, he slid his phone into his jacket pocket and rubbed his mouth and chin.

"What is it?" Lisa frowned, her arms folded across her chest.

"They're moving her."

"Amanda?"

"Yeah. The bets are split down the middle on this one. Half on the Boneblade coming from Brooklyn, the other half on The Bronx."

"Damn." She grimaced. "That doesn't leave much wiggle room if we choose the wrong one."

"It doesn't leave any room." Johnny glanced briefly at his hounds. "You don't have anything of the girl's to track, do you?"

"I wish I did."

"Well then, we have to make our minds up real quick and hope it's the right choice."

Lisa nodded and stared at the sidewalk. "Or we could head to Falcon Towers now. We could try to intercept them before they can get her inside for the Monsters Ball."

"It's too early to bring her out there now." He glanced at his watch. "We still have over five hours until that psycho auction kicks off and it's too much time for things to go wrong."

"Then what do you suggest?"

"Give me a minute, huh?" Johnny folded his arms in a mirrored pose and glared across the street. *If I had time to sit and think about it, I'd be having a fucking drink.*

Amanda Coulier sat in the back of the van, her hands and her ankles bound in front of her in handcuffs. The vehicle swayed uncomfortably as it increased speed on whatever highway they'd turned onto. She'd stopped counting the turns twenty minutes before.

"Yo, Max." The half-wizard who'd been shoved into the back of the van with her sniffed and ran a hand through his hair. The stink of his body odor assaulted her nose, and she grimaced beneath the black bag they'd drawn over her head. "Tony's asking about a pitstop."

"Fucking Tony doesn't call the shots." The driver growled his annoyance.

"Yeah, neither do you. What if I need a pitstop too, huh? Did you ever think of that?"

"Man, you should have thought about that before we left the goddamn warehouse," the gnome in the passenger seat grumbled. "I swear you're the dumbest asshole I ever met."

"Hey, fuck you, you little pissant."

Max chuckled in the front seat.

"What are you laughin' at?"

"You said pissant."

"So?"

"It sounds like pissin' ants. Like Carl's a fucking ant."

"Fuck you," the gnome added.

"Yeah, fuck you, Max." The half-wizard slumped into the seat across the back of the van from Amanda. She heard his rifle click against the unbuckled seatbelt. "So are we makin' a stop or what?"

"No. Tony can fuckin' hold it and so can you. We're about to reach the bridge."

Amanda took a deep breath. *This is it. I can do this at the bridge and they won't be able to follow me.*

"Fuck." The half-wizard grunted. "I'll piss in this bottle, then."

"Man, don't take your fuckin' Johnson out in the van."

"I'll be quick!" The sound of a plastic bottle top being unscrewed filled the space, followed by a zipper being pulled down. The van went over a pothole and rocked Amanda forward before her back slammed against the side of the van. "Fuck. Hey, take it easy, will ya? You want me to piss all over the place?"

"Not so quick, huh?" Max and Carl both sniggered in the front.

"You fuckin' morons," the half-wizard muttered. The sound of him relieving himself rose over the bump and occasional squeak of the van's failing suspension. He sighed. "Oh, yeah."

"Come on, Reggie. Save that shit for your bedroom."

Carl barked a laugh. "You still live with your mom, right?"

The magicals in the front burst out laughing.

Reggie grunted and screwed the lid onto the half-full bottle.

Now. It's now or never before he picks the gun up.

"Man, fuck you gu— What the hell?"

When Amanda shifted, the handcuffs around her wrists and ankles clinked to the floor. She yanked the bag off her head, leapt out of her clothes toward Reggie, and pounded him against the wall of the vehicle.

"Ah, shit! She's a goddamn—" His words ended in a tearing sound, followed by a gurgle.

Amanda had latched her wolf's jaws around his throat and ripped it out.

"Holy shit!"

Before Carl would reach for the gun at his hip, she bounded through the small space between the front seats and snatched the gnome's forearm between her jaws. Carl screamed.

"Get it off me, man! Get this fuckin' thing off me!"

"Shit!" Max tried to keep the van inside the lines of the road as they approached the Brooklyn Bridge and draw the gun at his hip at the same time.

"Max! What the—" The sickening laceration of flesh and muscle and crunch of bone filled the cab. The gnome shrieked mindlessly over and over, and she tossed her head to spit his detached forearm out.

Blood sprayed across the windshield a second before the bloody end of the gnome's forearm and hand thumped into Max's lap. "Oh, shit! Holy shit! What the fuck?"

The van swerved and he tried to correct it as he jumped around in his seat beneath his comrade's dismembered limb. Carl stopped screaming when her jaws closed around his throat.

Max shouted in surprise when the metal barrier before the start of the bridge raced up to meet them. He jerked on the wheel, the tires struck the curb and the barrier, and the vehicle launched into freefall before it rolled three times and stopped at the base of the bridge.

Tires squealed on the asphalt outside, followed by blaring horns and a few select shouts from New York drivers who barely managed to escape a pileup.

Amanda kicked against the dashboard behind her and realized she'd landed on the passenger-side window with the street directly below it. Max hung suspended above her, his hair dangling down the side of his forehead. He moaned and his eyelids fluttered open, and he immediately struggled to undo his seatbelt when he saw the small but deadly gray wolf growling at him, her hackles raised.

"Fuck. Fuck, fuck, fuck—"

She slashed his chest and throat with her front paws and rose on her back legs to reach as far as she could. When the blood dripped down his neck and face with a steady patter on the passenger seat below him, she stopped.

Get out of the van, Amanda.

With a growl, she vaulted over the passenger seat and scrambled to get her footing before she launched across the back of the van. The double doors at the back were badly dented on one side, and she charged forward to shove her shoulder against it. With a thump, she bounced back, lost her balance, and shook her head to clear the pain in her side.

Again. Only one more.

Backing up with a snarl, she crouched and surged toward the doors again. This time, they popped open with a squeal of bending metal and she tumbled out onto the asphalt.

"Gotcha!" A man with a red birthmark covering one side of his jaw threw himself at the young wolf and knocked her sideways.

Her claws scrabbled across the asphalt and she writhed in his arms before she managed to kick herself free. She turned and pounced on him to hurl him onto his back. The man's eyes widened when she attacked him again and ripped a chunk from his cheek.

"Ah! Fuck!"

"Get the girl!" Two other white, nondescript vans exactly like the one she'd forced to crash had pulled over on the shoulder and now, half a dozen Boneblade members raced after her as they drew guns and summoned spells. A dark-gray Chrysler stopped behind the last van and five more magical thugs spilled out of the open doors to join the chase.

Amanda spun, panting, and located the entrance to the pedestrian bridge of the East River. *No cars. Better option.*

She darted around the metal barrier and raced up the incline of the pedestrian bridge. A shattering blast of icy shards struck the side of the enclosed walkway on her right. Ice pelted off her coat as she surged forward, but she kept running. Bullets pinged off the concrete and metal to her left and right.

"Don't shoot her, you fucking morons! We need her alive!"

Footsteps pounded up the bridge in pursuit. She recognized the patter of four paws racing faster than anyone else on two legs and spun seconds before a massive black wolf launched at her. She ducked beneath the grown shifter's body and spun to clamp her jaws around his hind leg.

The black beast snarled and kicked her off. She impacted sideways against the pedestrian bridge's enclosure and shook it off before she scrambled to all fours again.

"What are you doing, Lenny?" a half-Kilomea shouted as his huge feet pounded up the bridge toward them. "Bring her the fuck down!"

As the black wolf leapt at her again, Amanda bounced against the metal gate lining the walkway and hurtled past its snapping jaws. She scrambled to get her footing again on the path and broke into a run.

A jogger pressed himself against the far side of the walkway as she raced past. He jerked his earbuds out as if that would somehow make more sense of the small gray wolf who raced up the bridge, the black wolf behind her, and almost a dozen huge men with drawn weapons barreling after her.

She darted away from the blast of crackling green magic that burst against the cement on her left. *I can't do this on my own. There are too many. If Brooklyn has any other shifters, I need to find them.*

Amanda pushed herself faster toward the top of the bridge that seemed way too far away and the young wolf raised her head to the sky and uttered a long, piercing howl. It was a call for help.

CHAPTER FIFTEEN

"I don't think we have a minute, Johnny." Lisa turned to look down the street but no one cared about a dwarf and a half-Light Elf arguing on the sidewalk.

"You're not helping." He studied the paving, then turned north. "I'm goin' with—"

"Johnny." Rex jerked his head up and his ears twitched to follow the sound.

Luther did the same. "That sound like a pup to you?"

"A scared pup. Johnny, that's her."

He stared at his hounds. "Are you sure?"

Lisa sighed and her shoulders sagged. "Please don't tell me you spent fifteen years retiring your sanity too—"

"Shh!" He raised a finger. "Boys?"

"Yeah, that's her."

"She needs help," Luther added. "South?"

"South."

"Let's go." The second Johnny gave the command, both hounds responded with long, baying howls of their own.

"Hang in there, kid!"

"We're coming!"

They raced down the sidewalk and passed Lisa in a blur of black and tan. Johnny sprinted after them, and the confused agent spun with a scowl of exasperation on her face. "What the hell, Johnny?"

"The girl's coming from Brooklyn!" he shouted without stopping.

"Shit." She broke into a run and didn't bother to ask more questions.

The hounds rocketed through the streets of Tribeca and sniffed the air as they ran.

"No scent of her yet, Johnny."

"We'll find her."

"I know." His boots pounded down the sidewalk after his dogs.

In typical New York fashion, the other pedestrians making their way down the streets didn't bother too much to move out of the way, even for two coonhounds and a scowling dwarf in black leather who raced toward them. Johnny skirted the corner of Broadway and Park Row after his dogs and collided with a man carrying a stack of melon crates out of his van before he muttered something and ran on.

"Hey, watch it!" The man gestured in protest and scowled as the melons scattered across the ground around him.

"FBI." Lisa panted and flashed her badge as she darted around the corner. "Sorry about the mess."

"What the fuck?" The man looked at the owner of the florist's shop next to his store and motioned to his spilled supplies. "Do you believe this shit?"

His neighbor shrugged and returned to work.

Johnny and Lisa darted after Rex and Luther, who hadn't slowed once since they began their race across Tribeca from the hotel. The hounds finally skidded to a stop at the park side of Chambers Street in City Hall Park and sniffed the air.

"Up there, Johnny!"

"On the bridge."

The dwarf adjusted his sunglasses against the brilliant glare of the sun striking the hoods and roofs of cars heading into Manhattan over the East River. "The bridge."

Lisa stopped beside him and took a moment to catch her breath. "Johnny, she can't be on the bridge. We'd see a pileup. Or at the very least, far more horns honking than usual."

"She's here." He scanned the racing traffic.

"Not on the road, Johnny." Luther sat and lifted his head, trying to point. "Higher."

"Higher?" The dwarf looked at the pedestrian walkway above the Brooklyn Bridge and scanned the thin crowd of people who walked slowly along it.

"There!" Lisa pointed at the top of the walkway as a tiny gray dot crested the highest point and barreled down the other side. A larger black dot followed, then a whole line of magicals who launched spells down the bridge toward the wolf. "She shifted."

"And she escaped. Good girl." He broke into a sprint toward the tunnel and staircase entrance to the pedestrian walkway off the park, his hounds loping at his sides.

"Here we go." Lisa took a deep breath and increased her pace to join them.

Rex and Luther bayed again and ran ahead of him. "We got it, Johnny!"

He retrieved another exploding disk from his belt with one hand and whipped his knife out with the other. A young couple pushing their baby in a stroller backed against the metal gates lining the walkway as the armed dwarf approached.

"Hey, man. We don't want any trouble."

"Yeah, me neither." He nodded at them as he raced past, and the couple stared after him in disbelief.

Amanda darted around two more unsuspecting joggers who shouted and stumbled against the metal sides. The black wolf snarled and surged after her to tackle her and drive her off her feet. She let out a sharp yelp and writhed beneath his paws, twisting and bucking.

"That'a boy, Lenny!" a Boneblade member shouted. "Hold her down so we can—what the fuck?"

Rex and Luther both launched themselves at the black wolf, and all three of them tumbled across the walkway toward the oncoming thugs, snapping and snarling.

"Who the hell lets their dogs off a leash?" a bald dwarf shouted and leveled his gun at the scrambling, twisting mass of hound and wolf in an effort to find a good shot.

"I do." Johnny launched his explosive disk as the other dwarf looked at him in surprise. The disk sailed over the bridge toward the unsuspecting Boneblade members who ran forward. It detonated a foot over their heads. Pellets of electrocuting mini-bombs caught five of the thugs, who jerked and bucked beneath the charge and fell to their knees. The pedestrians on the walkway screamed and evaded the explosion, raced away in the direction from which they'd come, and hauled their friends with them.

"Who's the goddamn dwarf?" a wizard shouted.

"It doesn't matter." The huge half-Kilomea spat through his unruly beard and oversized canines. "Kill him and catch the girl!"

Lisa drew her weapon, stopped four feet away from Johnny, and aimed at the oncoming gang members with both hands firmly around her weapon. "FBI! Freeze!"

A leering witch hurled a churning fireball at the agent. Johnny caught her arm and jerked her toward him and out of the way. "They don't care."

She clenched her teeth and rolled her shoulders. "Yeah, they don't care."

In response, she hurled a fireball at the bald dwarf, who ducked and would have caught fire if he'd had any hair. The Boneblade members behind him dodged her airborne attack and surged forward.

Johnny pushed on, dodged spells, and itched to get close

enough to the thugs to inflict real damage. He passed the small gray wolf who now crouched close to the walkway and jerked his head toward the Manhattan side of the bridge. "Go on, kid. We'll handle this."

Amanda growled, stared at him, and recoiled in surprise when Lisa darted past her on the other side. She launched herself up the last incline of the bridge and entered the battle with them.

The dwarf dropped and slid boots-first beneath a wizard's magical net that hurtled toward him. The magical sneered until he realized he hadn't captured the dwarf. When he looked down, Johnny's fist powered toward the underside of his jaw.

His next attack was released too late, and his spell erupted high above the Brooklyn Bridge as his feet lifted two inches off the sidewalk. He fell heavily, cracked his head sharply against the cement, and didn't move.

The half-Kilomea bulldozed forward and swung a huge fist studded with sharp thorns at the dwarf's head. The bounty hunter ducked and lifted his knife to slash at his adversary's fist. The blade stuck in the massive attacker's thick skin and jerked him forward before the handle was ripped out of his grasp.

They both stopped to stare at the blade embedded in the huge thug's fist, and the half-Kilomea uttered a deep chuckle.

"Right." Johnny glanced at the magical and inclined his head to study him. "I'll stick to blowing the huge fuckers like you up."

The thug reared and delivered a swift kick to his chest.

The dwarf grunted as he catapulted down the walkway and skidded on his ass with a grimace. "Shit."

Amanda's gray form streaked toward the witch. The young shifter vaulted at the woman's chest before she could unleash another spell and thrust her off her feet. A strangled shriek rose and ended in a gurgle before the wolf darted toward the other magicals who tried to capture her and fight her rescuers off.

The girl can fight. Okay.

Johnny pushed to his feet and yanked out a handful of his tiny explosive as the half-Kilomea lumbered toward him again and ripped the dwarf's knife out of his fist before he flung it on the ground.

He sighed. "Come on. Not even a little blood? Thick-skinned bastards."

Scowling, he crushed the tops of the large beads in each hand and felt the sticky coating ooze around his fingers as the explosives activated. He gestured at the half-Kilomea and smirked. "Do you want some?"

This time, he moved faster than the hulking magical, ducked under one massive sweeping fist after the other, and spun to stick an explosive bead on each of the thug's huge hands. He powered his fist into his adversary's gut and attached two more explosives there while he was at it. Grinning, he darted around the massive form and stuck two more on the backs of the thug's knees before he lobbed the other two at the broad back.

The bearded half-Kilomea whirled as quickly as possible for a guy his size and opened both hands like he meant to clap them against the sides of his opponent's head. With a smirk, the dwarf twisted and raced away from the giant magical, whose booming laughter followed him. "Aw, look at the scared little dwarf."

"Little?" He turned halfway and flipped his opponent the middle finger. "I almost felt bad for you. Not anymore."

The huge thug strode after him with a sneer. The bounty hunter ducked a globular maroon blood-spell unleashed from another magical's outstretched hands and ran toward the wizard instead before he could ready another attack. He swung a fist into his gut and knocked the wind out of him, then twirled and grasped the back of the man's jacket to use him as a magical shield.

His explosive beads detonated. The half-Kilomea lurched forward when the backs of his knees shattered with the explosion, followed quickly by the blast that ignited on his chest. It flung him back over his splintered legs, and the explosives on his hands detonated and sent thorn-covered fingers in every direction but mostly onto the wizard the dwarf held in front of him.

The large warrior roared and fell unconscious on the walkway.

Johnny poked his head out from behind the blood-splattered wizard who stared in wide-eyed shock at his fellow gang member. "Hey, look at that. He does bleed."

The man jerked away from him and yanked a pistol from the waistband of his pants. The dwarf snatched it out of his adversary's hands in one quick swipe, pounded the wizard on the side of the head with the weapon, and jammed his elbow into the guy's back as he fell. "Stay."

Lisa launched a fireball at a second witch, who returned fire with an equally strong fire spell. The agent lunged out of the way before the witch's attack arced over the side of the bridge and she raised her gun at the woman. "Hands up or I'll shoot!"

Her would-be assailant laughed and raised both hands into the air. Bolts of black lightning surged from her outstretched fingers and impacted with the walkway below, leaving huge divots in the cement.

"You had fair warning." Before the witch could retaliate with another spell, Lisa put a bullet in her chest and spun to aim at the second Boneblade dwarf who ran toward her with Johnny's knife. "That doesn't belong to you. Drop it."

He drew his arm back to throw the blade but she squeezed off a shot into his knee and he dropped with a scream. She stepped toward him and shoved him back with a kick to the chest. When she stamped on his forearm, the dwarf released the knife with a shriek.

Johnny darted toward them and stooped to pick his blade up before he delivered a swift kick to the other dwarf's head. "Good one."

He pushed into a sprint and past her to thrust his knife at a wizard who conjured a blade of sizzling yellow sparks.

Amanda darted from one Boneblade member to the next while they attempted to capture her. She snarled and snapped at their heels and occasionally savaged their pants and the legs beneath them.

A gnome with an electric cattle prod surged toward her. Rex jumped on him, flung him back, and buried his teeth in the magical's shoulder. "Get outta here, kid."

Luther skidded back and thunked against the metal half-wall on the side of the walkway. "This is us rescuing you. Get down the bridge." He snarled and leapt at the wizard who'd hurled him aside.

The black wolf they'd momentarily taken out of the game rose from a heap on the opposite side of the walkway and shook himself. He immediately ran toward Amanda as she attacked a gnome and caught her back leg in his jaws.

She yelped when he jerked her back and swung her against the metal barrier. The small gray wolf fell on the cement and shifted slowly into her human form, knocked unconscious.

The black wolf stalked toward her and snarled.

"Hey!" Lisa aimed her firearm at him. "You're not taking her, asshole."

He snapped at her and raced forward.

She fired one shot that grazed him in the shoulder when he dodged. With only a short yelp, he ignored the near-miss and gained speed and his large paws thumped on the cement.

"I would much rather arrest you," she muttered. "Fuck it." When she pulled the trigger again, the chamber was empty.

"Shit." Lisa fumbled with her jacket pocket and tried to access the extra magazine, but the wolf was almost on her. She shoved her hand out to hurl a fireball instead, but her attacker swatted her aside before she could summon the spell.

The agent impacted with the metal sidewall, her head clanged against the mesh, and her eyes rolled back in her head. The next thing she felt was the shifter's hot, metallic-scented breath rippling across her face. She groaned and tried to focus on anything but the blurry black shadow that loomed over her. *This is it. These guys don't take prisoners.*

A low snarl rose behind the wolf before the black beast was driven into the wall above her sprawled legs. The enemy howled in rage when Rex clamped on a huge mouthful of his shaggy fur and the flesh beneath. His brother got a full mouthful of shifter ankle and pulled fiercely as the wolf tried to turn and fight them. Luther leapt onto the wolf's back and snarled as he savaged the shifter's ears and neck.

Rex darted toward Lisa and examined her quickly before he licked her face.

"Thanks, buddy. I'm good. I'll be fine."

With a low whine, the hound darted away again to join his brother in overcoming the black wolf.

Lisa steadied herself with a hand on the metal half-wall and pushed to her feet. *I gotta check for concussions after this. And get a jacket with better pockets.*

She ejected the empty magazine, retrieved the new one, and thrust it in before she staggered up the walkway to aim at the magical thugs who continued to fight Johnny and his hounds. Almost half of them lay dead on the pedestrian walkway, and the other half walked backward up the bridge, defending the wizard with an unconscious Amanda draped over his shoulder and covered by another goon's oversized jacket.

"Dammit!" The dwarf raced after them and dodged the spells they hurled at him to keep him back. "I knew I should've brought a rifle."

"I'm on it." Finally regaining her balance, Lisa ran past him and aimed at the retreating Boneblade members.

The black wolf disengaged from Rex and Luther and hurdled over her head. He landed with a snarl and bounded up the bridge after the rest of his thug buddies.

"Stop!" she shouted and took a shot at the back of the wizard who carried Amanda. Rex and Luther raced past her after the wolf.

The retreating gnome stretched his hand out and raised a glittering magical shield that flashed bright yellow when her bullet bounced harmlessly against it. He cackled and reached into his jacket pocket. "Fuck you!"

As the rest of the gang members headed down the other side of the bridge toward Brooklyn, the gnome lobbed an enhanced magical grenade at the two hounds. The metal canister bounced once on the walkway and rolled toward them before it spun wildly. Both dogs skidded across the cement as they tried to pull up short and avoid the detonating device.

"Shit." Lisa lowered her gun and extended both hands as the magical grenade exploded.

Rex yelped and fell on his side in his scramble to escape.

"Johnny!" Luther shouted. "We're gonna die! We're gonna— Wait, what?"

Lisa's massive energy shield pulsed around the grenade's intended destruction. The stream of bright golden light streaked from her hands to fuel the shimmering wall that surged across the walkway and lifted high between the explosion and the hounds. She shouted at the effort and gritted her teeth as her hands shook.

Johnny emitted a shrill whistle, and both dogs spun away from the golden wall of light to lope to their master's side.

Come on... Lisa's hands burned with the intensity of her magic but she ignored it and pressed on the wall of light and the deadly explosion that blossomed beneath it. Her shield shrank, folded in on the eruption, and she couldn't hold it any longer. With a gasp, she stumbled forward and her spell snuffed out.

Dozens of metal shards from the grenade scattered onto the walkway and lay still. Smoke rose from the blackened edges.

She closed her eyes and staggered sideways. "I got it..."

"Yeah, you did." Johnny stopped beside her and held her pistol out. "Here."

"Thanks." She took it with a frown and turned to look at Rex and Luther as she holstered her weapon. "Are the dogs okay?"

"Hell yeah, we're okay!" Luther trotted toward them, his tail wagging. "That was awesome."

"I'd be happier if we had the girl," Rex added. "But I guess I'm cool with not being blown up."

The dwarf snorted. "They're good."

Lisa nodded. "I wish I could say the same for Amanda. She got so far and we almost had her."

"Yep." Johnny rubbed his mouth and sniffed. "They're not gonna take their eyes off her for two seconds after this."

"You can say that again. Not now that they know she's a shifter."

He closed his blade and returned it to his belt. "I fucking hate it when someone else brings a bomb."

She responded with a wry laugh and turned slowly toward him. "You're welcome, by the way."

"Yeah, that was good. Impressive." He hooked his thumbs through his belt loops and turned to look at his hounds, who sat obediently and waited for him. "You could have shielded yourself and probably caught up with those bastards, but you didn't."

"I know." Lisa ran a hand through her hair and nodded at the hounds. "Rex and Luther could have stopped the wizard scooping Amanda off the ground, but they didn't."

"Yeah, we saved her, Johnny," Luther said.

Rex barked. "We're awesome. No big deal."

"And we like her."

"Yeah."

Johnny scrutinized the agent with a flickering smile and nodded. "Anyone who lets scumbags get away—"

"Johnny, I didn't—"

"To put my hounds first earns some serious respect."

"Oh."

"Thank you." With a sniff, he turned and headed down the bridge toward Rex and Luther. "Come on, boys. Time to regroup. It looks like we're bringing the party to Falcon Towers tonight."

"Ooh, I love parties."

"Hey, Johnny. It's the kind with a buffet table, right?"

"Oh-ho-ho. Serious treasures under a buffet table."

CHAPTER SIXTEEN

In Johnny's hotel room, the bounty hunter sprawled on his bed and scrolled through his contacts again. *Maybe I should go back to Ernie's and ask him about the red boar now. I could get a lead or two if I can, then set it aside until after we get Amanda.*

Rex crawled on his belly across the king-sized mattress and lowered his head onto his paws beside his master's thigh with a whine. "Whatcha lookin' at, Johnny?"

He glanced at the dog and shook his head. *I'm not gonna talk about it now. And I can't go to Ernie now, either. I need to focus on the kid who still has everything to lose.*

Luther's tail thumped on the carpet where he lay at Lisa's feet, staring at her. "She's good with stuff, Johnny. Guns. Magic. Bombs. Computers. Real winner if you ask me."

The dwarf tugged on his beard and leaned back against the mountain of pillows behind him.

"Shit." Lisa pushed the rolling office chair away from the desk and her open laptop. "They made an update to the dark-web bidding."

He sat and scowled at her. "So now everyone knows?"

"Uh-huh. Listen to this." She turned to her laptop to read the updated description under Amanda's photo on the dark web. "'Unregistered shifter. Star of this year's auction and Belle of the Ball after all bids are placed.'"

"Motherfuckers." He gritted his teeth and thumped a fist on the mattress.

"Yeah. Now everyone knows and they're gonna make a huge spectacle of her at the Monsters Ball."

"Not if I have anything to say about it. What's the bid up to?"

Lisa blew out a frustrated sigh. "It tripled in less than twenty-four hours. Two hundred and twenty-five thousand."

Johnny grimaced and stared at the blank flatscreen TV mounted above the mini-fridge. "Put us down for three."

"Three—" Her eyes widened. "Hundred thousand?"

"Good guess." He nodded at her laptop.

"Johnny, that's—"

"Not even remotely what an innocent life is worth, Lisa. A child's life. Make the bid."

She raised her eyebrows and turned toward her laptop. "I guess it's pointless to ask if you're good for it, right?"

"Also a good guess. You're getting better." He scooted to the edge of the bed and leaned forward over his thighs. "Maybe these assholes will back off with this much money on the line."

"I don't know." Lisa typed quickly and entered their bid. "We're dealing with the East Coast's biggest crime lords. Even half a million's chump change to these guys."

"We'll see."

Two minutes later, the bidding updated again. She thumped her elbow onto the desk and rested her forehead in her hand as she stared at the screen. "Lemonhead."

"He outbid us again?"

"Yeah. It's up to half a million now. I guess I jinxed that one."

The dwarf ran his tongue over his front teeth and sniffed. "Seven-fifty."

"What?"

"Do it."

Shaking her head, she added their next bid of seven hundred and fifty thousand dollars. The price updated next to their Bulldog username, and the seconds ticked past slowly as they waited for Lemonhead to give up or raise the price again.

Johnny checked his watch. "Five minutes. That's a record for this guy, isn't it?"

"Yeah." Lisa stared unblinkingly at her laptop. "The auction doesn't close until the end of the ball, though. Who knows how long this guy's willing to sit around and—" She leaned closer and gaped at the screen. "Fuck."

He closed his eyes. "What is it now?"

"One and a half." She chuckled in disbelief and slumped in the office chair. "One and half million dollars."

"He's simply fucking with us now." The dwarf stood from the bed and went to the mini-fridge to retrieve a bottle of water.

"What do you mean?"

He chugged the entire bottle, screwed the lid on, and tossed the empty bottle across the room. It hit the trashcan with a ping and bounced around at the bottom.

"Nice one," Luther said, his tail thumping on the floor.

"Lemonhead doesn't give a shit how much he puts up. He wants Amanda. But more than that, he wants every other piece of shit who wants her to squirm."

Lisa turned in her chair to face him. "How do you know that?"

"It's what I would do. You were right. Money isn't an issue for this asshole. It doesn't matter how much we put down." he turned and gave the bed's thick wooden frame a sharp kick with his boot. "They're all the fucking same. They take and take and they won't stop at nothin' to rip away a girl's life simply because they can." The bedframe cracked with a hairline split when he kicked it again. "Like they fucking get off on it."

With his last kick, that side of the bedframe split wide and the whole thing tilted by an inch toward him. Rex jumped off the elevated side of the bed and trotted to the front to sniff the broken side. "I don't think it's supposed to do that, Johnny."

"Yeah, nothin's workin' out the way it's supposed to." The dwarf spun and strode down the short hall into the bathroom. The door slammed shut behind him, followed by the faucet turning on full blast.

Lisa looked at the hounds and muttered, "I think I know what this is about."

"Really?" Luther looked at her and thumped his tail on the ground. "You can tell us."

"Yeah. Come on, lady." Rex sniffed along the bottom of the bed frame and snorted. "He's not gonna talk about it in front of you but you might as well share what you got."

"Maybe it's time to open that can of worms. Carefully." She glanced at the door and slid out of the office chair. "I'll be right back."

"Aw, come on." Luther stood and took a few steps after her as she headed to the door. "I thought we were bonding here."

She flicked aside the bar used as a latch lock to prop the door open and disappeared into the hallway.

"She can't hear us." Rex sat and scratched behind his ear. "Did you forget?"

"Oh. Huh. Guess I did. Hey, you think he keeps any snacks in that fridge?"

"It is a fridge. Smaller means easier to open."

Luther sniffed the mini-fridge beneath the counter. "Worth a try."

The hounds hadn't made any progress when Lisa slipped quietly back into the room with her hands in her pockets. The dogs looked at her and moved out of the way as she sat in the office chair again. Two seconds later, the faucet turned off in the bathroom and Johnny jerked the door open before he smacked the light switch. With a grunt, he hiked his black jeans up and stopped halfway across the room before he wiped what was left of the dripping water out of his beard. "We need a legit way into that party tonight."

"I agree." She nodded. "But first, I think we need to talk."

He glanced at his hounds.

"Hey, don't look at us," Luther said and licked his muzzle.

"Yeah, she didn't tell us shit."

"It's not the time to bring feelings up," he muttered.

Lisa shrugged. "And that's still not my top priority. Mostly, I want you to hear me out. Or pretend to listen. Your call."

She pulled a mini-bottle of Johnny Walker Black Label out of her coat pocket and threw it to him.

Johnny snatched it in his fist and smirked at it. "Are you bribin' me for my attention?"

"That seemed like the best way to start, yeah." She gave him a small smile and leaned back in the chair. "Did it work?"

"It depends on what you have to say." Seated on the edge of the bed again, Johnny opened the bottle and downed the whole thing. "Go."

Lisa chuckled. "All right. Before I took this assignment, the department dropped a different file down on my desk and said I might wanna look into it. Your file."

The dwarf stared at her, his face devoid of all expression. *Goddammed Bounty Hunter Department.*

"I almost didn't," she continued. "But I don't like to leave stones unturned. Especially with an assignment that carries this much weight."

They stared at each other as she gave him a moment to respond, but his silence pushed her to keep going.

"You didn't wanna tell me what was up with the giraffe statue. I get it. So now I'm telling you I already know. And when all this is over—when Amanda's in FBI custody and safe again—I'll help you find the bastard behind the red boar. Only if you want my help, of course."

Johnny raised an eyebrow. "Is that it?"

MARTHA CARR & MICHAEL ANDERLE

"Yeah." Lisa laughed. "That's it."

"All right." He slid off the edge of the bed. "I think I know how to get us into Falcon Towers. Or at least who to talk to for the solution."

"Okay." She gave him a tight smile and glanced at the dogs. *He heard every word. Maybe he simply needs time to think about it.* "Then let's go."

"Yeah." He sniffed and strode toward the phone on the nightstand. "I gotta make sure the hounds are taken care of first."

"What?" Luther whined. "Are you kidding?"

"Johnny, you can't leave us here. You need us."

"Yeah, and who's gonna let us outside? You want us makin' a mess in this nice room?"

"It's less nice now that he broke the bed."

Johnny picked the phone up and dialed the concierge. "I ain't goin' anywhere dangerous, boys. But I need my hands free, and I reckon your instincts are gonna override your brains where Agent Breyer and I are headed."

"What the hell?" Rex responded with a quick growl and lowered his head to his forepaws. "That's the stupidest thing I ever heard."

Luther turned and sniffed Lisa's jacket pocket. "You got any treats in there for us, lady?"

Johnny hooked a thumb through his belt loop as he waited for the line to be answered.

"Greenwich Hotel Concierge. How may I help you?"

"Yeah." He cleared his throat. "This is Johnny Walker."

"Ah. Mr. Walker. How are you enjoying your stay?"

"'Bout as much as a wide-mouthed bass enjoys a hook through the cheek."

"I...I'm sorry, Mr. Walker. What was that?"

"Nothin'. I'm steppin' out for a spell and I need someone to keep an eye on my coonhounds."

"Um...I apologize, Mr. Walker. I can't—"

"Just Johnny."

"Oh. Sure, Mr…Johnny."

"So I need someone to keep an eye on my coonhounds. You know, check they're okay and take 'em out to do their business. Maybe toss a rawhide or two their way if y'all got any. Can you do that?"

A long pause followed. "It's… I'm so sorry. It's your accent. I can't seem to—"

"You need to pull the stuffin' outta your ears!" With a growl of frustration, he turned to look at Lisa.

"What?"

"It seems he can't understand a word I'm sayin'. He says it's my accent. I don't have an accent."

She pressed her lips together to keep from laughing and stood. "Why don't you put the phone on speaker. I'll see if I can help."

Scoffing, he stabbed the speaker button on the receiver and cleared his throat. "Are you still there?"

"Yes, sir. I'm still here. And I'm more than happy to help you with your request if I can understand what you're asking."

"Hello?" Lisa stepped up beside Johnny and leaned toward the receiver.

"Oh. Hello."

"Hi. This is Lisa Breyer. I'm right next door to Johnny."

"Yes. Hello, Ms. Breyer. I'm so sorry, I can't seem to—"

"It's fine. We need someone to take care of Johnny's dogs tonight while we're out. Only to come up here every…"

"Three hours," Johnny said.

Rex whined. "Three hours?"

"No. Make it two."

"Every two hours to let the dogs out."

"*Oh.* To let the dogs out." The Concierge chuckled. "Yes, of course."

"Thank you."

"Do they need to be fed as well?"

"No." Johnny and Lisa said it together and she tried to hide another smile as she glanced at him.

"Very well. Anything else?"

Johnny cleared his throat again. "That's it."

"That's all," Lisa repeated, which earned her a sharp glare from the dwarf. "Thank you."

"My pleasure, Ms. Breyer. What time do you plan to return to the hotel tonight?"

"Keep checkin' on my hounds until we get back," he grumbled. "Then you'll know."

Lisa leaned toward the phone again. "Did you catch that?"

"Yes. Yes, that came through with perfect clarity. Rest assured, Mr. Walker's canine friends will be adequately cared for until your—"

"Great." The dwarf thunked the phone down on the receiver and turned away from the nightstand to drag his duffel bag out of the closet.

She stared at the phone. "That wasn't very nice."

"What kinda Yankee moron can't understand what I'm sayin', huh? My accent. Please."

Nodding slowly, she turned away from the nightstand and folded her arms. "So where are we going?"

"Franklin Street Station." Johnny drew a long gold chain out of his bag and stuffed it into his pocket. He took two rawhide bones out and tossed one to each of the hounds. "That'll keep you occupied for a minute, boys. I'll come back in a few hours to feed ya, then you'll have to wait for the concierge." He wiggled his fingers and rolled his eyes.

"All right, Johnny!" Luther attacked his rawhide and settled onto the floor with it to start gnawing without delay.

"That's where you've been keeping the treats?" Rex glared at the door. "What the hell?"

"Is that how you say thank you, Rex?" Johnny cocked his head. "I thought I taught you better'n that."

Rex picked the rawhide up delicately in his jaws and added a muffled, "Thank you."

"That's better." The dwarf pulled a small square case covered in black canvas from his duffel bag and strapped it over his chest and shoulder. He nudged the duffel bag back into the closet with the toe of his boot and slid the door shut.

He nodded at Lisa. "Time to go."

"Okay." She shoved her hands into her pockets and followed him toward the door.

"Wait." Rex dropped the bone as his brother crunched his happily and trotted after his master. "Johnny. Don't leave us here alone like this. Come on."

"It's only for a few hours, boy." He raised his index finger, and Rex sat. "Stay and don't chew on anything that don't belong to you. I'll be back in a few hours."

"Wait, wait." Rex whined. "Johnny, you know dogs have no concept of time!"

Johnny shut the door with a grimace, and Rex responded with a high-pitched bark.

"Hey, if you don't eat that bone, I will," Luther said.

"Don't even think about it." His brother whined again and finally gave up. "I miss Johnny."

The dwarf exhaled a sigh as he and Lisa headed to the elevators. "They'll be fine. I'm not even worried about it. They're out in the Everglades by themselves all the time. This ain't nothin'."

They stopped at the elevators and he punched the call button. "Naw. They'll be fine."

Lisa darted him a sideways glance and bit her lip to hide a smile. "I didn't say anything."

He looked sharply at her as the elevator doors opened. "Yeah, keep doin' that."

CHAPTER SEVENTEEN

As they headed down the stairs at Franklin Street Station, Lisa looked quickly at Johnny and took her chances. "So where are we going?"

"To one of the best sources of information I know." He shoved his hands in his jacket pockets as they hurried down the stairs. "I should have thought of this sooner."

"And you're not gonna tell me any more than that, are you?"

"You'll see."

They reached the landing and he turned right to head to the end of the platform. She balked when he jumped onto the tracks and kept moving. "What are you doing?"

"The next train arrives in three minutes. We have more than enough time if you keep up."

As the dwarf's form faded ahead in the tunnel, Lisa glanced behind her at the New Yorkers milling around the station. No one paid them any attention. *I hope no one starts screaming and making a big deal out of it if they do see.*

Gritting her teeth, Lisa hopped off the platform and hurried to catch up with her partner, trying to steady her footing on the uneven tracks. "Johnny, you know how crazy this is, right?"

"I know you've never been down here, sure." He frowned and scanned the walls until he found a short set of stairs rising from the tracks toward an unmarked door. "You gonna tell me you don't trust that I know what I'm doin' at this point?"

"What? No." She followed him up the grated metal stairs to the door. "I know you know what you're doing. I simply don't see why we have to—"

The small explosive beads he had stuck on the door's lock detonated with a sharp pop that was completely drowned out by the rumble and squeal of the next approaching train. The door opened and he looked at her with a smirk.

"Break into unmarked doors in the subway," Lisa finished. "You used to do this all the time, didn't you?"

He shrugged and opened the door. "There's a better entrance at Spring Street but I don't feel like takin' a ride."

"Entrance to what?"

"You'll see." Johnny slipped through the door into the dark passage beyond.

All the light vanished as soon as the door closed behind Lisa. She pulled her phone out, meaning to bring the flashlight app up, but a sharp crack made her stop.

The dwarf turned and waved a thick red glowstick at her with a smirk. "This is better."

"You carry glowsticks in your pockets, too?"

"I carry a lotta stuff on me, darlin'. It shouldn't be that surprising." He hurried down the corridor until they reached another set of stairs leading into a darkness so thick, the glowstick only reached four feet in front of them. "You can put your phone away. That kinda light won't exactly get them rearin' to come say hi."

Lisa frowned and returned her phone to her pocket. "Is there anything else I should know before we reach— Wait, who?"

He smirked and moved quickly down the stairs. "You had no idea who I was talking about the first time, did you?"

"Johnny, you've completely lost me."

"I gotta hand it to you, Lisa. You have a damn good poker face."

"Thanks. I think."

The staircase seemed to descend forever before they finally reached the bottom. He cracked another red glowstick and stepped onto the set of tracks that ran miles below the active New York subway. "Did you know this was here?"

Lisa studied the abandoned subway tunnel, eerily quiet with no running trains or pedestrians milling around and waiting to catch their next ride across Manhattan. "I'd heard a few things. These tunnels were abandoned decades ago."

"Not completely."

The farther they walked down the empty tunnel, the more the air was filled with small, rustling echoes, thumps, and what sounded like claws scrabbling across the stone and dusty cement.

She turned and reached for her firearm when a pair of eyes glinted in the red light from the glowsticks before they disappeared. "Johnny..."

"Shh. Hold on." The dwarf scanned the darkness, then tossed one of the glowsticks down the tunnel. The red light jerked on and off as the stick sailed end over end and vanished in mid-air. "Bingo. Come on."

"Is that—"

"An illusion charm? Yeah."

"Who would need to put an illusion charm down here in an abandoned tunnel?"

"Merely a few friends who like to keep to themselves. My kinda magicals for the most part. Have you ever been to a kemana?"

Lisa walked along the raised tracks beside him and raised an eyebrow. "I'm a federal agent, Johnny."

"So no. You wanted to see the city, right? This should've been on your tourist list."

When they reached the place where the glowstick had disappeared, he stepped forward and vanished too.

"Hey!" She darted after him and stopped, momentarily blinded by the magical lanterns on the tunnel walls. The light was soft and dusty but intensely bright after the darkness behind them. Blinking rapidly to clear her vision, Lisa reached for her firearm again but stopped when Johnny clicked his tongue and shook his head.

"You won't need that. We're only here for a chat."

She lowered her hand and stared at the small shack-like homes built of metal scraps and boxes and old crates. Groups of three-foot-tall, brown, rat-like magicals stood and sat on piles of junk all over the tunnel, talking in low, scratchy tones. She turned to ask where the hell they were, but Johnny had already strode down the tunnel toward the encampment that looked more like parts of the Bronx in the 1970s without the skyline.

The agent hurried to catch up with him. "This is a kemana?"

"One of the run-down parts. You won't find a Willen in the busy places unless they're tryin' to lift something. But what they keep here? That's the real valuable stuff."

"All the junk, huh?"

"Naw." He tapped his temple. "It's all up here."

The Willens, dressed in a hodgepodge of incomplete outfits—one with mismatched shoes, another with only a pair of gym shorts, and two others wearing nothing but baseball caps—paused their conversations to stare at the dwarf and the half-Light Elf who walked down the alley of their camp in the abandoned tunnel.

"Hey! Johnny Walker!" A skinny Willen with an open bomber jacket over nothing else poked his head out of a precariously balanced stack of old packing boxes. "I thought you were dead."

"Well, now you know." The dwarf jerked his chin at the Willen and kept moving.

"You look like crap, Johnny," another rat-like creature shouted as he sorted through a pile of old computer parts in front of him. "It's good to see ya."

"Yeah." He raised his eyebrows and that was it.

"Not the friendliest, are they?" Lisa muttered.

"Being honest and being friendly ain't exactly the opposite." He grunted and returned the fading glowstick to his pocket. "You can't buy a Willen's flattery, either. Not for all the shiny shit in New York."

"Well, if they live like this, I wouldn't think they'd feel like flattering anyone."

He snorted. "It's 'cause they don't lie. Everything that comes out of a Willen's mouth matches exactly what they're thinkin'. That's why I'm a fan."

"I see."

Johnny studied her for a moment and shook his head. "It's like you've been livin' under a rock, Agent Breyer. Federal agent, sure, but you were a magical first."

Lisa cast him a disconcerted glance and swallowed. "Not everyone's been around as much as you have, Johnny."

"Huh. Ain't that the truth."

"Johnny Walker." A Willen wearing gold-and-black Nikes at least two sizes too big flashed the dwarf a snaggle-toothed grin. Gold-plated teeth glinted behind the magical's curling upper lip. "I heard you lost your mind and threw yourself into a pit."

"Only the Everglades, Brody." He stopped in front of the Willen and extended his hand. The creature shook it briefly and sneered at the dwarf. "It looks like you got yourself an upgrade."

"What, this?" Brody slapped a hand at the tinsel and round silver ornaments hanging over the extended roof made of two-by-fours that served as the front porch. "It's my Christmas present to myself. You'd be amazed at what can go missin' from Times Square without people noticin'."

"It doesn't surprise me at all." Johnny slid his hand into his pocket and paused. "I'm lookin' for information and decided you'd be the best magical to help an old friend."

"Aw. Ain't that sweet." Brody ran his tongue over his glinting gold teeth. "I'm not gonna lie, Johnny. I thought you was outta the game."

"I was. And I will be."

"We're trying to get into the Monsters Ball tonight," Lisa said. "It's down at Falcon Towers, and all the East Coast's biggest—"

"I know what the damn Monsters Ball is, lady." Brody's beady black eyes flicked toward her and his already wrinkled, rodent-shaped snout puckered even more. "I don't know you."

Johnny gestured vaguely toward her. "Agent Breyer with the Bounty Hunter Department. She's taggin' along."

She leaned away from him and raised her eyebrows. "Tagging along?"

He shrugged.

Brody scrutinized her and chuckled. "You got anything to pay for that little tidbit, sweet cheeks?"

She tilted her head warningly at the Willen. "Careful."

"Shit, I don't mean no disrespect, lady. But I gotta get what's mine, don't I? You know how things work down here."

"I honestly don't."

Johnny smirked. "She honestly doesn't."

"Huh. But you do, Johnny, don'tcha?"

"Yep." The dwarf drew his hand out of his pocket and let the end of the gold chain drop from his fingers.

"*Ooh...* Ain't that a nice piece a' shiny?" Brody reached for it, and the dwarf lifted it out of the way.

"Everything you know about the Monsters Ball tonight?"

"Yeah, yeah. Gimme." The Willen grinned when the gold chain fell into his outstretched clawed hand. He pulled aside a fold of brown skin below his ribs and secreted the chain within before he gave his belly a quick pat.

Lisa wrinkled her nose and stared at the creature's bare stomach. *I don't even wanna know what else he has stashed away in all that skin.*

"Like your lady friend said, Johnny. The party's goin' down at Falcon Towers in the penthouse. Kicks off at eight thirty and probably goes until two or three in the mornin', if you ask me. Those bastards know how to party. But it's invitation-only, and all those pretty little invites have already been sent out. Pure gold, Johnny? You believe that? All engraved and shit. Good luck gettin' anywhere near that ball without one a' them cards."

The dwarf nodded and folded his arms. "Who has the invites, Brody?"

The Willen uttered a high-pitched giggle and stared at the watch on the dwarf's left wrist. His tongue ran over his gold teeth again. "That'll cost you extra, Johnny. It's a whole different ball-game. You know how it works."

Without looking away from Brody, he unfastened his watch and dropped it into the cupped paws.

"Ha! You always bring the good stuff. Yessir." The watch vanished into another fold of brown skin on the left side of the creature's chest this time, and he grinned. "I know one guy who got hisself one a' these gold invites. Mid-level thug who married up into high society. What a douche. You could take his. The guy strides around callin' hisself the Artful Dodger. He made his mark as a cat burglar, yeah?"

"I reckon he's got nothin' on you, though," Johnny muttered.

"Damn straight he don't!" Brody cackled. "But the Artful Dodger ain't snaggin' the same pretties I got comin' my way. It don't mean he ain't a wily bastard, though. He's never been caught. I hear he used his burglin' money to buy into that Monsters Ball. If you want one a' them gold cards, Johnny, you go through him. The guy's in Queens at the Three Brothers Munic-ipal Waste Company."

Lisa slid her hands in her jacket pockets. "If you're so good at stealing things—"

"Stealin'? *Stealin'*?" Brody leaned away from her and patted the folds of skin at his chest where Johnny's watch wasn't even visible anymore. "Lady, I'm a collector."

"Right. Is there any chance you could collect this golden ticket for us?"

The Willen shivered. "No way. That type barbeques Willens for fun. Uh-huh. I ain't shimmyin' down no hidey-hole to so much as touch the guy. You're on your own."

She glanced at Johnny. "What if we had a few more shiny things for you?"

"Nope. There ain't enough watches on either of yous to get any Willen to snag that card for you. I'm done talkin', Johnny. I hope you don't die." Brody spun away, slapped the tinsel and Christmas ornaments hanging off his roof, and dove into the dark hole of his home.

"Come on." The dwarf nodded toward the illusion charm at the entrance of the Willen camp. "We'll take a taxi when we get up top."

"Do we need to stop at the hotel first?"

"For what?" he nodded at the other gathered Willens who studied them as they headed down the abandoned tracks. "You have enough ammo on you, don't you?"

"Well, yeah. I only meant if you need to get anything."

"Nope." He patted the black case the size of a lunchbox that thumped against his hip. "I have everything I need right here and I'm takin' it to Queens."

CHAPTER EIGHTEEN

They had the cabbie drop them off ten blocks from the Three Brother Municipal Waste Company and walked the rest of the distance. The commercial building was set far enough away from the surrounding neighborhoods that anyone could walk around the place doing whatever they wanted and not draw any attention.

The two partners crouched behind the open gate in the multi-layered chain-link fence surrounding the building.

"It looks like the Willen's information was accurate," she muttered.

"'Course it is. Brody used to be a second pair of ears and eyes for me back in the day." He sniffed and leaned sideways for another glance at the front of the building. "It feels like back in the day's catchin' up with me damn quick."

She counted the magicals and low-level thugs who moved in and out of the building. "It's hard to get a good read on them when they all move around like that. But I count at least thirty-five."

"Did you? I had twenty-nine but wish it was thirty, though. I like a nice round number."

She frowned at him as they drew back behind the gate. "There are probably more inside. Either way, they're heavily armed."

"Yeah, so am I." Johnny squatted on the cement and pulled the strap of the black case over his head before he unzipped the top.

"With a knife and those exploding beads? I don't think that's gonna be enough."

"All that's simply the icin' on the cake, darlin'." His hands moved quickly as he took piece after metal piece from the case and attached them one after the other. "I brought a little somethin' extra this time."

Lisa folded her arms. "A telescope?"

He clicked the last component into place and lifted what looked very much like a telescope with both hands. "It's not your fault you haven't seen a masterpiece like this before. It's one of mine."

When he flicked the safety off and took two extra magazines out of the case to store in his jacket pocket, her eyes widened. "You built a gun."

"Yeah." He zipped the case again and slung the strap over his head and shoulder before he stood. "They won't know what hit 'em."

"You won't either firing something like that." Lisa smirked. "Your high-tech potato gun must have a hell of a recoil."

Johnny snorted and patted the side of his weapon. "Not for me."

"Okay, can't we simply slip in and out this time? You know, use a little magical finesse without blowing anything up?"

Shaking his head, he adjusted the components of his highly portable weapon. "You obviously don't know how this is done."

"Fine. I'll go around back and keep an eye out for the target. If he is as artful a dodger as he thinks he is, that's where he'll head first. You distract the muscle."

"Sure. A hole in the chest is a hell of a distraction."

She stared at him. "Is that seriously your plan?"

Johnny smirked. "Maybe."

"Give me a little head start, okay?" With a small smile, she shook her head and moved around the side of the fence to head to the back.

Hefting his weapon, the dwarf stepped through the open gate and strode toward the magical thugs who carried heavy fire-power of their own. *Not as heavy as mine.*

He got halfway to the front door before a Crystal rose from behind a stack of crates and noticed him. "Hey! What the hell do you think you're doin'?"

As the creature turned to aim a huge gun at the dwarf, Johnny lifted his weapon and grinned. "It's playtime."

He squeezed a shot off before his adversary had taken aim. The stacked crates exploded in a shower of splintered wood and icy fragments as the Crystal was launched back with a roar. Two seconds later, the charge fired from his blast detonated a second time. The area erupted in a column of fire and smoke, and the other magical thugs outside turned their weapons onto the bounty hunter.

"Don't move, dwarf!"

"I don't know who you think you are, asshole, but—"

Johnny switched the setting on his portable firearm and unleashed a spray of automatic fire. The bullets themselves were slightly modified—not to punch through flesh but to leave his targets stunned and breathless before the rounds detonated on their own. One by one, the dozen thugs still out front were hurled against the wall as he swept his weapon's fire across their scattered line and the tiny explosives did what they were designed to do.

One wizard managed to raise a shield in front of him before the exploding bullets could hit home. With wide eyes, he hurled a fireball at the dwarf before the bullets exploded on his shield, then turned and raced through the door.

The bounty hunter ducked the fireball and drew an extra

magazine from his pocket. "Yeah, keep runnin'. I was takin' this party inside anyway."

He marched toward the door, which was now shut and locked. Squaring his feet, he switched the setting to rampant explosion and fired a shot at the barrier. The metal squealed and collapsed, careened through the doorway, and clattered to the floor in a cloud of dust, smoke, and metal shards. His expression smug, he inserted the new magazine into his weapon and headed inside.

The wizard who'd tried to lock him out lunged at him and another fireball materialized in his hand. Johnny ducked beneath the attack and cracked the end of his heavy modified rifle against the side of his opponent's knee. The magical fell with a shriek, and he elbowed him in the side of the head.

As the wizard sagged, the sound of two dozen firearms locked and loaded and aimed at the bounty hunter filled the room.

He jerked his chin at them, raised his gun, and switched the setting again quickly. "How's it goin', assholes?"

His weapon fired faster than any of theirs and this time, sprayed real bullets that didn't explode but drilled through stacked crates and folding tables piled high with locked brief-cases. A money-counter exploded and rained hundreds of fifty-dollar bills all over the thugs who took cover behind pallets and the steel support beams spaced evenly through the main room every twelve feet.

In the next moment, the thugs returned fire.

Johnny dove behind an overturned table and took one of the flattened black disks from his belt. He pressed the button on the top to activate it and lobbed it across the room. It exploded in the air with a crack and boom far bigger than an explosive that size warranted. Magicals of every size, shape, and race were launched away from the detonation and slid across the floor to ram into more stacked crates.

A shifter woman was halfway through a shift when the blast

hurled her against a half-full vending machine. The clear pane shattered and bottles of water, Gatorade, and soda tumbled over her. She slipped into her human form a second before the destroyed machine toppled forward onto her with a crunch and the sign at the top flickered on and off.

Johnny laughed and lifted his weapon before he stood from behind the overturned table. "Do you want more?"

Shots were fired by the thugs who hadn't been in the direct line of his last explosion. He fingered the trigger and let his automatic firing do the work for him. Bullets thunked into supplies and chairs and tables, pinged off the support beams, and ricocheted off the walls.

A witch summoning the shimmering wall of an attack spell in front of her outstretched hands screamed and fell to one knee. Her spell snuffed out and she immediately clutched both hands around her thigh above a bullet hole. "Motherfucker!"

"Maybe don't stand so close to the metal, huh?" the bounty hunter shouted in response.

A stream of icy shards hurtled toward him from the back of the wide main room. He spun and pressed his back against one of the steel support beams to check his ammo. *Okay. Light 'em up a few more times and if Lisa takes long enough, you can have some real fun.*

He stepped around the other side of the beam and sprayed automatic fire at the Crystal at the back of the room. A stormy blizzard kicked up around the enemy's body as he pelted another stream of jagged ice that passed his target and exploded against the steel beam. *The fucker can't see what he's aimin' at when he goes all snowy. Come on.*

A gnome with a machine-gun almost as big as he was thunked the weapon on an overturned table and opened fire. Johnny ducked and slid across the floor as the bullets whistled overhead. The report of someone else's automatic weapon's fire echoed through the room. Attack spells in blazing colors followed.

Before he finished his slide toward the next steel beam, the dwarf ejected the magazine of regular bullets and retrieved the last one from his pocket before he thrust it into place. The machine-gun sprayed bullets into the already cracked cement at his feet before he scrambled upright and pressed his back against the next beam. "Yeah, we'll have some fun."

He twisted and fired the single dart from the magazine into the center of the room. It split apart in mid-air and launched four separate pieces toward the four closest steel beams. The highly charged magnets clung to the beams after four thumps in quick succession and detonated with a massive magnetic charge. The shockwave spread outward from the beams, then sucked in all at once and drew every piece of metal in a thirty-foot radius with it.

Guns were ripped from the thugs' hands and clanged against the steel girders. Watches and rings and thick chain necklaces were yanked off their owners too. A half-Kilomea launched toward the closest beam, dragged by his belt buckle, and roared when his belt and his crotch caught the corner of the support. He sagged against the thick metal and tried to wrestle himself free from the beam that had become one of the four strongest magnets in Queens.

A half-wizard shrieked and became airborne, carried by the rifle strapped around his neck and shoulders. He struck the closest beam with a thump that knocked him out cold and left him to dangle by his weapon strap. Even the machine-gun was dragged from the gnome's hand in mid-fire and it lurched after the stream of bullets redirected toward the far-right beam. The bullets clanged against the metal to leave small dents but none dropped.

Two thugs were knocked in the head by their neighbors' flying weapons and sprawled on the floor, groaning.

Johnny ejected the empty magnetizing magazine and stepped out from behind the beam a good ten feet outside the magnetic field. Holding his multi-purpose launcher-rifle with both hands like a bat, the dwarf grinned at what was left of the Artful Dodger's cronies. "I kinda like goin' old-school, yeah?"

A dwarf woman and the Crystal exchanged a confused look, then darted toward the Level Six bounty hunter with the dozen other criminals still on their feet. Spells streaked toward him and he ducked and dodged around them before he swung his heavy weapon into a wizard's gut. He spun, whipped his knife out, and slashed a Light Elf's thigh before the magical could conjure more than a spark in his hands.

"Who the fuck are you?" the elf snapped.

He walloped his weapon against the elf's back and thrust him forward onto his face. "I'm back. Who's next?"

Lisa slipped through the back door of the waste management company's main building, her service pistol drawn as she cleared one room and section of the back hall at a time. She reached the rear of the main warehouse the Artful Dodger and his thugs used as their operations base as Johnny's magnetic pulse erupted from the four steel beams in the center. *That's one hell of a toy to lug around. Now, where's our guy?*

As her partner pounded heads and leapt off stacked crates, his knife flashing under the overhead lights, she peered through the open double doors in the back and scanned the magicals. *If he's never been caught, there's no way he stuck around for this.*

The thugs raced toward the dwarf and got more than they bargained for in a serious ass-kicking from the bounty hunter. Lisa caught sight of a man with long, stringy black hair who vaulted onto a stack of crates on the left. He paused, crouched there, and looked over his shoulder at the dwarf, who quickly dispatched the other criminals as he circled the room. A thick strand of the man's hair lifted toward the melee before it settled over his shoulder again. He leapt off the crates onto the metal shelving unit along the back wall, then scurried across the shelves toward the open double doors farther back.

So the Artful Dodger's an Atlantean buying his way up the criminal ladder. No wonder he's never been caught—until now.

She slipped into the hallway again and pressed her back against the wall. When she heard the soles of two light rubber shoes meet the floor, she raised her pistol and focused on the doorway.

The Artful Dodger walked swiftly through the open doors and flicked the collar of his brown suede jacket up with a smirk. He didn't see Agent Breyer's pistol come down on the back of his head or the floor coming up to meet his face. The Atlantean hissed and scrambled onto his back as he reached into his jacket pocket.

Lisa kicked his hand away and placed her shoe dead-center in the Artful Dodger's chest. The only thing that stopped him from throwing her off was her pistol aimed at his head. He hissed at her again and one eye twitched. The dozens of snakes attached to his head where hair should have been raised and hissed at her too.

"If I see one of those so much as wiggle the wrong way, I'll kill you."

His hair was silenced and fell limply away from his face instead.

"And don't even think about sending a stowaway."

The Atlantean snarled at her. "What do you want?"

"Your invitation to the Monsters Ball tonight."

He chuckled. "Fat fucking chance, lady. I bought that fair and—"

Lisa squeezed off a shot two inches from the man's head and severed the head of one of his snake-hair creatures. The others squeaked in agony and hissed at her again as the magical they served growled. "That's your second warning. I usually don't have to go to three."

A shifter catapulted through the open doors behind them, snarled, and scrambled to gain purchase on the cement floors before he thumped painfully against the far wall. As he pushed to his feet, the gray wolf snarled, shook the pain aside, and lurched into the fight as Johnny's bellowed laughter and a, "No, fuck you!" echoed in the main room.

Lisa looked at the wolf, intending to shoot him if she had to, and the Artful Dodger seized his opportunity. He pounded his fist against the side of her knee and rolled clear when she shouted in surprise and staggered sideways and away from him. The man broke into a run down the hall, zig-zagging to keep her from settling her aim with her weapon.

Gritting her teeth, she holstered her gun as she raced after him and summoned a fireball. The Atlantean reached an open metal staircase and launched onto the edge to pull himself up by the railing. She released her fireball at his hand and knocked his hold loose. Then, she jumped after him, wrapped both hands around one of his legs, and pulled.

They both toppled into a heap, and she scrambled to her knees at the same moment he did. Her vicious right hook caught him in the jaw. His hair whipped sideways with him, and the snakes hissed again in fury.

She hissed in response and drove her other fist into the Artful Dodger's stomach. He swung wildly at her, his eyes wide, and she blocked each attack before she pushed off her knees and into a crouch to deliver a swift kick at his chest. As soon as his back hit the floor, she stood over him to deliver two more swift punches to his face. His eyes rolled back in his head and the snakes fell limp around him. She swiped her dark hair out of her eyes before she yanked his jacket open.

The first pocket was empty, but the second held a thin, metal square that she jerked out with a grin. The engraved gold invitation winked at her under the caged lights overhead, and she secured it in her jacket pocket. Drawing her weapon again, she kept her eye on the groaning Artful Dodger and sidestepped toward the double doors into the main room. "I got it!"

Johnny leapt off a table to deliver a flying double-kick at the half-Kilomea's gut. The hairy, growling magical staggered away, his belt loops frayed and sticking out around the waistband of his cargo pants. Pushing off his back, the dwarf snatched his empty rifle-launcher and dove through the massive warrior's legs. His weapon cracked against the back of the magical's knees and he darted toward the back of the warehouse with his knife between his teeth.

A wizard lurched at him and caught the dwarf from behind. He doubled over, threw the man over his shoulder and into another folding table, and dropped to punch the guy in the face. Spells streaked toward him and Lisa, and they ducked beneath the crackling magical attacks before he took another exploding disk from his belt.

"I had a great time, fellas, but won't be doin' it again!"

The disk detonated with a shockwave that blasted the last handful of still-conscious thugs across the room. It launched Johnny and Lisa forward against the far wall of the back corridor too. Laughing, he slapped the wall and turned to look at her. "After you."

"Right." Grimacing, she rubbed her smarting forehead and darted the Atlantean on the floor a dismissive glance. "Let's get outta here."

The dwarf followed her the way she'd come toward the back of the building, and by the time the thugs in the main room recovered from the blast, their attackers were gone.

"Oh, shit." A gnome raced down the hall toward the Artful Dodger, who now pushed off the floor to sit upright. "Are you good, boss?"

The Atlantean slapped his crony's hand away. "Don't touch me."

"My bad." The diminutive thug stepped back and studied his boss cautiously. "It's the first time I ever seen you take a beatin'."

"And the last time." The Dodger ran a hand through his snake hair and felt the loss of the one head severed by the woman's bullet. "That fucking bitch."

The Crystal staggered through the doors and his ice-covered feet crunched across the floor. The millions of ice crystals encasing him tinkled against each other and glittered as he moved. "Who the fuck were those guys?"

"They're probably workin' for one of the Monsters if you ask me," the gnome said.

"Yeah, well, they didn't exactly leave a note." The Dodger straightened his suede jacket, paused, and checked his inside pocket. "Fuck."

"Who did we piss off this time?" the Crystal asked. "I thought we were good with Mattheus, boss."

"It wasn't Mattheus." Their leader rubbed the side of his swelling jaw and spat out a bloody glob. "Whoever it was doesn't want me at the fucking ball. Get back in there and clean that shit up."

The Atlantean turned and stormed down another hallway toward the room he used as his private office. None of his underlings said a word. They all knew the Artful Dodger wasn't a real mob boss, not like those East Coast yuppies going to the Monsters Ball that night. He'd only bought his way into their party with the fortune he'd amassed by stealing, and a good portion of it had most likely been from them.

CHAPTER NINETEEN

At the hotel, Johnny shrugged into his new dinner jacket that matched the dress slacks and stared at himself in the mirror of the closet's sliding door.

"What are you supposed to be, huh?" Lying across the king-sized bed, Luther raised his head from his forepaws and tilted it in confusion. "I don't get it."

"Yeah, Johnny." Rex padded toward his master to sniff the hem of the dwarf's pants. "Halloween was six months ago."

"We have a ticket into that party tonight, boys." He sniffed and combed his fingers through his thick auburn hair. "I gotta play the part."

"The part of a dwarf with a stick up his ass?"

Luther's tongue lolled out of his mouth as he panted in amusement, and his laughter filled his master's head. "Good one."

He lowered his hands and turned away from the mirror to focus on his hounds. "What, you want me to find a couple of hound tuxedos? I bet we could pass you off as my magical bodyguards."

Rex sat and stared at his master. "For real?"

"No. Y'all get to stay here."

"Again?" Luther whined. "Johnny, you just got back."

"Yeah, an hour ago."

A knock came at his hotel door. When he opened it, Lisa stood there in a skin-tight maroon dress with the functionless but alluring shoulder straps draped across her upper arms. He raised an eyebrow.

She studied him slowly and pursed her lips in a small, coy smile. "Wow, Johnny. You clean up much nicer than I expected."

With a grunt, he turned away from the door without holding it for her to enter and returned to studying himself in the floor-to-ceiling mirror. "I shouldn't have let you talk me into the monkey suit. This is not my gig."

"Maybe." She let the door swing shut behind her and joined him in front of the mirror. "From where I stand, this looks very much like your gig."

She smiled at him in the mirror's reflection and pulled the silver-sequined clutch out from under her arm to hold it with both hands. Her three-inch stilettos only turned their height difference into a glaring discrepancy. He came up to her shoulders.

Johnny glanced at her heels. "Are you tellin' me you can run in those if you have to?"

"I wouldn't wear them if I couldn't."

"Uh-huh." He studied her reflection in the mirror. *Drop-dead sexy. That ain't gonna help none.* "Are you packin'?"

Lisa took a step back and spread her arms. "Can't you tell?"

Where the hell' is she keepin' it? The corner of his mouth twitched into a crooked smirk and he turned away from her to retrieve the remote from beside the flatscreen TV on the dresser. "As long as you can draw a weapon from wherever you're stashin' it in that outfit, we'll be fine."

"You'd be surprised by how much I can do in this."

Johnny paused with the remote aimed at the TV and grinned at her. "Not surprised at all, darlin'."

On the bed, Luther stopped panting to lick his muzzle and utter a low whine. "Oh, man, Johnny. You're in for it now."

"If she was a dog, Johnny, she'd be wagging her ass in your face and tellin' you to come and get it."

"Ha-ha. Yeah, she is—"

The dwarf cast Luther a withering glance and snapped his fingers. "Hush."

The hound lowered his head to his forepaws again and Rex settled on his belly on the carpet in front of the nightstand.

Lisa narrowed her eyes at her partner and smiled. "What do they want now?"

"Merely to be a pain in my ass." The dwarf sniffed disdainfully and lifted the remote toward the TV again to turn it on. "I'm gonna leave them with somethin' that at least sounds like they have company."

As he flipped through the channels, Luther stretched his back legs out on the bedspread. "Johnny. Put on one of those huntin' shows."

"Yeah." Rex responded with a sharp, excited yip. "Like *Duck Dynasty*."

"Like—" Johnny turned to glare at the dog. "Boy, you must be outta your mind."

"What? That show's awesome."

Luther's tail thumped against the bedspread. "There's a smokin'-hot Frenchie on there too. She's the best part."

"Ugh. Don't lower your standards like that, bro."

"Oh, come on. First you say the city poodle's outta my league, and now you tell me I can't even like watchin' the French Bulldog on the TV?"

"I didn't say she was out of your league, Luther. I said it would never work—"

The dwarf snapped his fingers and the hounds' bickering ended abruptly. "There. Y'all can watch Discovery Channel and maybe learn a few things about… What's that?" He squinted at the TV. "Australia. Sure. Broaden your horizons."

The remote clattered onto the dresser and he headed toward Lisa. "Do you have the time? The Willen took my watch."

Smirking, she pointed at the digital clock on the nightstand. "Eight o'clock."

"Great. So we'll either be fashionably late or who-gives-a-fuck early. Let's get outta here."

"What about room service, Johnny?" Luther asked.

"Yeah. You said we'd have dinner in forty minutes. It's been like a million minutes already."

"Do the dogs have everything they need?" Lisa asked and looked over her shoulder at them as she headed to the door.

He raised an eyebrow. "What made you ask that?"

"The way they're staring at you."

There is no way she can hear them. Maybe she simply knows dogs better than I thought. "I ordered a few big-ass steaks, no sides, and told the guy to slip the trays through the door and hightail it out again."

"Oh, good." Chuckling, she opened the door. "They're gonna think we're having some kinda private party of our own in there. Or that we're keeping a dangerous, rabid creature in the hotel room."

"Let 'em think whatever they want, darlin'. Someone's gotta serve those steaks and we gotta go."

"You're the best, Johnny!" Luther called.

"Wait, wait, wait." Rex stood and trotted toward the door. "Aren't you gonna say goodbye—"

"Holy shit! Rex! Check this out!"

"What?"

"This dingo looks exactly like that bitch you picked up in Goodland."

"Are you kidding me?" Rex spun and raced toward the bed for a flying leap.

"Woah! Did you see that? She took down a whole—"

Johnny pulled the door shut and turned to head down the hall. "They won't even know I'm gone."

He drove their rental to Manhattan's Financial District and pulled up to the curb at 8:36 pm. The valet in front of Falcon Towers took his tip and widened his eyes. "Sir, did you mean to—"

"Yep. Keep the change." He closed the door, turned toward the building, and his eyes narrowed. The valet pulled their SUV swiftly into the lot and the street grew quiet. "Does it seem weird to you that no one else is steppin' outta their cars?"

"If you were one of these assholes wanting to get in on the bidding, would you run the risk of being late?"

He snorted. "Nope."

"There you go." Lisa's heels clicked on the front walkway toward the building. "I'm kinda glad there's no one else to see us roll up driving our own car. Everyone else would've had a driver."

"Yeah, so did we. And he's cheaper too 'cause he'd simply be payin' himself. I'm talkin' about me, by the way."

She smirked as the doorman opened the door. "I meant private drivers."

"I know what you meant, darlin'. I still don't see the difference."

"Welcome to Falcon Towers," the doorman said, inclined his head, and glanced from the dwarf to the well-dressed, fit woman who stood so much taller than him. "Are you visiting someone this evening?"

"Yeah." Johnny cleared his throat and glanced at the elevators. "We're goin' to the penthouse."

"Ah. Yes. May I see your invitation?"

He drew the engraved gold card from his pocket and flashed it at the doorman.

"Very well. If you'll make your way to the last elevator, Dennis will take you up."

"Thank you." Lisa grinned at the man and batted her lashes as Johnny slid the invitation into his pocket again. The doorman nodded and watched them move down the lobby toward the last elevator.

"Are you Dennis?" Johnny asked the man standing behind the open elevator doors.

"Yes, sir. That's me. Do you have your invitation?"

The dwarf flashed it again, and the elevator operator clasped his hands behind his back with a small nod. "I merely need to authenticate it, sir. If you don't mind."

"I kinda do, yeah."

"We were invited, darling." Lisa smiled sweetly at him. "Let the man do his job."

Gritting his teeth, Johnny handed the invitation over and sniffed. *She's playin' that one a little too far if you ask me.*

The elevator operator took the invitation graciously and inserted the end of it into a small card-reader he took from his pocket. The device emitted a soft beep and flashed a green light, and the stolen invitation was returned to him. "Up to the penthouse."

"Uh-huh." After pocketing the golden card, the dwarf tugged on the lapels of his dinner jacket and stared at the floor counter ticking up to the top floor and the penthouse above it.

"Have you heard anything about what's waiting for us up there?" Lisa asked.

The man frowned at her in surprise but recovered quickly. "No, ma'am. I think those details are meant to remain in the penthouse. But all the other guests did seem particularly...excited."

"Well, that's a relief."

Johnny turned slowly to frown at her. Lisa's only reaction was to give him another sickly-sweet smile before she stared at the floor counter, holding her clutch in both hands.

When they finally reached the top, the door opened and the operator gestured with a white-gloved hand toward the entrance of the penthouse. "Enjoy your evening."

"Thank you very much." She stepped out first, and he forced himself to not adjust his dress slacks as he followed her.

"Did you ask the elevator guy for information?"

"It's not a big deal. Do you have any idea how much information the concierges and doormen and even elevator operators hear during a regular day?" She shrugged. "He's good at his job, though. He didn't offer any info but still gave us something to look forward to. Assuming we were here to have fun."

"Oh, we'll have fun. Then, we'll hightail it to the hotel with the girl."

Two half-Kilomea security guards in matching tuxedos and with heavy-duty assault rifles stood on either side of the foyer entrance. They regarded Johnny with contempt, and their oversized eyeteeth protruded half as much from their hairy faces as their full-blooded cousins'.

The dwarf jerked his chin at them. "Hell of a night, huh, fellas? Do they give you a shift drink during this gig?"

The guard on the left grunted and glanced at the black, steel-toed boots he'd refused to switch out for dress shoes. "Invitation. Sir."

Johnny slid his hand into the inside pocket of his dinner jacket and flashed the golden card at the guards. "What if you gotta hit the john? Do you need to sign off on that, or you go in shifts when nature calls?"

The guard on the right couldn't pull his gaze away from the relatively modest neckline of Lisa's dress that only left about half her figure to the imagination. The rest of the skintight ensemble took care of the other half. The bounty hunter pointed at him and looked at the other guard. "He doesn't talk much, does he?"

She chuckled and caught his forearm to lower it to his side. "Don't pay attention to him, gentlemen. He gets like this when he's excited."

The left-hand guard grunted again and nodded toward the penthouse behind him. "You're good."

"Yes, we are." She tugged her partner along with her as the other guard turned to look over his shoulder as she walked away. His counterpart punched him in the arm and shook him out of his stare. "If you talk to everyone like that tonight, Johnny, you'll blow our cover."

"Please. Everyone in this building is an asshole at some level. An asshole who doesn't pretend to be a fucking saint? That's refreshing."

"Maybe rein it in a little. We still have a long night ahead of us."

He grimaced. "Don't remind me."

They stepped into the sweeping main room of the penthouse, which was already filled with the East Coast's widest selection of crime bosses, syndicate owners, and drug lords. Scantily clad women with frilly, ruched bonnets walked around serving hors d'oeuvres on glistening silver trays. A champagne tower rested against the far-right wall.

To the left of center against the wall of windows that looked out over Times Square was a stage, and black curtains had been hung between the side of the stage and another door leading to the penthouse's more private rooms. The bar was set up in the kitchen to the right of the foyer, and Johnny headed that way first.

"There's something we forgot to cover," Lisa muttered as she walked gracefully beside him in killer stilettos.

"I don't think so."

"I don't think we should use our real names. Call me Candace, okay?"

He chuckled. "Do you know how many times some

douchebag lookin' at you in that dress is gonna think he's so smart by callin' you Candy instead?"

"Go with it. What do you want me to call you?"

He turned slowly to look at her. "Johnny."

"That's not—"

The dwarf waved her off. "The only name I'm usin' is my own, darlin'. I don't think these are the kinda folks who worry about rememberin' first names."

She smiled at two Azrakan who walked past. The female's crown of horns was much smaller than the male's, and she glared at Lisa while her partner examined the agent from head to toe and flicked a forked tongue between his lips. The female snarled and pulled him along with her across the penthouse.

Johnny stepped up to the bar laid out on the eight-foot-long kitchen island's granite countertop. "What're you drinkin', darlin'?"

"Oh. Gin and tonic, please."

The dwarf rapped his knuckles on the counter. "Extra lime for her. I'll have a Johnny Walker Black. Double. Straight."

The bartender nodded, already looking sweaty and hot beneath the high, stiff collar of his shirt and the heavy, well-tailored black vest over it. He set the glasses down in front of them when he finished and nodded. "Enjoy yourselves."

"Open bar?"

"Yes, sir."

"It's gonna be a good night." The dwarf raised his drink in a silent toast to the man and took a long sip. "Let's go get our mingle on, huh?"

Lisa finished squeezing the extra limes into her drink. She turned to face the magical mobsters entertaining themselves with low conversation and stuck the tiny cocktail straw into her mouth. "Let's."

They headed toward a group of three Kilomeas without illusion charms who stood beside the champagne tower. The biggest one wore no dress shirt beneath his leather vest made to look like a suit vest, but at least he'd donned a pair of brown slacks almost the same color. *I don't care how hairy those bastards are. They should cover up like the rest of us— Oh, shit.*

Johnny settled a hand under her elbow and steered her away from the Kilomeas.

"What are you doing? Isn't that Garreth Browel?"

"The big motherfucker? Yeah." He cleared his throat. "But the two-legged wildebeest on his right is Malek Ordus."

She shook her head. "Who?"

"Does New Jersey's Fang ring a bell?"

"Oh…"

"No, no." His hold on her elbow tightened slightly. "Don't look at him. I collected a bounty on him in '97. While I didn't expect him to be out livin' the life so soon, they don't pay me to keep tabs on these assholes after the fact."

"Right. So the Kilomea are off limits tonight."

"Only those." He nodded at an Atlantean woman in a black dress cut so low it might as well have been a light robe she'd shrugged onto her naked body and forgotten to close all the way. She sipped a drink of something black-green and viscous and looked incredibly bored as the males around her of multiple different races vied for her attention with stories of their exploits and monetary values in the billions. "But there's Ameyna the Heiress."

"And she looks like she'd appreciate a distraction. That's Clyde Ambrose next to her. He runs the import-export smuggling off the eastern seaboard."

Johnny chuckled. "Is that what your bosses call heavy munitions these days? Import-exports?"

"I'm trying to keep a low profile, Johnny."

He smirked and glanced meaningfully at her outfit. "You should've worn a different dress, then."

"What's wrong with my dress?" Her tone took on an unexpected harshness but the small smile that bloomed on her lips was completely real.

"Absolutely nothin'."

They drifted slowly toward the group of crime bosses gathered around Ameyna the Heiress. Johnny raised his whiskey to his lips and gestured toward the chandelier. "You know, I like what they've done with the place. I woulda put a rack up myself. I got a sixteen-pointer at home over my ballroom, but I guess they were goin' for a more open feel."

Lisa pressed her lips together and looked at him in surprise. "You never cease to amaze me with your eye for interior design."

"What can I say? It's a gift and a curse."

She took a long sip of her gin and tonic to keep from laughing.

He stared at the chandelier. *Yeah, she didn't see that comin'. I can shit-talk my way into snobbery like the rest of 'em. And I wanna rip that fucking monstrosity from the ceiling.*

One of the hors d'oeuvres girls walked past with a silver tray in her hand. "Beluga caviar?"

"Oh. Thank you." Lisa stretched to take one of the delicate crystal saucers beneath each hors d'oeuvre, glanced at Johnny who stood a foot below the server's tray, and handed him the saucer before she took another.

The server's frilly lacy bonnet fluttered on top of her golden curls as she nodded at them and continued her rounds through the penthouse.

The agent almost burst out laughing when she saw her partner scowl at the gooey black pile on the saucer. "What's wrong?"

"What is this? It looks like shit on a fancy plate."

"It's Beluga caviar, Johnny—"

"I know what it's tryin' to be. But trust me, this ain't fresh."

"And you know that simply by looking at it?" Smirking, she

lowered her head to sniff the tiny pile with four artisanal crackers spread along the saucer beside it.

"Lemme tell you somethin', Candace." Johnny sniffed. "The only way to eat caviar is to slip a hook through the fish's cheek and slice the belly open yourself. I don't care what kinda fish it is. That's fresh. This was canned and shipped from Italy or somewhere crazy like that. Untaxed too, I reckon. No one in this room took the time to fish and slice for this pile of— Uh-uh."

With a soft chuckle, Lisa slid her clutch under her arm and held both her drink and the crystal saucer deftly in one hand so she could scoop a mound of Beluga caviar onto one of the crackers.

"Oh, come on. Did you hear what I said?"

The cracker crunched in her mouth and her eyes widened. "It's perfect."

Rolling his eyes, he lifted his drink to his lips and set his saucer on the tray of a passing server returning to the kitchen. "You're only doin' that to get a rise outta me."

"If that's what you wanna think, go ahead. I'm taking the little enjoyments where I can get them."

"Uh-huh." He looked at her and raised a finger to the corner of his mouth. "You got a little somethin'…"

"Oh." With a self-conscious laugh, she wiped the stray cracker crumbs and fish eggs from her mouth and scanned the penthouse. Quickly, she leaned toward him until her lips were inches from his ear. "We should start pretending to have a real conversation and listen to what these strutting peacocks let slip to the Heiress. I heard one of them say auction."

Her delicate perfume smelled like she'd watered it down before she put it on—barely strong enough that anyone close enough would get a hint of something sweet. He took another sip of his whiskey and watched a group of wizards in silk suits and a compact man with a hooked nose and a diamond-studded watch who stared at him and the gorgeous woman who stood over a foot taller than him. *That perfume wasn't part of the plan.*

"I've been listenin', darlin'."

Smiling sweetly, Lisa moved away from him and straightened before she took another sip. "Good."

CHAPTER TWENTY

Reynaldo chuckled. "I wouldn't go so far as to say that. Even if they did provide much more fleshed-out descriptions, I doubt they've had enough time to discover everything about each lot. What are there? Two dozen?"

"Twenty-seven," Ameyna replied in a low, drawn-out hiss.

"Like I said. Practically two dozen."

"And there are more of us than that here tonight." The half-wizard who stood beside the Atlantean Heiress raised his drink and smirked at her. "And many more who bid before this little get-together began. How many do you think will go home empty-handed when the night's over?"

"You mean other than you, Marco?" A shifter with a long, thick black ponytail tied back with an emerald-studded brooch lifted his glass. "We'll see."

Marco's face took on a deep red flush and he swirled the champagne in his wide-bottomed glass quickly. "You're placing your bets in the wrong pool, Cal."

"That's rich coming from the man who's supposed to fix the Preakness." Cal darted the man a feral grin. "How much did you lose last week?"

"Not enough to keep me from bidding." Marco sipped his champagne. "I haven't seen your name up on the auction board since, what? Two nights ago."

"I'm merely biding my time. Trust me, wizard. I didn't come here simply to watch the rest of you have all the fun."

Ameyna sipped her sludgy drink and the glittering black snakes of her hair wove constantly as they watched the other crime lords in the penthouse for her. Each of them had a half-carat diamond affixed to their sleek foreheads above their eyes. These cast a halo of glinting white dots across the Atlantean's plunging neckline and the lapels of the other bosses standing around her.

"And what about you, Heiress?" Reynaldo asked. "I heard business is good for you in the Houses. I'm interested to hear what you're looking to find tonight."

She gave him a sideways glance but didn't move her head. "I'm not telling you which lots I'll bid on, human."

Ignoring the slight against his non-magical lineage, Reynaldo chuckled softly. "I merely wondered why the East Coast's most successful and alluring madam comes to bid on this particular auction."

The snakes in her hair closest to the man stretched toward him with a chorus of hisses. "A few of my regulars have asked for something to fulfill some of their more...acquired tastes."

Cal uttered a low, growling chuckle. "Like that shifter girl?"

Marco's eyes fluttered closed as he took a slow, deep breath through his nose. "Can you imagine? I hear the bid's been at two million since this morning. It's not surprising if you ask me."

"Two point three," Ameyna replied.

"Oh." Reynaldo grinned and leaned away from her. "So you have kept an eye on the little shifter peach."

"I keep an eye on all of it. Don't presume to understand my motives, Reynaldo. False intelligence doesn't look good on you, but I suppose we all have to work with what we have."

Marco and Cal snorted into their drinks. Reynaldo's lips twitched into a sneer, and he adjusted the collar of his dress shirt without being able to come up with a reply.

"If you were to bid on our Belle of the Ball," Cal said, "do you think you'd manage to outbid Lemonhead"

Ameyna's dark, glistening gaze flicked toward the shifter, and her eyes widened slightly. "If he even appears. In-person attendance is still required to place a winning bid and take the prize home, is it not?"

"I wonder if he knows that. It's about time we put a face to that stupid name."

Marco sipped his champagne. "You saw that Bulldog trying to give Lemonhead a run for his money, didn't you? Like a bad episode of *Bidding Wars*."

"Whoever that chump is, he dropped out after a million and a half." Cal stroked his beard. "My bet's on Bulldog being a mid-level monster with delusions of grandeur."

"Or he merely didn't think the girl would provide enough of an ROI." Reynaldo raised an eyebrow. "If you ask me, I'd say she's worth more than two point three million."

"Then why don't you bid when they bring her up on stage?" Cal asked.

"Maybe I will."

"I've had my eye on those Guatemalan twins," Marco added. "The things one could do with a matching pair of devout and terrified immigrants. What do you think?"

The conversation turned away from Lemonhead and the bid on Amanda and didn't circle to them again. After three more minutes of listening to the infuriating exchange, Johnny placed his hand on the small of Lisa's back and guided her farther across the penthouse. "Let's keep walking."

She looked at him in surprise but didn't shy away. "I didn't take you for the handsy type."

He removed his hand and slid it slowly into the pocket of his slacks. "I ain't."

They canvassed the penthouse and the dozens of mob bosses both magical and human and listened in on any conversations that even hinted at information about Lemonhead or Amanda. Many of the usernames they'd seen on the dark-web bidding were thrown around—along with exorbitant amounts of money for various lots —but no one knew who Lemonhead was, what he wanted, or if he would even make an appearance at the Monsters Ball.

Halfway through their wide circle around the penthouse's main room, Johnny had mapped each and every criminal asshole he'd felt staring at both him and Lisa—mostly Lisa, though. By the time they returned to the bar at the kitchen island, he suggested they go back for another drink.

The bartender looked at them with well-honed apathy and no hint of recognition.

The dwarf cleared his throat. "Yeah, we'll have another—"

"Gin and tonic for the lady," the bartender said. "Extra lime. And Johnny Walker Black for the gentleman. Double. Straight."

He smirked at the man and rapped his knuckles on the granite counter again. "You're good."

"Thank you, sir."

As the bartender moved swiftly to pour their drinks, Johnny turned to Lisa and found her tangled in conversation with an overweight wizard in a pinstriped suit and a golden monocle.

"A beautiful thing like you? Come on. Of course you're interested. Let me get you a drink and we'll talk."

"I'm already getting my drink, thank you." She shook her head firmly. "And I'm not interested."

"Don't say that, honey. Look at you." The wizard stepped toward her and his eyes bulged as he stared down the front of her dress. A thin sheen of sweat glistened on his forehead. "This isn't the kind of offer that gets passed around every day." His thick-fingered hand slid onto her hip as he stepped closer and chuckled. "There's a private room on the east side. Grab your drink and I'll tell you all about it."

Lisa looked slowly at his hand on her hip and stuck her clutch under one arm. "You need to—"

"Clean out your fuckin' ears, bub." Johnny caught the wizard's hand and jerked it away from her hip. Bones crunched in the dwarf's vicelike grip, and the wizard shrieked as his knees buckled beneath him. His other hand slapped the granite countertop and he gaped at his crushed hand.

"My hand! W-what are you? Crazy?" He shrieked again. "Y-you can't—"

"I just did. No means no. That's been a thing for a while." He released the wizard's hand and the magical staggered to his knees with a gasp. His monocle fell from his eye and the end of the attached chain pulled free from its pin as he cradled his hand to his chest and groaned.

The dwarf turned toward the counter for their waiting drinks and offered Lisa her gin and tonic. "Let's go."

She scowled and took her glass quickly, but she wasn't happy about it.

Pausing beside the sniveling, oversized wizard, he sneered at him and muttered, "Don't let me catch you doin' that again. Douche."

His boot crunched on the fallen monocle as he stepped away with his partner at his side.

"That does not count as keeping a low profile, Johnny."

"Neither was he. The bastard needs to learn—"

"Hey." She stopped and turned toward him. "Next time, let me take care of it."

He studied her face and his eye twitched. "You're pissed."

"I can handle myself in almost any situation, Johnny. I thought we covered that already."

"All right. My bad. No means no even when you're turning help down, huh?"

"We're a team but I don't need your help with that."

"Yeah." He sipped his whiskey and heaved a loud, contented sigh. "How's your drink?"

Taking a deep breath, Lisa stared at him over the rim of her glass as she slipped the cocktail straw between her lips. "Exactly the way I like it."

"Good. Do you want me to let you order your own drink next time too?"

She rolled her eyes and couldn't help a small chuckle. "You can keep ordering my drinks."

"Great. We're finding boundaries. Now, let's go—"

"Ladies and gentlemen. Monsters and men." The MC's high-pitched voice shrieked over the loudspeaker, and all attendees paused their conversations to be picked up later and turned to face the stage. The gnome who stood there in a glittering, emerald-green smoking jacket jerked the microphone out of the stand and gestured expansively with his other arm. "Now that you've all had some time to build a little more excitement for tonight's event, it's time to open the auction for the last round of bids. And do we have some exquisite lots to present to you tonight, ladies and gentlemen. Absolutely exquisite. So let's begin, shall we?"

A round of polite applause and a few whistles drifted toward the stage as the gnome marched toward his list on the podium. The only sign that any of these criminals were more excited than they let on was the fact that no one said a word and all eyes stared hungrily at the sheet of paper fluttering in the gnome's hand.

"Here we go," Lisa muttered into her glass.

Johnny downed the rest of his double Johnny Walker Black and grimaced. "Fuck."

CHAPTER TWENTY-ONE

"Up first, Lot 13725." The MC gestured toward the black drape stretched between the stage and the back corner of the penthouse.

It whipped aside and another Kilomea security guard in a tuxedo yanked a terrified young girl onto the stage. She stood with her shoulders hunched, her thick black hair hanging around her face like a curtain as she shuddered with silent tears.

"Jesus," Lisa muttered.

"Beautiful girl from Chinatown, ladies and gentlemen. Seventeen. Looks can be deceiving when she's standing like that. Chin up, girl." The MC chuckled. "Size two. The virtual bidding closed at five o'clock this evening with the winning bid at fourteen thousand. Do I hear fifteen thousand? Fifteen? Fifteen thousand to the wizard up front here. How about seventeen and a half? Do I hear seventeen and a—"

"Twenty-five." The bid came from the shifter Cal with the long dark ponytail.

"Twenty-five thousand to Cal Pelfer and Queens' very own purveyor of mind-elevating alternatives." The gnome winked at the shifter mob boss and tittered. "Do I hear thirty? Thirty thousand? How about twenty-seven and a half? Do I hear twenty-seven and a half? Bid will go to Mr. Pelfer at twenty-five thousand. Going once. Going twice. Sold."

A silver ball of light launched from the MC's outstretched index finger and burst beneath the high penthouse ceiling like a glitter bomb before the magic dissipated into the air.

"Thank you, Mr. Pelfer. Your lot will wait for you in the back until you're finished with tonight's auction. Harvey, please hand the gentleman his ticket." The gnome nodded vigorously and grinned as a half-Kilomea security guard handed Cal Pelfer his claim ticket. "We're getting off to a wonderful start tonight, ladies and gentlemen. A wonderful start indeed. And now I'd like to turn your attention to Lot 13726, all the way from Jamaica!"

The guard who still held his hand around the terrified young girl's arm jerked her backward across the stage with him. They vanished behind the black curtain two seconds before another one appeared dragging a tiny Jamaican girl behind him by the back of her shirt. She cried out when he jerked her around to stand on her feet and she whimpered on the stage.

"Now look at this one," the MC cried. "Ten years old. And she's come a long, long way to be with you tonight, ladies and gentlemen. Look at that potential. Bidding closed this evening at thirty-three thousand dollars. Do I hear forty?"

The dwarf's grasp tightened around the empty rocks glass until it cracked.

"Johnny," Lisa whispered and leaned toward him. "I'm not gonna ask if you're okay but we can't start breaking things now."

"I know," he all but growled in a low tone.

"We have to lay low until they bring Amanda up—"

"I know," he snapped and leaned to the side to clink the almost shattered glass on a passing server's tray. His fist clenched and unclenched as he forced it down to his side again. "I'm fine."

She gave the surprised server a reassuring glance, then raised her chin as she forced herself to look at the stage. "I know."

Johnny sniffed. The muscles of his jaw worked beneath his bristling red beard as he endured the spectacle and couldn't do a damn thing about it. *Rein it in, Johnny. You're not here for these girls tonight but you will be there for them. Play it smart. These mother-fuckers are goin' down eventually.*

As girl after girl was brought onto the stage, bid on, sold, and whisked away again to await being claimed by their monstrous buyers, he made a mental note of each and every one of them—what the girls looked like, which magical fucker bought them, and for how much. If he didn't recognize a buyer right away, he paired them with a name he knew he wouldn't forget. Fuckface in the Cravat. Stringy Bitch. Dickless Wizard with the Scar. Dickless Human with the Tattoo. Pencil-Thin Douchebag Beard.

Lisa noticed his lips moving under his red mustache as each girl was sold to the highest bidder and the crime lord was handed their claim ticket. "Do I need to be worried?" she whispered.

"No. They should be, though. I'm comin' for every last one of these sons of bitches later. Personally."

She returned her gaze to the stage and sipped her drink slowly. *He says 'later' like he's coming out of retirement. The Depart-ment's gonna piss themselves in excitement if that's what he plans to do.*

After twenty-six kidnapped, terrified, and weeping young girls were brought onto the auction stage and purchased like fucking cattle, Johnny's head throbbed from how tightly he clenched his jaw.

"Look at that." The gnome MC turned to watch the last girl dragged off the stage after she fainted. "What an incredible lineup, huh? And you've been so patient, ladies and gentlemen. So patient and so generous with your bids. But of course, that's why you were invited, isn't it?"

A round of eager chuckles issued from the crime lords scat-tered around the room. The feigned amusement died down quickly, however, so they could hang on the gnome's every word.

"And now, ladies and gentlemen, the moment you've all been

waiting for. The moment I've been waiting for too. I can't lie to you. Lot 13752, the Belle of this season's Monsters Ball!"

The crime lords and mob bosses drew closer to the stage to get a better look, muttered to their neighbors, and sipped their drinks. A Wood Elf stepped too close to Ameyna the Heiress and earned a face full of snake-hair bites before he staggered away with a snarl. Another scuffle broke out between a dwarf and a wizard who wouldn't let the shorter magical step in front of him despite being able to see well over the shorter man's head.

Johnny sneered and stared at the black curtain and the small scuffle rising behind it. "Here we go."

"How are we gonna do this?" Lisa asked.

"It'll come to me. Just back me up."

"You got it."

The sharp smack of flesh on flesh came from behind the curtain before a full-blooded Kilomea whipped the curtain aside and stepped onto the stage. His huge, shaggy feet made the platform tremble so much that the MC stumbled and righted himself hastily using the podium for balance. With a grunt, the Kilomea jerked a short chain of heavy metal links. "Move it, bitch."

The chain grew taut in his hand and a brilliant blue flicker of light and the zap of an electric cattle prod illuminated the darkness behind the stage. The chain slackened again, and the Kilomea hauled on it while whoever worked behind the curtain shoved the next lot onto the stage.

Amanda snarled at the Kilomea, her hands cuffed behind her back. The chain was attached to a heavy metal collar around her neck. When her hairy, snaggle-toothed handler pushed her forward, she snarled again and snapped at him with very human teeth.

"Woah-ho-ho!" the MC shouted into the microphone. "Look at the fight in this one, ladies and gentlemen."

The Kilomea jerked on the chain, and a collective gasp of amused excitement rose from the bidders. Amanda gritted her teeth and stared at the faces of so many strangers waiting to see who would pay the most money to take her home tonight. Her small fists clenched tightly at her sides as her chest heaved with rapid, heavy, furious breaths.

That's it, girl. Johnny couldn't look anywhere but at the young shifter's determined, unbroken strength. *We're gonna need that fight in you soon.*

"Twelve years old, ladies and gentlemen," the MC continued gleefully. "And a spitfire at that, isn't she? You've all read in the description that she likes to bite, and you've seen it for yourselves. No one's looking for this one, folks. We also came upon some new details in the last twelve hours, which if you haven't already guessed by the collar... Well. This one's a shifter. Bidding closed this evening at two point three million dollars. Do I hear two point five? Anyone with two point five—ah. Yes. Two point five to the Heiress. Very nice. Do I hear three million? Three million for this firecracker of a young shifter, and only twelve years old! Still time to mold her, eh? Three million? Three million to the gentleman in the back. That's fantastic, sir."

Heads turned toward a gray-skinned magical who stood at the back of the gathered crowd. Johnny didn't bother to look but Lisa caught a glimpse of the hulking giant in the tailored white suit. *The guy looks like he was burned all over and painted in ash.*

"Do I hear three point five million? Anyone?" The gnome was grinning now, breathing heavily as he almost pressed the head of the microphone against his glinting teeth. "Three and a quarter? Do I hear three and a quarter million for this fine young shifter in the collar? They don't make 'em like this anymore, no sirree. No? Very well. Three million dollars to the gentleman in the back with the impeccable white suit. Going once. Going twice—"

"Four million!" Johnny shouted and folded his arms.

Lisa balked as the rest of the crime lords turned to stare at the dwarf who hadn't bothered to wear proper footwear for the occasion.

"Well." The MC chuckled in surprise. "This is certainly a surprise, Mr…"

"Let's simply go with Bulldog, huh?"

Lisa fought to not roll her eyes. *Oh, now he wants to use an alias.*

"Mr. Bulldog. Magnificent. Do I hear four and a quarter?"

"You!" The scarred, gray-skinned magical in the white suit roared and shoved other crime bosses out of the way to get to Johnny.

"He doesn't sound very happy about this," Lisa muttered.

"Why would he be? He can bid or get the fuck outta here." The dwarf stared at Amanda, who frowned at him from the stage like she tried to place his face. *That's right, kid. You've seen me before.*

"Do I hear four and a quarter?" the gnome shouted. His eyes widened as the magical in the white suit tossed anyone out of his way who didn't automatically move for him.

"Five million," the burned magical roared.

The spectators murmured their acknowledgment. A few of them clapped in approval, fully impressed by this unnamed attendee to the Monsters Ball who put five million dollars on the line to get what he wanted.

"I'm so sick of your bullshit," he shouted. "Bulldog! I'm talkin' to you! You've hiked this up for two days. What's your fucking game?"

Johnny's smile widened as he unbuttoned his dinner jacket, folded his arms, and slid his hands inside it.

Lisa turned for a brief glimpse of the magical who stalked toward them in undisguised fury. "That's him, Johnny. That's Lemonhead."

"Five million. Well, I never." The gnome rubbed the top of his head vigorously and regained his composure. "Mr. Bulldog? Do I hear five and a quarter from you? Five and a quarter for the young shifter with enough life in her to…ha. Well, to do anything, really. Five and a quarter, Mr. Bulldog?"

"Yeah. I'll raise the stakes." Johnny drew two massive pistols from the shoulder holsters strapped beneath each arm and aimed them at the MC. "For you."

"Johnny!" Lisa took a long step back, hiked the bottom of her dress up, and drew her service pistol from a thigh holster.

The dwarf fired a monstrously loud shot from one gun that splintered the podium into a million pieces. Lemonhead reached for him with both meaty hands and roared so forcefully in his rage that spit flew from his open mouth. Johnny turned to aim the gun at his attacker, but the hulk smacked his arm and the shot went wild and ricocheted off the penthouse's marble floors.

The venue erupted into chaos. Some of the mob bosses drew their weapons or summoned spells to aim at Johnny and Lisa. Most of them headed toward the back to claim their purchased girls or hurried to the front entrance, the Monsters Ball be damned.

Johnny ducked another swing from his adversary's fist— which was three times the size of a regular man's—and fired his weapon into the magical's foot. Lemonhead roared and lunged at the dwarf with both arms to catch him. Ducking again, he side-stepped the man, dropped one of his guns into the body holster, and withdrew a small metal bar strapped to his belt.

He threw it at his opponent, and the bar unfolded into segments before it landed on the magical's enormous shoulder. The device unraveled further into the shape of a spider and climbed along the huge man's shoulder and up his neck until it latched itself onto his face, poked one long metal leg into his mouth, two more into his nostrils, and two more at his eyes.

Lisa launched a fireball at the wizard Marco and struck him solidly in the gut. His champagne glass spun from his hand and shattered on the floor. She squeezed off two shots at one of the half-Kilomea security guards and disabled him with a well-placed bullet in each of his kneecaps.

Lemonhead flailed at the mechanical spider on his face— which elongated its legs and swung its body out of reach each time, keeping its sharpened legs embedded in the soft parts of the magical's marred and wounded face. Johnny took a black disk from those he'd replenished on his belt and lobbed it at the stage. It detonated before he could tell Amanda to take cover, but the girl didn't need his help.

As the Kilomea holding her chain leash staggered under the explosion, roared, and clapped his hands over his ears, the girl shifted. The collar clinked onto the stage with the empty hand-cuffs and her torn, tattered clothes a second before the small gray wolf buried her fangs in the back of her guard's ankle. With a snarl and two quick jerks of her head, she ripped her bastard handler's Achilles tendon out and he fell with a bellow, his foot dangling awkwardly from what was left of his ankle.

Without pause, she pounced on his chest and knocked him onto his back. Her swift jaws and the strength of her rage made quick work of his throat. A thick spray of blood arced over the back of the stage and spattered against the wall of windows to obscure the view of Times Square. Amanda bounded off him and spun toward the crowd with a snarl, then threw her head back for a blood-curdling howl of victory.

As Johnny retrieved his exploding beads from his pants' pockets and crushed the tops, he caught a quick glimpse of the small gray wolf with blood matting the hair of her muzzle as she growled at the gnome. The MC shrieked and darted away before he flung himself ignominiously off the stage.

The kid has bigger stones than half the goons in this place. I'll give her that.

Johnny ducked another swing from Lemonhead before the man ignored him in favor of trying to pry the spider off his face. By the time he finally succeeded, the dwarf had already thumped half a dozen explosive beads onto the back of his white suit jacket. He vaulted up and slapped another on the side of the magical's beefy neck.

Lemonhead crushed the metallic spider in one hand. Sparks

and shards of metal erupted and he hurled it across the room. He spun and batted his adversary with a forearm as hard as a brick.

The dwarf catapulted away and landed with a grunt. "I could have done without the bruised ass, shitface." He drew his second pistol again and aimed with both. "You're not goin' anywhere with the—"

The magical roared when the explosive beads detonated and thrust him forward in a burst of light. The bead stuck to his scarred, gray neck whipped his head dangerously and he toppled like a felled tree.

Lisa incapacitated the second security guard with a bullet in his trigger hand and a fireball she'd meant to aim at his gut. A Wood Elf woman attacked her with a strobing pulse of lightning-like energy that raced through the agent's body and made every muscle momentarily rigid. As a result, her fireball caught her target guard in the groin and he dropped then and there with a bugle-like scream that resembled a rutting elk.

Johnny shot the Wood Elf in the shoulder with his massive pistol and she spun away from the agent with a cry of rage. Ameyna the Heiress floated smoothly past at the same moment and landed a backhanded slap against the elf's cheek that knocked her out cold. The Atlantean woman hissed at Johnny, her hair snakes hissed at him, and in moments, she was at the other side of the room and getting the hell out of the penthouse.

The elf's spell on Lisa ran its course and she staggered forward with a gasp. "Wood Elves and their fucking lightning." She whirled and raised her service weapon toward the wizard who tried to play Catch That Shifter like an idiot. He never saw the shot coming.

Amanda flinched at the clap of gunfire and snarled at the woman until she recognized her.

Johnny's pistols clattered to the marble floors as he stood and raced toward Lemonhead, who lay face-first on the ground. He drew his knife, straddled the huge magical's back, and brought his knees down hard on his adversary's triceps. The knifepoint pressed against the side of Lemonhead's thick neck, and his other hand forced the guy's face against the marble floor.

"You came out of hiding on the wrong fucking night, Lemonhead. You shoulda stayed under your rock where you belong."

The magical froze and his massive back rocked up and down beneath the dwarf as a dark, careless chuckle rose from his thick throat. "Lemonhead? That sonofabitch won't come up for air again any time soon."

Johnny thumped the side of his fist against the back of the gray-skinned man's head and cracked his cheek against the marble again. "What the fuck are you saying, asshole?"

"I'm saying he's dead, you moron." The giant burst into laughter despite the fractured cheekbone and the heavy dwarf who crushed his back and arms. "He has been for years."

"You killed him."

"Yeah, I'll take the credit." The man's next laugh came out as a wheeze.

"So who are you, shitstain?"

The magical grinned and his eyes rolled to the corners to get a glimpse of Johnny's face. "The Red Boar rises, dwarf. And this time, I'm here to stay."

Johnny's chest tightened. *This is him. This is the fucking piece of shit who—*

"Johnny!" Lisa wiggled a small radio at him that she'd taken off one of the fallen guards. "They're sending backup."

"Give me a minute."

Amanda uttered a sharp yelp as another half-Kilomea goon working for Boneblade caught her by the scruff of the neck and threw her across the room. She struggled to rise to her feet and snarled and snapped at him, but she now favored her front right paw and limped while she prowled tensely as her attacker lumbered toward her.

"Johnny, we have to go," Lisa shouted and squeezed off two

more shots at the witches who summoned a group spell. The spell winked out when two of them were eliminated and the rest of them were thoroughly pissed. "Now!"

The half-Kilomea stalked toward Amanda, backed her into a corner against the wall, and sniggered. "If I have to physically break you to break you at all, you little bitch, I'm happy to do it."

Dammit.

Johnny turned to reach for one of his pistols on the ground, and the Red Boar fucker roared and threw his assailant off him fully. The dwarf rolled, managed to snatch up one of his pistols, and aimed it at his daughter's killer. The gray-faced magical kicked up a silver tray abandoned by a fleeing server and caught it in time to deflect the bullet. He staggered back, the tray dented toward his chest, and snarled.

The bounty hunter aimed his massive gun at the chandelier and sneered. *Fuck this.* Two shots were all it took to sever the chandelier from its bolts in the ceiling and the crystal pieces tinkled as it fell.

One of the extended iron arms drove into the Red Boar's back and snagged his white suit. The magical fell with a howl as the chandelier landed on top of him. Crystal shards sprayed everywhere and peppered the penthouse walls. The champagne tower exploded and fell to the marble floor in a shower of glass and bubbly.

Johnny raised his arm to shield his face, turned, and got one foot under him for the momentum to hurl his knife. The half-Kilomea choked on a wet gurgle when the blade pierced the side of his neck and he sagged. Amanda pounced on him, ignored her tender paw, and closed her jaws on his face to tear off a huge chunk of beard and the flesh beneath it. She shook her head and the piece flew across the room. Finally, she sat on her haunches and licked her bloody muzzle as she stared with amber eyes at the dwarf.

He snorted and yanked his knife from the half-Kilomea's

neck. "That's one hell of a way to send a message, kid. Let's get outta here."

Lisa darted toward them, stopped, and stripped her stilettos off quickly before she hurried after Johnny and Amanda with a heel in each hand.

"So much for running in heels," he muttered and directed another shot at a gnome who raced toward them with a machete in hand. "Who the fuck keeps a machete in a penthouse?"

"Didn't you see me fighting in these heels?" She turned and drove the sharp end of one heel against the temple of a wizard who tried to sneak up on her from an open doorway into another private room. The heel punctured the soft spot there with a wet thump and she jerked it out again to let him slump to the floor.

Johnny stared at her with raised eyebrows.

"I ran out of ammo, okay?"

A small smile played at the corners of the dwarf's mouth. "I could watch you do that all day."

"Uh-huh. Let's move."

CHAPTER TWENTY-TWO

Johnny tossed the keys to the valet in front of their hotel with a nod. "Feel free to ignore the blood in the back seat," he said with a grunt. "It's not ours."

The man's eyes widened but he was good at his job and slid into the front seat of their rental without comment before he drove it smoothly and calmly toward the valet lot.

Lisa walked beside him, her stilettos hanging from one hand with both heels cracked and crooked. "Walking barefoot in Manhattan wasn't exactly something I had planned for this trip."

"Eh. There's a first time for everything." He ran a hand through his hair and nodded at the twenty-four-hour doorman who opened the door for them.

The man studied each of them in quick succession—the dwarf with a ripped dinner jacket hanging off one shoulder, the attractive woman in a fine cocktail dress with broken stilettos in her hand and mussed-up hair, and a medium-sized gray dog that looked more like a wolf—blood-matted fur and all—but trotted obediently at the couple's side. "Looks like a fun night."

"Somethin' like that, yeah." The dwarf glanced at Amanda,

who panted and trotted three feet away from Lisa. *She's stronger as a wolf. And I wouldn't wanna shift into being naked right now either.*

They headed to the concierge desk first and he rapped his knuckles on the high counter. "How's it goin'?"

"Mr. Walker. Lovely to see you. And Ms. Breyer." The man had done this for so long, he didn't bat an eyelid at the disheveled appearance of his odd guests with even stranger requests. "Did you have a pleasant evening out?"

"More or less," Lisa said.

"Excellent. Your four-legged friends have been taken outside a total of six times since you made the request, Mr. Walker. Fine dogs, I must say."

"Did you walk 'em yourself?"

"Beg pardon?"

Lisa smirked. "He asked if you walked them yourself."

"Ah, yes. Unfortunately, I have a duty to remain at my station here during operating hours. But the same young man from our staff has been up to see those dogs each and every time. He's grown quite fond of them in the last eight hours if you ask me."

When the concierge noticed Johnny's confused frown, he took a chance on his years of experience in reading his guests' expressions to also read their thoughts. After twenty-five years in his position, he'd maintained a ninety-five-percent success rate with this.

"And no, Mr. Walker, I do not man this concierge desk twenty-four-seven as a regular occurrence. But I thought it prudent to remain here at the hotel until you returned. So many things can get lost in translation with a change of staff, you understand."

The dwarf nodded and reached into the deep pocket of his slacks for his wallet. "Much appreciated. Listen, there might be a few stuck-up assholes rollin' around asking for me and Ms. Breyer over here. Maybe even our new friend."

The man leaned over the desk to peer at Amanda. "I see. Quite docile for a stray."

"She ain't a stray." He cast the man a quick glare.

"Of course not."

"If anyone comes askin' for any of us, tell 'em we ain't here. You never saw us, we never talked, and you have no idea what they want. Understand?"

The concierge didn't bother to glance at the stack of twenty-dollar bills he had slipped out of his wallet and placed on the desk. He did, however, offer Lisa an apologetic smile.

"To thank you for your dedication," she translated and nodded at the stack of twenties. "And we'd appreciate it if our stay here was kept under wraps."

He nodded and slid the stack of bills slowly toward him across the desk before he secreted them with a deft hand. "I will forget this conversation and all others the second you leave the lobby, Ms. Breyer. We always put our guests' wishes first in this establishment."

"I have no doubt. Thank you." Giving him a knowing smile, she nodded and turned toward the lobby elevators.

"You honestly can't understand a thing I'm sayin' to you?" Johnny asked and squinted at the concierge.

"Enjoy the rest of your night, Mr. Walker," the man replied. "You know who to call if you need anything else."

"Huh. Yeah." Narrowing his eyes even further, he jerked his chin at the concierge, then turned to follow his companions across the lobby toward the elevators. "Yankees."

When they reached their adjoining rooms, Lisa pulled her keycard out and flashed it in front of her door. She smiled at the small gray wolf sitting patiently between the doors. "Come on, kiddo. I bet you could use a nice hot shower and I might have a few extra things in my bag that'll fit you."

Amanda looked at Johnny with wide amber eyes.

"Go on. We'll pick this up again in the mornin'. My dogs are achin' too. And I reckon my hounds haven't got a wink since we left."

Lisa snorted and immediately wiped the smile off her face when he fixed her with a confused frown.

"Is somethin' funny?"

"Not at all. Good night, Johnny."

"Night." With a sniff, he unlocked his hotel door and cast a final glance at Amanda as she trotted into Lisa's room and disappeared. *Yeah. She'll be all right.*

He opened the door and both hounds leapt off the bed to race toward him.

"Johnny! Oh, my God. Johnny! You're back!"

"You were gone forever, Johnny. Like…years!"

Rex and Luther leapt onto the dwarf and one of their paws hung over each of his shoulders as they licked his face.

"Years, huh?" With a chuckle, he gave their sides a vigorous rubdown before he pushed them both off and snapped his fingers. "That's enough."

Luther's tail thumped madly against the carpet. "You bring us anything, Johnny? Huh? We've been good."

"So good." Rex's tongue lolled from his open mouth. "The best."

Johnny eyed the scattered fragments of rawhide bones littered all over the hotel room floor, interspersed with pieces of bone from their steaks. "How about the guy who took you out?"

"He took us out often, Johnny." Rex followed his master toward the closet. "He was nice. Gave us treats—"

"He what?" He spun toward his dogs and glared at them. "Say that again."

Luther leapt onto the bed and turned in three tight circles before he curled on the bedspread. "The rawhide, Johnny. Endless supply. Every time he came in here, he magically found another one on the floor and gave it up."

Rex panted and sat as his master kicked his boots off. "Ha. What a sucker."

The dwarf smirked and didn't bother trying to explain that the hotel employee had only thrown them the pieces of one rawhide for each of them. *I thought I was gonna have to break someone else tonight for feeding my hounds.*

He unbuckled his belt and removed the last explosive disk from his previously full artillery before he let his blood-stained and tattered dress slacks fall to the floor. After retrieving his wallet and tossing it on the bed, he shrugged out of the torn dinner jacket and ripped the button-up shirt away from his chest. Buttons scattered and bounced across the floor.

"Ooh." Rex ignored his master and turned to sniff the buttons. "How's the girl?"

"Yeah, we can smell her. Why didn't she come say hi, Johnny? It's not like she's afraid of dogs, right?"

Rex chuckled. "Wouldn't that be seriously confusing?"

"She's fine." Wadding up the dress attire he'd cringed at spending almost three hundred bucks on earlier that afternoon, Johnny strode to the small trashcan in his boxers and shoved everything into the bin. That done, he yanked his black jeans and a black t-shirt out of his duffel bag and pulled them on. "She's a tough kid, I tell you what. Out of all the—"

He stopped and gritted his teeth as the faces of twenty-six other young girls he hadn't been able to save tonight flashed through his head.

"All the what, Johnny?"

"Yeah, you can't cut off in the middle of something like that."

His expression grim, he stepped toward the mini-fridge and searched inside. Any other night, he might have smirked when he saw the four mini-bottles of Johnny Walker Black stocked neatly beside the bottles of water and the craft beers. Tonight, he merely grunted and swiped two bottles before he kicked the door shut with a black-socked foot.

"She did all right, boys. That's all that needs sayin'."

"So when do we meet her, huh?" Rex sniffed a larger chunk of destroyed rawhide and lay on the carpet, his back legs kicking out behind him as he began to gnaw it.

"You already met her on the bridge," he muttered. He opened both mini-bottles and tossed the lids at the trashcan that overflowed with his party clothes. The plastic lids caught in the fabric and remained stuck there.

"He means for real, Johnny." Luther crawled across the bedspread on his belly until his snout settled inches from his master's thigh. "Like talking. That's how you make friends."

"Talking and sniffing." Rex paused his chewing to sniff the slobber-covered rawhide. "And sometimes humping."

"Yeah, humping. That's how you know your real friends from all the posers." Luther's tail thumped on the bed as he stared with drooping eyes at the mini bottles in Johnny's hand.

"We'll see her in the morning, boys. And no humping."

"What?" Rex raised his head and looked over his shoulder at the bed with a low whine. "She's only a pup. What are you thinking?"

"You are one messed-up two-legger, Johnny."

The dwarf sniffed and stared at the blank wall next to the TV. "Tell me somethin' I don't know."

He upended both mini-bottles into his mouth at the same time and drained them in two seconds.

CHAPTER TWENTY-THREE

Without any word from Lisa or Amanda the next morning, Johnny ordered room service—complete with another steak for each hound—and set to work cleaning the massive pistols he'd brought with him. *These aren't the best for hunting. They're good enough for crashing Monsters Balls, though. And monsters' balls.*

He snorted and finished wiping the outside of the second pistol's barrel with the cloth before a knock came at the door.

"It's Lisa. And Amanda."

"Yeah, hold on." He wiped the gun, set it on his duffel bag on the bed, and went to answer the door.

It took him completely by surprise to see the young girl standing beside Lisa in an oversized t-shirt and navy sweatpants that fit around the waist but were too long and bunched at her ankles. Amanda gave him a small smile. Her long dark hair had been washed and brushed and hung over her shoulders in a brown sheen. Hazel eyes stared expectantly at the dwarf who'd rescued her.

And now this kid gets to go...where? Not back home. Not to the place where her twin and parents were ripped to shreds in the living room.

"Johnny?" Lisa raised her eyebrows and smiled. "Can we come in?"

"Yup." He sniffed, stepped aside, and glanced at the white trainers on Amanda's feet. "Nice shoes."

"Oh." The girl shrugged. "Lisa and I have the same shoe size. Weird, right?"

Johnny looked at the agent as she slipped through the door and gave him a knowing smile. "How you feelin', kid?"

"Hungry." Amanda scanned the hotel room and cocked her head. "You're much tidier than she is."

"Is that right?" He cast Lisa a sidelong glance.

She looked at the floor and tucked her dark hair behind her ears as she fought a smile. "I have different priorities."

"Oh, Johnny!" Luther raced around the other side of the bed and skidded to a stop in front of Amanda. "She's here! You're here! Johnny, Johnny. Tell her we like her. Tell her we saw her fight."

"Hey, buddy." The girl leaned forward, propped her hands on her thighs, and grinned at the hound. "Luther, right?"

"Holy shit! She knows my name. Johnny, how does she know my name?"

Rex trotted across the hotel room after his brother. "Heya, pup."

Amanda chuckled. "I never had a chance to thank you guys for helping me on the bridge yesterday. So thanks."

She held her hand out toward Luther and he sniffed her fingers once before he gave them a quick experimental lick.

"She thanked us, Johnny. No wonder everyone wants this kid on their side."

A small frown creased the girl's forehead but she wrinkled her nose and shook it off. "But now I have you to help keep me safe from here on out, right?"

"Oh, yeah." Rex sniffed the girl's borrowed shoes, then walked around her to sniff her backside before he joined his brother again and sat. "We got you covered, pup."

"Thanks for that."

Johnny glanced at Lisa, who stood with her arms folded and watched the girl pet the two coonhounds like the last four days of her kidnapping and all the horrors she'd gone through didn't exist. *Coincidences happen. But it sounded a hell of a lot like she's having a conversation with them.*

He shook himself out of that line of thinking and cleared his throat. "You said you're hungry. There's, uh…half a room-service pancake left. A little eggs if you want 'em—"

"Yeah, thanks." Amanda flashed him a winning grin and stepped around the hounds, laughing when they followed closely at her heels.

Lisa gave him a playful frown. "Half a pancake?"

He grimaced and shrugged. "It gets too sweet after that."

"Watch for the eggs, Rex. Scrambled eggs fall like rain."

"On it. I'd take some of that pancake, though. They put so much butter on it."

"Ooh, yeah. Butter. Hey, is there any bacon left?"

The girl lifted the lid of the silver tray and gave the dogs a playful frown. "Didn't you guys have steaks already?"

"Well, yeah. Johnny always gets us steaks." Rex sat, licked his muzzle, and looked over his shoulder at his master. "Wait. How does she know that?"

The girl met the dwarf's gaze and raised her eyebrows. "They did have steak, right?"

He narrowed his eyes at her. "Yeah. How did you know?"

She shrugged. "I can smell it."

"Woah-ho-ho…Johnny! She can smell it."

Rex cocked his head at his brother. "She's a shifter. What did you expect?"

"She's not shifting now, is she? What if there was a difference? You know, two legs versus four."

"Obviously not." Rex lifted his head and sniffed at the half of a pancake Amanda lifted in both hands like a syrupy, soggy pizza. "How about some of that cake from the pan, pup? Huh?"

She smirked and looked at Johnny again. "Can I?"

The dwarf folded his arms and stared at her.

Lisa shook her head. "He doesn't like anyone to feed his—"

"Go ahead." Johnny shrugged and nodded at the hounds. "But only a little."

The agent leaned away from him in surprise. "Changing your rules now, huh?"

He shrugged. "Some of us deserve an exception now and then."

She took a deep breath and he completely missed the concerned frown that crossed her features.

"Johnny, you're the best." Luther's tail thumped on the carpet, then swung between the side of the dresser and his brother's hindquarters. "Like for real. The total best."

"I don't know, man." Rex stared at the pieces of pancake in Amanda's fingers. "The pup might have you beat, now. You never feed us pancakes."

The girl smiled at the hounds and regarded them sternly. "I'm trusting you guys. Be gentle. Stay sitting. Deal?"

"Deal." Luther shifted his front paws in excitement. "Definitely deal."

"Pancakes!"

The girl fed them both a small piece before she crammed the rest of the pancake into her mouth and still managed an intelligible, "That's it. No more. Go lay down."

"Oh, man. Syrup. Butter. I can't even…" Rex licked his muzzle, sniffed the floor, and returned to the strip of open floor between the bed and the window.

Luther stayed where he was and stared at the girl.

Amanda laughed and forced an escaping mush of pancake into her mouth. "Didn't you hear me?"

Johnny snapped his fingers. "Luther."

"Yep. Got it." The hound uttered a low whine and hopped onto the bed.

She can definitely hear them. I don't know if it's kids or shifters or what, but I'd set my watch and warrant on it.

The dwarf cleared his throat. "Did you hear that?"

When the girl looked at him, he glanced briefly at the hounds.

Amanda smiled as she lifted a handful of scrambled eggs to her mouth. "Yep. All of it."

I fuckin' knew it.

"Hear what?" Lisa looked up from her cell phone and glanced from the dwarf to the young shifter.

"Siren about ten blocks north," Johnny said off the cuff.

"Twelve." Amanda grinned at him and shoveled the eggs into her mouth.

Little smartass too, huh? Okay.

Lisa frowned. "I don't hear anything."

"I'm tryin' to make sure she's still workin' the way she's supposed to. We don't want her goin' home with any issues we should have caught beforehand, yeah?"

"The only issue I have is this empty plate." Licking her fingers, Amanda scanned the breakfast tray and glanced around the room. "Do you have anything else?"

Johnny shook his head. "I reckon you'll get as much food as you want on the way out. You're gonna have to settle for water now."

He pried the mini-fridge open with his boot, retrieved a bottle of water, and tossed it to her.

"That'll work." She opened the bottle and downed almost all of it in one breath. Her loud gulps filled the silent hotel room. She lowered the mostly empty water bottle, shook what was left, and drained it. "Thanks."

The dwarf watched her intently as she stuffed the empty water bottle into the trashcan, turned, and flopped onto the bed beside Luther.

She's somethin' all right. Exactly like Dawn. Maybe a little too much.

He rubbed his hand over his face as Amanda patted Luther's head and closed her eyes.

"Johnny, can I talk to you out in the hall for a minute?" Lisa's wide eyes betrayed her concern, although she kept her voice calm and even.

"Yeah." He pointed at the hounds. "No jumpin', boys. And keep an eye on this one."

"Why?" Rex's head popped up from the other side of the bed. "Look at her, Johnny. She's not goin' anywhere."

Amanda smiled, her eyes still closed. "We're good."

"Uh-huh. I bet you are." The dwarf turned to follow Lisa out of the room and slapped the bar forward to keep the door propped open. *I'm gonna have to sit and talk about this with the hounds eventually.*

The door thumped against the metal bar to leave an inch of space in the doorway, and he folded his arms. "What's up?"

"I just got word that another team's on their way to take Amanda into protective custody. They should be here in about twenty minutes."

He stared at her. "You don't look happy about it."

"Probably because I'm not." She shrugged. "Words matching facial expressions, right?"

"Sure."

She glanced up and down the hall, then leaned toward him. "Look, Johnny. I'm…risking a lot by telling you this. My career at the very least. Maybe more. I don't think—"

"No way!" Amanda shouted. "Are you serious?"

"Yeah." Luther's higher-pitched voice filled Johnny's head. "He makes all kinds of things. Bombs. Guns. Little crawling doohickies. And these collars. Check it out."

"Cool…" The awe in the girl's voice made his throat tighten.

"So it's not only you," Rex added. "Johnny can hear us too. And we can hear him, obviously."

"Obviously."

He gritted his teeth and swallowed quickly. *Great.*

"Man, these other hounds have no idea what they're missing, you know? I mean, canines aren't exactly the best conversationalists."

"What?" Amanda laughed. "I think you guys are doin' fine."

Lisa frowned and leaned toward the slightly open door. "Is everything okay in there?"

"Yeah, we're good." The mattress creaked under the girl's shifting weight. "I'm watching TV. Some of this stuff is nuts."

"Okay." The agent turned toward Johnny and frowned at him. "I hate to even think it, but what if the Boneblade...you know, did something to her we can't see? She's talking to herself—"

The volume on the TV turned up and the sound of braying zebras beneath a narrator's voice filtered into the hallway.

Johnny fought back a laugh. *Damn, she's smart. She covers Lisa's questions and keeps me from hearing those coonhounds talkin' about me. I'm not sure I can get behind that one.*

"Johnny?"

"She's fine." He shook his head and sniffed. "Kids are kids, right? They talk to the TV sometimes. Big deal."

"Right." Lisa glanced at the time on her phone and grimaced. "I think we need to get outta here."

"What about protective custody?"

"Yeah, that's what I'm trying to tell you." She slid her phone into her pocket and glanced at the ceiling. "I don't think protective custody covers the full extent of...what the Bureau has planned for her."

He raised his eyebrows. "That's new."

"Yeah, it's... She has so many connections. Or at least Bruce Coulier did. And there's still so much for these senators to lose if

Amanda is taken by the wrong people again. Not to mention the shifter part. There aren't many shifters in the Bureau."

He scowled and nodded slowly. "So what are you thinkin' here? More like a house-arrest-forever type deal or moldin' an FBI war hound by convincin' her she owes them everythin'?"

Lisa gestured helplessly. "Take your pick."

"Nah. I'll go with Option C. Get your stuff." Without waiting for her to reply, he shoved the door to his room open and stormed inside with a sharp whistle. "Look alive, boys. We're hittin' the road."

Amanda sat quickly and stared at him with wide eyes. She thumped the remote and the TV blinked off. "What's wrong?"

"Nothin' yet. But something will be if we don't get a move on."

Luther hopped up and leapt from the bed. "What d'ya need, Johnny? Want us to bite off a few hands?"

Amanda pointed at the hound. "Hey. I haven't tried that one on a hunt yet."

"Real fun." Rex trotted around the bed and sat in front of the nightstand to watch the dwarf packing his things into the duffel bag on the bedspread. "Especially when they scream."

"It's the way the bones snap that gets me every time," Luther added.

"Are you guys messing with me?"

"Nope."

"Uh-uh."

"We don't mess around, pup. Not when it comes to huntin' game."

"Yeah. Wild game. Monster game. Same thing."

Amanda chuckled and ran a hand through her hair. "Well, whatever you're hunting, I think—"

A brisk knock came at the door, and all four of them turned to look at it.

"It's me," Lisa called.

"'Course it is." Johnny jammed his cleaning box into the duffel bag and zipped everything with a quick jerk. "Hey, kid."

"Yeah."

He looked at her and lowered his voice. "Let's cool it on the whole talkin' to the dogs thing, huh?"

"Why? They have so many cool things to say."

"Johnny, I like her."

The dwarf snapped his fingers and the hounds shut up. He darted another glance at the door. "Because until twenty minutes ago, I was the only one who could hear 'em. And they were the only ones who knew it."

"Oh... Why haven't you told anyone?"

He snorted. "That's a loaded question."

"What about Lisa? She's your partner, isn't she?"

He swung his duffel bag over his shoulder and whistled at the dogs. "She's not my partner."

"But I thought—"

"Let's leave the questions for after we get outta here. This isn't the time."

Amanda slid off the bed and stared after him. "They're coming for me again. Aren't they?"

"Not the assholes you're thinkin' of, kid. But it don't matter who it is. I ain't about to let anyone take you unless you give the go-ahead first."

"Good idea."

Johnny opened the door and nodded at Lisa. "Time to split."

"Amanda?" Lisa peered around the half-open door. "Are you ready?"

"Not yet." The girl stood beside the foot of the bed, her arms folded as she stared expectantly at the dwarf.

He turned and snorted. "What are you doin'?"

"Waiting."

"For what?" He made an exaggerated sweeping gesture toward the hall. "We don't exactly have much time, kid."

Amanda raised an eyebrow.

"Hey, Johnny."

"Shh."

Luther uttered a low whine. "But Johnny, you said no one was taking her without her go-ahead first."

Amanda glanced at the dog, then looked at Johnny and raised her chin.

"Christ on a crutch." Rolling his eyes, he extended a hand toward her. "All right, kid. Do I have your ever-lovin' permission to take you with me out of this damn hotel so we don't get caught in the crosshairs of a few chumps whose ugly mugs I'd rather not look at today or what?"

"Yes." The girl hurried toward the door and slipped into the hall with them before he slammed the door shut. The hydraulic hinge rendered his attempt completely unsatisfying as it slowed itself and shut with a click.

"We're takin' the stairs." He strode down the hall with Rex and Luther at his sides.

Lisa looked at the girl beside her and muttered, "What was all that about?"

"Nothin'." Amanda shrugged and gave her a small smile. "I like him."

Fighting back a laugh, the agent tightened her grasp on the handle of her rolling suitcase and watched the dwarf moving ahead with his dogs. "Yeah. Me too."

CHAPTER TWENTY-FOUR

Two federal agents in matching black suits and dark sunglasses neither one of them bothered to take off stepped through the front doors of the Greenwich Hotel when Benny the doorman opened it for them. "Good morning, gentleman. Looking to—"

"FBI." The agent with a double chin as the only sign of excess weight on his body flashed his badge. "We'll be quick."

"Of course." Benny stepped aside as the agents headed toward the concierge desk. He looked at Alexander, who'd seen the quick flash of the badge but didn't give any indication that he knew why the gentlemen were there. *That's why they pay him the big bucks, ain't it? Old man's got balls of steel under all that posh.*

Then he saw the wicked-looking metal collar hanging from the back of the other man's belt. *Nothin' about that looks good.*

"Good morning, gentleman." Despite the four hours of sleep he'd had between his extended shift the night before and the start of his regular shift this morning, Alexander was wide-eyed and as gracious as ever. These days, he could only sleep five hours a night anyway. "Welcome to the Greenwich Hotel. Are you checking in?"

"No." The man with the double chin whipped his badge out of

his interior jacket pocket again, let it drop open, and flipped it closed quickly. "Federal business. You understand."

"Oh."

For the first time in fifteen years at this gig, Benny saw surprise and confusion on Alexander's face. *No way. After everything he's seen here, a couple of feds ain't nothin'.*

The concierge's eyes widened and he watched the agent tuck the badge into his jacket pocket. "My apologies, gentlemen. I... don't understand."

"You don't need to." The other agent with a scar running down the side of his upper lip just off-center rested a forearm on the desk and leaned forward. "We're here to meet a few associates. Johnny Walker and a fellow agent, Lisa Breyer."

"I'm sorry." He shook his head with an apologetic smile. "I haven't heard or seen either of those names. How long have they been here?"

The man with the scar shrugged. "A few days."

"Hmm. They must have checked in during the night shift. Let me see..." He typed on his computer, then shook his head. "I'm afraid I don't see either of those names in the system. Are you sure you have the right hotel?"

The other agent scoffed and turned away from the concierge desk. "Do you think she used another name?"

"Why the hell would she? No one's looking for her."

At the far end of the lobby, Johnny poked his head around the corner of the adjacent hall and growled his annoyance. "Shit. They're here and not interested in playing nice, either."

Lisa's eyes widened. "What?"

"They have a damn collar." He grimaced at Amanda. "I'm not gonna let 'em use it."

She clenched her eyes shut and shook her head.

"We can go out back, right?" The girl tried to peer around the corner too but he guided her back gently.

"That's still the plan." Slinging the strap of his duffel bag across his chest, he glanced at his hounds. "No squirmin', got it?"

"What? Why would we—woah!" Luther uttered a low whine as Johnny squatted and wrapped an arm around each dog's back.

Hefting the hounds, the dwarf sniffed again and gestured across the back of the lobby. "No whinin' either."

"Johnny, we can walk." Rex licked his master's beard. "What are you doin'?"

"Johnny..." Lisa frowned at him. "What are you—"

"I ain't cut their damn nails once since they were pups." He adjusted the hounds under each arm. "And they're easily distracted."

"Oh... You want us to be quiet." Luther panted. "Yeah, yeah. I get it."

"Johnny, I'll be quiet. Promise. I don't like this—"

"Shh." He looked at Amanda. "Not a sound."

She nodded slowly and hurried across the open area at the back of the lobby with him.

The two agents were still too busy interrogating the concierge to notice the first sign of movement behind them. The man with the scar nodded at Alexander. "Maybe you've seen them around and didn't know who they were. Tall, leggy brunette who looks good in almost anything."

Lisa scowled as she listened to the conversation from around the corner. Johnny and Amanda were almost at the other side.

"And the guy's a dwarf," the agent added. "He wears a lotta leather. You can't miss the accent, either."

Alexander cleared his throat. "I believe the more appropriate moniker these days is little person."

"What?" The man wrinkled his nose. "No, he's an actual—dammit. Never mind. How about any guests with two dogs, huh? Basset hounds or somethin'."

Safe on the other side of the lobby, Johnny froze when he

heard the wildly inaccurate description of his dogs and whirled again. *That bastard.*

He saw Lisa across the way instead. She shook her head slowly with a warning frown. His upper lip twitched in irritation and he turned toward the end of the hall and the back exit.

"No, I'm sorry." Alexander shook his head. "We don't allow dogs here. That wouldn't happen."

"It would if you'd met this guy." The man with a double chin stroked it and grimaced. "How about a kid? They had a girl with 'em. Twelve years old with long brown hair."

For the first time during this conversation, the young man didn't have to feign surprise or cluelessness. "No young girls. I wish I could help you, gentlemen."

Lisa chose that moment to make a quiet dash across the back of the lobby, but her timing was off.

Rubbing the side of his face in agitation, the man with scar started to turn toward the back.

Benny leapt into action without thinking. "You mean that girl?"

Both agents spun toward him and hurried toward the front doors, eager to see where the doorman was pointing.

Clasping his hands behind his back, Benny turned quickly toward Lisa and gave her a quick thumbs-up. She returned it and hurried across the open space as fast as she could without making a noise.

"Do you see her?" the first agent asked.

"No." The man with the scar turned toward Benny. "You saw a girl out there?"

"Yes, sir. Walking down the sidewalk. I think she had some beagles on leashes."

The agents squinted through the glass front doors and scanned the sidewalk.

One of them pulled his phone out and dialed Agent Breyer's number. "This is ridiculous."

As soon as he put the phone to his ear, a low ringtone came from the back of the lobby. The agents looked at each other and hurried toward the sound, picking up speed.

"Is there anything else I can help you with, gentlemen?" Alexander called after them. He received no reply.

"Shit." Lisa located her phone and switched it to silent. "Go."

Johnny thumped his back against the door, turned, and dropped the hounds to their feet. "The fucking keys are with the valet."

"Well, we'll have to be fast." She closed the door and tilted her head at a huge rock on the sidewalk. *Way too convenient, but okay.*

She wedged it against the door, then hurried after Johnny, Amanda, and the hounds.

As the two agents who'd come to take the young shifter into FBI custody—protective or otherwise—fought to open the back door, the concierge retrieved the radio from under his desk and pressed the call button. "Vince? Would you be so kind as to bring Mr. Walker's car to the front? Quickly."

"You got it, Al."

He replaced his radio and looked at Benny. "Over here, Mr. Frolish. If you please."

Benny cleared his throat, jerked his doorman's uniform jacket down, and glanced at the front door before he approached the desk. "Did I get that wrong, Al?"

"Not at all." Alexander counted the bills out without looking, his hands hidden beneath the desk, then slid them across the surface toward the doorman. "You did very well. I value a man who can think on his feet."

Glancing from the stack of bills to Alexander and back again, Benny opened his mouth but couldn't get a word out.

"Take it, Mr. Frolish. You've earned it."

"Yes, sir." His hand moved discreetly over the bills and he thumbed through them with wide eyes before he shoved them into his pocket. "Two hundred bucks?"

"There's more as long as you maintain that level of quality customer service." Alexander smirked at the doorman and nodded toward the front again. "Much more."

"Yeah, I like the sound of that." With a disbelieving chuckle, he returned to his post.

The two agents raced past the front doors of the hotel toward the valet as a large black SUV drove down the street in the opposite direction. From the open driver's window, a large hand with thick red hair along the wrist emerged to raise a middle finger. The agents didn't see the fugitives drive past.

Benny did and grinned.

Lisa leaned back in the front passenger seat and thumped her head against the headrest with a sigh. "Sorry."

"For what?" Johnny slipped his sunglasses on and his other wrist dangled over the wheel of their rental.

"I almost cost us this whole mission, Johnny." She glanced in the rearview mirror to see Amanda in the back seat between the hounds. The girl stared at Luther and grinned, then turned sharply to look at Rex and laughed. "It almost cost her more than I want to admit."

"Naw." He shook his head. "I don't care what you say, darlin'. There's no way a half-Light Elf Fed who bashes skulls in with her fancy heels can't take on a coupla suits. It'd be a complete waste, anyway. Those two ain't got a sense of humor."

Lisa snorted. "No, I guess they fit the fed stereotype very well."

"Or you're merely the exception." He gave her a hasty sidelong glance she didn't see through his black sunglasses. "You put a lot on the line by sneakin' us outta there."

"I know." She closed her eyes with a quick sigh. "And I'll answer for it when I have to. But after what we saw in that penthouse, Johnny, I know I couldn't live with myself if I simply handed her over to—"

"I know. Believe you me, darlin'. I feel ya." Looking into the rearview mirror, he smiled. "Hey, kid."

Amanda's crooked smile greeted him when she looked at his reflection.

That damn smile's gonna break a lotta hearts one day. Mine first, I reckon. "Have you ever been to Florida?"

"What?" The girl grinned beneath a confused frown. "No. Isn't that where all the old people go to retire?"

Lisa laughed and ignored Johnny's quick scowl.

"No, there's much more' than that down there. The Everglades, for one. Big ol' beautiful swamp. 'Gators. More huntin' than you'd know what to do with."

"I can hunt?" Amanda's eyes widened.

"Down there? Sure."

Rex pressed his nose into her hand and lifted it onto his head. "Yeah, yeah. Scratch right there."

Luther whined. "Hey, no fair."

With a short laugh, she scratched behind his ears too. "I've never hunted before."

"No?" The dwarf looked at the rearview mirror again. "That's a shame."

"Yeah. My parents don't—" She swallowed. "They didn't let me. Said it wasn't safe."

"Well, not in New York. I tell you what, kid. There's more than enough to get your goat down where I'm from. Best damn fried catfish too."

She wrinkled her nose. "You can eat that?"

"Ha!" Luther's tail thumped against the back seat. "You hear that, Johnny? The pup doesn't know what a catfish is."

Rex laughed. "But it sure as hell isn't a cat. Am I right?"

Luther and Amanda both gave him blank looks before the girl cracked up laughing. "Catfish!"

Johnny smirked and turned to look at Lisa. "I guess I'm buyin' one more ticket to the Everglades, the sweetest place on two planets. Are you comin' with us?"

She folded her arms, shrugged, and stared out the windshield as they headed to La Guardia. "What the hell. I'm already on vacation."

"I think they call that suspension, darlin'."

Rolling her eyes playfully, she shook her head. "I choose to call it something else."

"Well, hot damn." With a gruff laugh, he reached toward the dashboard and punched the radio on. A King Diamond song burst through the sound system.

When she turned toward him with a raised eyebrow, the dwarf threw her the devil horns with one hand and didn't take his eyes off the road.

CHAPTER TWENTY-FIVE

"Damn, it's good to be home." Johnny strode through the entrance of his cabin and took a long, deep breath through his nose. "It smells good too."

"Hey, pup." Luther trotted into the cabin next to Amanda, staring up at her and panting. "Wanna see the swamp?"

"Lotsa huntin'," Rex added. "Water. Mud."

"Ooh, mud. Nothin' like swamp mud."

"Ain't that the truth. Hey, pup—"

Johnny's piercing whistle silenced the dogs immediately, and they looked obediently at him while their tails wagged. "Go on out back, boys. I'm givin' the kid the grand tour."

Luther whined. "Can't she come with us, Johnny?"

"Come on—"

The dwarf's only response was to point a finger toward the back of the house. "Git."

The hounds' claws scrabbled across the floor as they raced through the small, tidy house toward the dog door in the back. "Come find us when he's done torturing you, pup!"

"Yeah, look for the birds. I haven't seen birds in years! Get 'em!"

The dog door clacked open and shut and Amanda laughed. He raised an eyebrow at her, and she harnessed her amusement into a smirk before she shrugged. "They are good dogs."

"Uh-huh."

Lisa closed the front door behind her and dusted her hands off as she stepped down the short hallway. "For some reason, I appreciate this place far more than I did the first time."

"Yep." Johnny hooked his thumbs through his belt loops. "Absence makes the bullshit flush itself out and all that."

The young shifter laughed and clapped a hand over her mouth. "That's not how the saying goes."

"That's how my saying goes." He jabbed a thumb against his chest and grinned. "Come on. I'll show y'all to your room."

"Um…" Lisa gestured toward the door. "I was gonna get a hotel down here—"

"You what?"

"I was gonna get a room—"

He shook his head. "I don't think so."

Folding her arms, she inclined her head in a challenge and stared at him. "Excuse me?"

"You know what I'm sayin'."

"No, I don't, honestly. It sounds like you're telling me I can't decide for myself where I'll stay for the night. On my vacation."

Johnny's mustache bristled when he gave her a tight smile that was more of a grimace. "I ain't sayin' that. I'm sayin' it's a bone-headed move to go traipsin' all over—"

"Let me stop you right there." She raised a hand and glanced at Amanda. "Did anyone ever tell you that being an ass to women isn't the way to get them on your side?"

He snorted. "It usually works well for me."

When Lisa didn't dial down the intensity of her warning stare, he frowned and slid his hands into his pockets.

"It ain't workin' now, is it?"

"Not really, no."

"Well, what do you want me to say, darlin'? It's a long shot to think any of those bastards from the Burroughs are gonna come hightailin' it out here after the ass-kickin' we gave 'em last night, but it's still a shot. And I assume your FBI buddies ain't too happy with you right now either. Maybe they'd like to scoop you up themselves, huh?"

Lisa's lips twitched into an unamused smile. "They are not my buddies, Johnny."

"Well, whatever. It's a helluva lot safer for both of you right here in my home. It's beautiful. Good food. Friendly folks. You don't need anythin' else."

A slow smile spread across Amanda's lips when she looked at the agent but he missed it completely.

The half-Light Elf stared at him without a word.

"Dammit. What?"

"If you want me to stay because you enjoy having your partner around, Johnny Walker, that's all you have to say."

He flung his hands in the air and spun in a tight circle. "All this about a partner. That ain't what I'm sayin'—"

"Maybe it should be," Amanda said. Both adults looked at her in surprise, and the girl shrugged. "Or whatever."

Johnny's thick red beard moved when the muscles of his jaw worked over and over. "I guess...I don't mind if you stay." He pointed sharply at Lisa. "But if you decide to say screw it and end up in some nasty-ass motel in Medley where I can't reach you, don't blame me."

"The thought never crossed my mind, Johnny."

"All right." He sniffed and nodded toward the hallway and the two bedrooms across from his workshop. "Now come on so I can show y'all where to put your heads. Then I need a drink."

As the dwarf trudged off down the hall, Amanda paused next to Lisa and muttered, "He didn't say he wants you to stay."

The agent shrugged. "He did. In a Johnny Walker kinda way." She looked at the girl and winked. "It's good enough."

"I don't get it." Shaking her head, the shifter followed Johnny into the single guestroom after he jerked open the door and it swung against the wall with a bang.

"It ain't a penthouse suite or nothin', but—what?"

Amanda bit her lower lip and studied him.

"Aw, shit. That's my bad, kid." He grimaced and gestured toward the room. "All I meant is there's a bed and a dresser and a closet. Y'all might hafta share."

"I don't mind." Amanda turned and jumped onto the bed. The mattress bounced violently and squeaked beneath her. "It's cozy."

"Yeah." Johnny scratched the back of his head and scowled at the bedframe. "Cozy."

"I'll stay for one night." Lisa raised her index finger and nodded. "Then I have to get to the office to clean up my mess."

"Sure thing." He rubbed his hands together and turned toward the bed. "Are you good here if we—"

A loud, contented snore rose from Amanda's open mouth, her arms spread beside her and her legs dangling over the edge of the bed.

"Cozy. Okay."

Lisa stepped into the room with a knowing smile. "I'll get her settled—"

"Nah. You go on and take a load off." A small, pained smile flickered at the corners of Johnny's mouth when he looked at her without a hint of sarcasm. "This ain't my first rodeo."

"Right." Nodding slowly, she turned away from the room and pointed down the hall. "I'll be…"

She left without finishing the sentence, mostly because she didn't want him to hear the lump in her throat. *What are the odds? He lost his twelve-year-old daughter and now, there's a girl the same age lying in that... Was that his daughter's room?*

Johnny glanced at everything around the bedroom except the snoring Amanda and walked slowly toward the dresser. He slid the bottom drawer open and pulled out a thick weighted blanket in a purple-toned camo pattern. *I knew there was a reason I kept this.*

Walking slowly toward the bed, he frowned at the idea of dragging Amanda toward the head of the bed. He grasped her legs instead and turned her sideways until her small frame stretched across the mattress horizontally. She didn't stir once, even when he settled Dawn's favorite blanket on the strong-willed girl who'd fallen asleep in this bed like she'd already been doing it for years.

Once he'd tucked the blanket under her chin and made sure it covered her outstretched arms, he stared at her. "Right at home here, ain'tcha? Shit."

The dwarf rubbed his head and moved silently out into the hall. He left the bedroom door cracked slightly and wandered into the living room.

Lisa sat on the black leather couch opposite the empty fireplace, her arms folded and one leg crossed over the other. "That's a hell of a trophy."

He turned to look at the boar's head mounted above the mantel and his antique rifle collection. "Yeah. I aim to switch that one out with a new boar's head soon enough."

"You'll find him, Johnny."

"I already found him." The dwarf swallowed thickly and glared at the game trophy he'd brought home from one of the hounds' first real hunting trips. "I coulda slit his throat too if I didn't have someone a hell of a lot more important to pay attention to."

"What do you mean?"

"Nothin'. Come on. We're goin' for a drive." He headed toward the front door again and she frowned at the boar's head before she followed him.

"We probably shouldn't leave her here on her own."

"A kid who passes out that fast? She ain't slept in a hot minute. We'll be back before she's up, I guarantee."

"But on the off-chance that we're not..." Lisa paused at the door and peered inside. "If I'd been through what she's been through, I wouldn't wanna wake up in an empty house."

"The boys will take care of her, darlin'. Trust me. They're better company for her right now than either of us."

When Johnny stepped out onto the front porch and caught the screen door before it could slam shut, she pushed the bedroom door open enough to peek inside at the sleeping girl. The sight of the purple blanket over Amanda's body made her chest tighten. *I can't imagine what she's been through. Or him.*

The sound of a diesel engine roaring to life outside ripped her from the moment, and she closed the door most of the way again before she hurried out to join the dwarf.

She smiled, feeling lighter out in the warm spring air a little less muggy than it would be in two months from now, even in the Everglades. She stretched a hand to the passenger door of Johnny's red Jeep, but it popped open before she could touch it.

"Get on up, darlin'." Johnny pulled his sunglasses out of his jacket pocket and donned them quickly.

"We could take the rental, you know."

"Are you kiddin'? When I pull up in Sheila, everyone knows who's about to step inside." He snorted and nodded behind her at the sky-blue Acura parked on the dirt drive. "I thought I was gonna have to change my name and move to Wisconsin or some shit if anyone saw me in that."

"But no one did."

"And a good thing, too. Come on."

Chuckling, Lisa hauled herself into the passenger seat, which bounced alarmingly beneath her when she sat. "So this is Sheila, huh?"

Johnny clicked his tongue. "Now why are you askin' questions you already know the answer to?"

"For fun, I guess." She buckled her seatbelt and smirked at him.

"You're lookin' for fun, huh? Just you wait, darlin'. You ain't seen nothin' yet." He shoved the gear shift into reverse, accelerated across the drive in a spray of dirt and fine dust, and spun the wheel until they faced the dirt road leading away from the house.

She caught her breath. "Maybe don't—"

The gear shift was pushed into drive, Johnny stepped on the gas, and Sheila rumbled away from the cabin. She pressed herself back against the seat and shut up.

CHAPTER TWENTY-SIX

"What'd I tell you, huh?" Johnny scrambled out of the Jeep and swung the door shut, grinning as he whipped his keyring around his finger.

Lisa stumbled out and steadied herself with a hand against the Jeep. "You told me that would be fun."

He stopped when he stepped around the hood and saw her standing there as if collecting herself. "You'll get your land legs back in a shake. Speakin' of which, I should take you out on the airboat—"

"Why don't we...stick to roads and tires for now, huh?" Running a hand through her hair, she straightened and gave him a warning look.

Johnny's eye twitched and he burst out laughing, doubling over to smack his knee. She couldn't help but chuckle with him. "Tell me you know how to swim, darlin'."

"I know how to swim, Johnny."

He wiped a tear from the corner of his eye and smirked a little as he studied her curiously. "So what is it? Are you afraid of boats or somethin'?"

"Only if you're driving it." They both laughed and he jerked his head toward the unmarked trailer on stilts on the opposite side of the gravel lot. "Come on. This is how we have fun in the Everglades."

"A trailer."

"Looks can be deceivin' down here, darlin'. I thought you already realized that." After another brief chuckle, he sniffed and thumbed his belt loops as he trudged across the gravel. "We'll start small and then I'll get you on that airboat. Just you wait."

"Uh-huh." Lisa turned to search the mostly empty lot—two other trucks not nearly as big as the one parked in front of Johnny's house, another Jeep, and a station wagon with a small fishing boat on a trailer hitched to the back. She squinted and took a few steps back before she turned to follow the dwarf. *What's he up to now?*

"Are you gonna tell me what we're doing here, Johnny?"

"Why?" He stopped at the bottom of the stairs leading to the trailer and nodded at the door. "I'm about to show you."

"Of course." Lisa rolled her eyes. "I don't know what I was thinking. Johnny Walker doesn't do surprises. He's as straight-laced as they come. I have nothin' to worry about."

"Well, I'll say you got one outta three there." Still smirking, he trudged up the stairs, which shivered under his boots as he climbed. "Roll with it, darlin'. You ain't gonna find this on any tourist map, that's for damn sure."

He waited for her to reach the top landing attached to the side of the trailer and wiggled his eyebrows at her as he took hold of the door handle.

"I'm not sure I like that look."

"And I'm not sure I need you to." He opened the door and stepped into the dimly lit trailer.

Lisa looked over the side of the railing and scanned the empty lot in the middle of Nowhere, Everglades. She took a deep breath and followed him inside.

The door creaked when it shut behind her, and she frowned

at the inside of an actual diner that stretched the length of the trailer in front of her. The full-sized bar in the back was long enough for eight bar stools, three four-top tables filled the main space, and a two-top stood on the far end of the trailer beneath the only window that wasn't covered with black-out curtains. "Wow."

"You know it."

"This is where you take someone for a date?"

He looked sharply at her and frowned. "This is a date?"

"Well, no. But if it were..." Lisa gestured toward the diner-trailer. "Seriously, come on."

"Huh." He shrugged casually, gave her a half-smile, made his way slowly across the Formica floor until he reached the end of the bar. "Heya, Darlene."

"Johnny." The round, red-faced woman behind the bar raised an eyebrow at him as she wiped a freshly washed rocks glass dry with a bar rag. "Who's your friend?"

"Darlene, Lisa. Lisa, Darlene. This woman makes the best damn fried catfish in...psh. What d'ya think? Two hundred square miles?"

Darlene pursed her lips and her head wiggled on her squat neck as she twisted the glass repeatedly. "Did I do somethin' to offend your sensibilities, Johnny? Or you puttin' on a show?"

"The best in the whole damn state," another patron offered.

The bartender glanced at the man with the white handlebar mustache and dark denim overalls seated at a four-top by himself. "Thank you, Arthur."

He raised his beer toward her in appreciation.

"Hell, the best damn place in the South!" The man at the far end of the bar lowered his head and raised a sloshing glass of clear liquid as he swayed somewhat on the bar stool. "Ain't no one can fry up any damn thing like you, Darlene. Not those fancy chefs, not my mama—"

"You hush your mouth, Fred." Darlene smacked her rag on the

bar and Fred jerked his swaying head up to look at her. "Anyone who comes in here bad-mouthin' their mama can keep on walkin'."

"Yes, ma'am." The man lowered his head again and scowled at his glass.

Johnny chuckled and climbed onto the second barstool over, leaving the first open for the agent. "I've been tellin' her about that catfish, Darlene."

"Mm-hmm." The woman glanced at Lisa and nodded. "Have you ever had catfish before?"

"In Illinois once, I think."

"Ha!" The proprietor set the clean glass on the bar and tossed the rag over her shoulder. "Girl, that ain't catfish. You watch. I'll go fry you up somethin' that'll make you never wanna leave. What are you drinkin'?"

Even as she asked, the woman had already pulled a bottle of Johnny Walker Black out and poured four fingers into the rocks glass before she slid it toward the dwarf. She didn't look at him once.

"Oh." Lisa tried to peer over the edge of the bar and only saw a fridge filled with glass Coke bottles, Cheerwine, and Sprite. "What kinda beer do you have?"

"No beer." Darlene pointed at the trailer roof and the small overhanging runner across the ceiling. "Don't have a license for any booze."

Lisa looked at the printed non-certificate in fading, hand-written ink that announced the lack of a license to sell alcohol. She turned on the barstool to look at Arthur as he guzzled the rest of his beer from the bottle. "I... Did I miss something?"

"Get her an Everglades Iced Tea, Darlene." Johnny nodded at the bartender, who responded with a coy smile as she reached beneath the bar.

"Now that we do have." The crack and hiss of a bottle opening filled the trailer, followed by the clink of a metal cap bouncing across the floor. Darlene set a frosty beer bottle in front of the agent and winked. "Catfish for two, Johnny?"

"I wouldn't have it any other way." He raised his rocks glass at the woman, who patted the bun of brown hair streaked with gray at the back of her head as she turned and stepped through the door behind the bar. The dwarf chuckled as he raised his glass to his lips.

"So this is where Johnny Walker spends all his time when he's not hunting in the swamp with his coonhounds, huh?"

"You forgot to mention the workshop, darlin'."

"Oh, that's right. Someone's gotta put in all that time to make all kinds of high-tech bombs that look like portable speakers for a voice assistant. I almost expected to hear Alexa telling you to repeat the song request as you crushed monsters' heads."

Johnny lowered his glass slowly and leaned forward over the bar before he turned his head toward her. "A portable what?"

She fixed him with a disbelieving look. "Seriously?"

"And who the hell's Alexa?"

With a chuckle, she raised the beer to her lips and muttered, "Forget it."

He shook his head and stared at the bar with a small smile. "I don't spend all my time here, anyway. That's Fred's job."

The man jerked his head up and blinked blearily at the back of the bar with a grunt. "Pay's shit but the coffee's good at least." He swung his rocks glass of whatever clear liquid he was drinking toward the two of them before his eyes fluttered closed again and his head dropped to his chest.

"Huh." She shook her head. "I guess every bar has one."

"This ain't a bar, honey." Arthur slid out of his chair, dropped a wad of bills onto the table, and wiped the beer foam off his mustache. "Darlene has a heart a' gold openin' her house and home up to any bastard lucky enough to find the place."

He winked at Lisa and hiked the pant legs of his overalls up before heading toward the front door. "Be good, Johnny."

"Johnny, be good!" Fred shouted and waggled a finger in the air.

Everyone ignored the man.

The dwarf smirked at the wall behind the bar. "Any time you want me to take a look at that rifle, Arthur…"

"Man, if it ain't broke, I ain't tryin' to fix it. And I don't want you tinkerin' with my stuff anyhow." Chuckling, Arthur opened the trailer's single front door. The hinges squealed and he let it clap shut behind him.

Lisa could feel the vibration of the man's footsteps down the exterior staircase through her barstool.

The trailer fell silent enough that the clink of a metal spatula and the hiss of food on the grill and in the fryer rose behind the back door.

She sipped her beer. "So now what?"

"We wait for the catfish. Then we eat it. Then we leave."

She turned toward him with an exasperated smile. "I meant with Amanda."

"Yeah, I know."

"Do you have any plans?"

Johnny snorted. "I'd have thought after forty-eight hours on a job with me, you would have realized the answer's no across the board."

"She's not a job, Johnny."

"Don't I know it." He took another sip. "I guess I'm lettin' the kid stay with me for as long as she wants to, at least."

"What are you gonna do with a kid?" Lisa regretted the question as soon as it left her mouth. *She's not the first kid he's taken care of but you'd never know simply by looking at him.*

"Well." He scowled and his mustache bristled above his upper lip. "I reckon I'll raise her the way *I* was raised. In the Everglades."

"That's a start. I guess."

He responded with a sharp laugh and shook his head. "Did

anyone ever tell you that gettin' smart with a dwarf isn't the way to get him on your side?"

The door from the kitchen opened and Darlene stepped out with a paper-lined basket of red plastic in each hand.

Lisa grinned at him and raised her beer. "I don't know. Is it working?"

Johnny glanced at her, then clicked his tongue and knocked his rocks glass gently against her bottle. "It might be."

CHAPTER TWENTY-SEVEN

When Rex and Luther saw Sheila barreling up the dirt road onto Johnny's property, they both uttered long, baying howls and darted around the side of the house.

"Come on, pup!"

"Yeah, keep up if you don't wanna miss all the fun!"

Amanda hurried after them, her bare feet flying across the low crabgrass and small stones that studded what served as a yard beside the cabin.

"You can move faster than that!"

"Not on two legs," she shouted in response. *And I don't even know what the rules are around here about running on four. This'll be weird.*

Sheila slid to a halt at the end of the dirt drive and the driver's door opened a second after the diesel engine sputtered to a halt.

"Johnny! Hey, Johnny! She's up."

"We heard her snoring even from out back." Rex sat and his tail swung across the dirt to flurry sprays of red-brown dust. "And now she's up."

"And now you're here."

"And now we get to do something fun, right?"

"Right, Johnny?"

As he shut the Jeep door, Johnny ignored his hounds' rapid-fire questions and looked at the girl, who slowed to a jog past the front of the cabin. Out of all the things he could have said to her in that moment, his mouth decided on, "What happened to your shoes?"

She glanced at her bare feet and shrugged. "They made too much noise. And this feels better."

"Huh." He scratched the back of his head and glanced at the hounds. "Did you take her out in the swamp, boys?"

"No way."

"Not without you, Johnny."

Rex's tongue lolled out of his mouth. "Anyway, she just woke up so it's not like we had time to—"

"Hey, you're not supposed to tell him that."

"Why not?"

"Great. I have my hounds playin' me."

"What's that?" Lisa slid out of the passenger door and closed it behind her with a sigh.

"Nothin'."

"You bring us anything, Johnny?"

Luther raised his head toward the dwarf and his nose wiggled frantically as he sniffed all over. "I smell catfish."

"Aw, come on. I bet it's in his pocket."

"Yeah. Yeah, good thinkin'."

He snapped his fingers. "Y'all don't need anythin' else until suppertime. Go on."

The hounds trotted away from their master, their tails wagging as they sniffed the dirt. "He's got something in his pockets."

"It's catfish."

"Maybe fries."

"Maybe steak."

"We should go through his clothes. That's a lotta pocket steak pilin' up."

Luther's head whipped toward the house and he froze. "Yeah, yeah. Let's go."

Clouds of dirt kicked up as the hounds raced past Amanda and down the side of the cabin to reach the dog door in the back.

The girl gave Johnny a mocking grimace that turned into a quick smile. "They're crazy."

"Not crazy if it's your instincts." He gestured toward the door and turned to look at Lisa. "Let's have us a—what?"

The agent grinned at him and gestured vaguely. "Only...the stuff that comes out of your mouth sometimes."

"Instincts are funny?"

"Never mind."

Johnny shook his confusion off and nodded at the front porch. "Come on, kid. I think it's time for a little sit-down. We have a few things to go over with you."

As he opened the screen door, Amanda looked at Lisa with wide eyes. "What happened?"

"Nothing."

"So why did he say we need to talk? That always means something happened. Usually not good."

The agent put a gentle hand on the girl's shoulder and guided her toward the porch. "Everything's fine. I promise. And I don't think you'll be disappointed."

"Also something that means the complete opposite." The girl gritted her teeth and stepped through the open screen door and the front door Johnny hadn't bothered to shut behind him. "Does he have a rule about bare feet or something? 'Cause I can put the shoes on again."

"Give him a chance, okay?" Lisa nodded down the hall toward the living room. "Go on."

"You're coming too, right?"

She nodded. "Sure."

The dwarf was already slumped on the leather couch and his

boots rested on the coffee table with one ankle crossed over the other. He stared at the boar's head mounted over the fireplace as the two women entered the room and he slapped a hand onto his belly. "Boy. That catfish sure sticks around, huh? Go ahead and take a load off."

"Okay…" Amanda glanced nervously at Lisa, who gave her an encouraging nod. The girl crossed the living room slowly to take the high wing-backed armchair beside the fireplace. Her shoulders slumped as she waited for him to say something. "You're telling me I have to leave, aren't you?"

"What?" He jerked his boots off the table and leaned forward. "What made you say that?"

"Well…we're having a talk." She shrugged. "And you haven't had a kid around here in a long time. Most people don't want to start all over again after that. Especially not halfway through."

"Halfway." He snorted in amusement and an attempt to cover up his embarrassment. *If she can see through my bullshit and solid walls, I'll eat my foot.* "Look, kid. I don't know what you've heard about me—"

"Enough." Amanda frowned and sighed heavily. "How old is she?"

"Who?"

"The girl with you in the picture. It's the only one you have. That's your daughter, right? She looks like your daughter."

Johnny wheezed out a slow breath and pointed at her. "You went in my room."

"You left me alone in your house." She leaned back in the chair. "If you didn't want me to go into your room, maybe you should have left a note."

The dwarf glanced at Lisa, who stood with her eyebrows raised at the growing tension in the living room. *There's an I-told-you-so waitin' for me after this.*

"All right. Let's start over." He kicked against the floor to scoot farther back on the couch and folded his arms. "First of all, no. I ain't sayin' you have to leave."

"You're not?"

"Not yet. But we gotta lay down ground rules, and that comes after we—"

"Yeah, yeah. Whatever you want. I'll do it."

He gritted his teeth. "Can I finish?"

"Uh-huh." Amanda pulled both bare feet up onto the cushions of the armchair and wrapped her arms around her bent knees. Her hazel eyes glistened in the low light as she stared intently at him.

"Man." He ran a hand through his hair, stroked his beard, and opted for folding his arms again. "Before anything else, kid, I gotta ask. Do you have any extended family somewhere?"

The girl shook her head slowly.

"Right. So at least I won't have any—"

"Do you?"

"Huh?"

"Have family around?" Amanda tilted her head. "You know. Extended."

"Er…" Johnny grimaced and his tongue moved around his mouth like he tried to get rid of the bad taste in there. *Even the taste of this chat isn't goin' anywhere near the way I wanted it to.* "No, kid. It's only me."

"And your daughter. Obviously." The girl gave him a completely innocent smile and shrugged. "So where is she?"

He swallowed.

Lisa cleared her throat and pulled her phone from her jacket pocket to wave it at them. "I'm gonna…check some emails. Outside. Better reception."

She turned away without waiting for a reply and he didn't move until after the front door shut behind her.

"Listen, kid—"

"Do you even have reception out here?" Amanda frowned and

looked around the room. "I heard people all the way out in the boonies don't have anything. Even magicals."

"The boonies." Johnny shook his head. "We have much to go over."

"I don't see a TV, either. Is that like a personal choice or 'cause you can't get cable?"

"Amanda."

She jerked her head toward him and widened her eyes. "Yeah."

"Can we stick to one question at a time?"

"Sure. Let's start with the first one, then."

Johnny rubbed his mouth and muttered, "You mean the one about cell reception?"

"No. I asked where your daughter is."

"Yeah, I didn't think so." He took a deep breath to reply but she beat him to it.

"It's kinda weird to think about you having a daughter but kinda cool too. Like, does she hunt? I bet she's good with guns too, huh? That could be a genetic thing. Like how Claire and I—" She froze and the daydreamy smile filtered away from her face as she scanned the floor and realized what she'd almost said. "Well. I only wanna know everything about your kid."

The dwarf stared at the coffee table, breathing heavily through his nose as he stroked his beard in a tense but absent gesture.

"Why aren't you saying anything?"

"I will. Gimme a minute."

Amanda pressed her lips together and stared at him so intently, his forehead started to itch.

"I don't talk about this much, kid. I got a little rusty because of it, understand?"

"Not really, but okay."

He responded with a wry laugh. "If we're gonna do this— whatever we're tryin' to do— I need you to sit tight, open your ears, and keep your mouth shut until I'm done. You can do that, right?"

When he looked at her, Amanda raised her chin and mimed zipping her lips.

"Right." *Fuck, I'm not ready for this. I probably never will be.* He cleared his throat twice before he felt like he could start. "Her name was Dawn."

"Oh." The girl leaned toward her bent knees and rested her chin on them.

"I haven't said her name out loud in…a long time." His next sigh emerged as another wheeze. "And I wouldn't normally lay all this out for a kid, but after what you've been through and after seein' what you can do… Hell, it might be good for both of us."

She stared at him and studied him from head to toe without moving a muscle.

"I lost her when she was your age," he muttered, his gaze fixed on the coffee table. "I did everythin' I could to bring her up right and I'd like to think I did. She was…huh. She was somethin' else, that girl. Much like you in some ways. Minus the wolf part."

They both uttered nervous, semi-humorless chuckles.

"The one mistake I made was in not bein' there when she needed me most. Now, I ain't sayin' you wouldn't be fine without me or that you owe me a damn thing." Slowly, he raised his gaze to meet hers and nodded. "But I don't aim to make that mistake a second time."

"Okay." Amanda nodded. "So far so good."

Johnny snorted. "You got some way of lookin' at the world, kid. I tell you what."

"But I can stay with you, right?"

"Only if you want to."

"I do."

The dwarf narrowed his eyes and nibbled on the inside of his bottom lip. "You do?"

"Yeah. You can teach me stuff, right? I don't know about guns or anything but, like…how to fight. You know, as a girl and not a wolf."

"Huh. If the truth be told, I don't know much about fightin' girls."

She snorted a laugh and rolled her eyes. "Whatever."

"Have you ever been on a boat?"

"Well, my dad has a yacht. Had a yacht—"

"Naw, that ain't the same. What about fishin'?"

The girl wrinkled her nose and shook her head. "I've never done it but I could learn. And hunting, too. I like that part."

"Yeah, I bet you do." He leaned forward over his lap and wagged a finger at her. "I mentioned ground rules."

"Yeah. Sure."

"If you're gonna live here, you stay outta my room."

Amanda swiped both hands through the air. "Off-limits. Got it."

"And don't touch my guns."

"Yeah, I won't."

He turned slightly away from her and squinted again. "And if you go anywhere, you tell me about it first. I ain't buyin' a cell phone for a twelve-year-old, so I best be able to trust that I can find you if I have to 'cause you told me about it first."

"Seriously?" The girl's eyes widened. "Like I can leave the house? By myself?"

He chuckled. "The concrete jungle ain't nothin' like the Everglades, kid."

"Yeah, okay. Deal. That's…that's awesome."

"All right." Johnny slapped his thighs and pushed to his feet with a grunt. "Now go on and tell that half-Light Elf pretendin' to check her email on my front porch that we had our little chat and we're good to go."

"Okay." She bounded from the chair, darted toward the living room, then stopped and turned.

Johnny didn't know what hit him when she threw her arms around his neck and gave him a tight squeeze.

"Thanks, Johnny. For everything."

"Uh-huh." His hands moved like molasses toward her back to give her two awkward pats. "Kid, I ain't...uh, that much of a hugger."

"Right." She released him, searched his face, and punched him in the shoulder. "Me neither."

The girl's bare feet pounded across the floor toward the front door.

The dwarf's bushy eyebrows danced up and down as he watched her, unable to decide which fucking emotion he felt right now. "All the wrong damn ones."

He slapped his forehead, rubbed his eyebrows, and turned in a confused circle. The only option he had left was to sink onto the couch and stare blankly at the coffee table again.

The dog door clacked open and shut in the back and the hounds' nails clicked across the hardwood floors.

"Wow, Johnny. That was...intense." Luther stopped in front of his master and sat to look at the dwarf with glistening, puppy-dog eyes.

"You could've told us." Rex sat in front of Johnny's other leg and rested his chin on the dwarf's knee with a low whine. "We didn't know you had your own pup, Johnny."

"I sure did." Johnny's eye twitched as he stretched absently to pat his hounds on the head. "It looks like I got another one now."

Right on cue, laughter from both Amanda and Lisa filtered through the screen door, although Johnny couldn't make out any words. *They are probably laughin' at me but who the fuck cares?*

"She's a good one, Johnny." Luther thumped his forepaws onto the couch beside the dwarf's thigh and wagged his tail. "Good for you."

"Good for us."

"Just good."

"I know." With a sniff, he let his hands linger on his hounds' heads. "I'm only hopin' I can be the same for her."

"Come on, Johnny. You're good for us. And we're a lot more work."

"No opposable thumbs. I can't even put on my pants by myself."

Johnny looked at Rex and raised an eyebrow.

The hound's thin chuckle filled his head. "Kidding."

"Oh, I get it. Pants. 'Cause you don't—" Luther stopped and whipped his head toward the door before he uttered a sharp bark. "He's back."

"Johnny." Rex raised his head and spun hastily. "Johnny, it's him. The salty two-leg."

"Asshole alert!"

Both hounds raced across the living room at the same time and scrambled across the hardwood toward the front door.

"Great." With a scowl, Johnny stood again and headed toward the door. "If he ain't here to pat me on the back and hand me a drink, he can move right along."

CHAPTER TWENTY-EIGHT

"Johnny! Open the door!" Rex barked.

"We'll get rid of him for ya." Luther couldn't hold still and pranced enthusiastically in front of the screen door.

"What's going on?" Amanda appeared in the doorway and looked at him with wide eyes. "Who's here?"

"The Fed with a hole in his pants," Luther said.

Rex barked again. "Yeah. And his butt."

She gave them a confused smile. "Um…"

"You can let 'em out," Johnny called as he strode toward the front door. "They get too excited and forget about the damn dog door."

As soon as she opened the creaking screen door, the hounds rocketed out of the cabin like two bullets, baying loudly, and raced up the drive with a flurry of dust behind them.

Johnny stepped outside onto the porch and let the door close with a soft thud. He stopped beside Amanda and folded his arms. "This'll be a joke and a half."

Lisa frowned at him. "Johnny?"

He nodded at the end of the drive as the black SUV came into view, trailing a cloud of dust. The hounds circled the vehicle continuously as they barked, snapped their jaws, and bayed like they'd flushed a gray fox. "Nelson."

"Damn." Lisa wrinkled her nose. "I thought I had more time."

"Don't write your vacation off yet, darlin'. He ain't here for you."

"You don't know that."

"He's the only liaison with enough balls to step onto my property. If your bosses wanted you, they would have called."

"Hmm." She frowned as Agent Tommy Nelson's SUV rolled to a stop in front of the folding lawn chairs again.

Rex and Luther barked and snarled outside the driver's door, their heads low and hackles raised.

Tommy opened the door, jerked his ankle away from a pair of snapping jaws, and shut the door again.

"Johnny!" His voice was muffled from inside the car. "Johnny, call 'em off, huh?"

The dwarf cupped a hand around his ear and leaned forward. "I can't hear you, Nelson. Come on up."

"Come on, Johnny." Tommy lifted a briefcase from the passenger seat and grimaced at the hounds who bounded up to claw at the window. "Your dogs are gonna rip me apart."

"I already did, dummy," Rex shouted. "Remember? You taste like ass."

"Ha." Luther dropped to all fours and panted. "Funny. 'Cause that's where you bit him."

Johnny whistled and the hounds turned toward him. "Give the agent space, boys. Only for a minute."

"Yeah, yeah." Rex backed up across the dirt. "We'll watch him."

"He won't get past us, Johnny."

With a sigh, Tommy opened the door again slowly and set his shiny black shoe gingerly on the dirt. The hounds backed away but growled as the agent pulled the briefcase out carefully after him and shut the door. Rex barked and the man jumped. "Jesus. Do you bark at every loud noise?"

"Only when you're the one makin' it," Rex replied. He bared his teeth and continued to growl. "Better be careful."

"Look at him shaking, Rex." Luther's laughter flooded Johnny's mind over the admittedly terrifying growls and snarls. "Yeah, that's right. Keep walkin'."

"And don't make any loud noises." Rex sniggered. "Who knows? You might fart too loudly and set us off."

"Ha-ha. Good one."

The dwarf snorted and fought back a laugh. Beside him, Amanda tried to hide a smirk.

Lisa studied them both and shook her head. "I missed the joke."

"Come on, darlin'. Look at the guy."

Tommy stumbled across the dirt drive and almost fell when he ran into one of the lawn chairs. He righted himself and looked over his shoulder every two steps to keep an eye on the coonhounds.

"Ooh, you stink when you're scared," Luther taunted.

"They all do. Nothin' special about this one." Rex barked sharply and the agent almost tripped over his own feet again as he scrambled toward the front porch. "Look at him go, Johnny! Like a rabbit out of his hole."

"Rabbit tastes way better, though."

"For sure."

The man finally caught his balance again on the porch and spun, clutching the briefcase in both hands and breathing heavily. "What did you do to your dogs, Johnny?"

He shook his head. "Nothin'. They merely don't like you."

"Why? I didn't do anything."

Amanda shrugged. "Maybe you smell funny."

Tommy whipped his head toward her and scrutinized her for a long moment. "Huh. It looks like you're fittin' right in."

"Like a glove, Nelson." Johnny inclined his head and fixed him with a stern look. "Do you need somethin'?"

"Yeah." The agent jerked his tie from side to side to loosen it and glanced at the hounds who continued to growl at him from the bottom of the stairs. "A quick debriefing. And a few other things."

He gestured toward Amanda. "I'm debriefed if you ask me."

"Come on, Johnny. Let's cut the shit. Oh. Sorry about the language, kid."

The girl shook her head. "Like I give a fuck."

All three adults stared at her.

"What? Not okay?"

"You're fine."

Tommy scoffed. "Johnny…"

"Nah, she earned that one, Nelson. Trust me. But hang onto the next one for the right moment, huh, kid? It's all about timing."

She nodded. "Got it."

The dwarf snapped his fingers. "That's enough, boys. Our stiff friend in the monkey suit got the point. Didn't you?"

The man tugged the rumples from his standard Fed suit jacket. "Yeah. Sure."

Johnny opened the screen door and stepped inside. "You have ten minutes, Nelson. I'm feelin' generous today."

With a long-suffering sigh, Tommy caught the screen door and hefted the briefcase inside after him. Lisa and Amanda followed, and the hounds didn't make it onto the porch in time. "Aw, come on. Johnny! Let us in!"

"Hey, Rex. Back door."

"Yeah, dog door."

"Hurry."

The visitor shook his head as he watched Amanda follow Johnny into the dwarf's workshop. Lisa caught up to him, and the man leaned toward her to mutter, "How much of a nightmare were the last forty-eight hours for you?"

She grinned at him and gave him a condescending pat on the back. "Not nearly as much as you hope, Tommy."

He paused in the doorway to the workshop and frowned as he wrinkled his nose. "Come on. It's not an image I needed."

"I don't know what you're talking about." She stopped beside Johnny on one side of the worktable and batted her eyelashes at her fellow agent.

The dwarf snorted. "Neither do I. 'Cause you ain't sayin' nothin'. Nine minutes, Nelson."

"Yeah, yeah. But…Christ."

Amanda leaned over the head of the worktable and lowered her elbows onto it to prop her chin in both hands. She watched Tommy with wide eyes as he took his place across the table from Johnny and Lisa.

He swung the briefcase onto the surface and looked at the young shifter. "This is probably not a conversation for a kid. You know."

She shook her head. "Not really."

"Johnny, a little help here?"

"She's earned a place here too, Nelson." He rapped his knuckles on the table. "You know."

"Whatever." With a heavy sigh, the agent flipped the locks on the briefcase up, spun it sideways, and opened it. "It's time for your next job, Johnny."

"Uh-uh." He shook his head. "This one was a one-time deal. I'm out."

Tommy ignored him and whipped the top sheet of paper out of the briefcase without trying to make him read it this time. "You'll like this one, Johnny. It's in your back yard."

"I don't think you heard me."

Another array of pictures thumped onto the table. Johnny didn't look at any of them.

"Some Oriceran monster's made a big fuss around many tourist areas. And by monster, I mean of the creature variety. You used to take these on by the truckload back in the day." He threw two more photographs down and stabbed his finger at each one in turn. "It struck a five-star resort in the Keys three weeks ago. We thought that one was a disgruntled employee playing with homemade bombs. Boy, was that poor bastard surprised."

"Nelson."

"Four days later, a gas station off one of the roads through the Everglades—don't ask me which one 'cause they all look the same to me—was demolished and burned to the ground after a gas leak. Shit happens sometimes, right? Except that we found the same purple goo at both the resort and the gas station. And at a waterfront bar and music venue five days ago. It was undoubtedly the same substance. I think maybe it's some kinda biological flammable. Or the monster likes to take a shit after it destroys its target. I'll leave that up to you to decide."

Amanda tilted her head and stared at the photos. "You want him to go after this and you don't even know where the gas station is?"

Tommy leaned away from her and scoffed. "It's all in the file. Johnny knows how to read." He turned toward the dwarf and nodded. "Plus, if you take this case, Agent Breyer gets a clean slate. Which is saying a hell of a lot after she broke rank like that and helped you smuggle Amanda Coulier out of Manhattan instead of doing her job."

"Are you for real?" The young shifter glared at the man.

"What?"

"They're not the ones who smuggled me anywhere. Do you even know what you're doing?"

"Oh." The agent glanced at her and shrugged. "Sorry. Slip of the tongue."

Johnny rubbed his mouth. "All right, asshole."

Tommy thumped a fist on the worktable and nodded. "All right. Should I take that as a yes?"

"Maybe."

"I knew the bug would hit you again sooner or later, Johnny." The man chuckled. "You were made for this work and we don't clear a whole lotta Level Sixes in the Department. You're damn valuable."

"No shit." The dwarf sniffed and scanned the photos again. "I'll take the job."

"Yes." Agent Nelson pumped a fist in front of him, caught Lisa's smirk, and lowered his hand quickly to his side again.

She shook her head slowly. "Unbelievable."

He ignored her. "Great. If you have any questions, give me a call, and we can—"

"On one condition," Johnny added.

All the energy seeped out of Tommy at once. "I should have expected that."

"And it happens by the end of the week."

"Well shit, Johnny." The man glanced at Lisa and laughed nervously. "You gotta tell me what it is first."

The dwarf folded his arms and glared at him. "I want all the files on my daughter's case."

"What? Johnny, you have all the files. Or the copies at the very least."

"No, I don't." He pressed his fingertips onto the tabletop and leaned forward. "I found him, Nelson. He calls himself the Red Boar."

"You...you what?"

Lisa stared at the dwarf with wide eyes. "Johnny?"

Tommy shook his head. "I never heard of him."

"'Cause he's been playin' house with Lemonhead. Look, I don't need to explain to you what I know or how I found it. But your people have been holdin' back for fifteen years, Nelson. I know there's more and I want those files in my hand by the end of the week. Then I'll go huntin' for your creature."

"It's not my creature, Johnny." The man glanced at all the photos on the worktable and nodded. "I swear I don't know anything about holding information back on her case either. But you have yourself a deal. I'll get you those files."

"By the end of the week."

The agent nodded and proffered his hand. "End of the week."

Johnny waved him off. "I'll shake your hand when you deliver."

"Huh. Yeah, okay."

"Do you think you'll need a partner for this one, Johnny?" Lisa asked with a small smile.

"It's too soon to tell." The dwarf shrugged. "But someone did offer help to track the one sonofabitch I couldn't find on my own. So if you wanna stick around…"

"Well, that's essentially a requirement if she wants to clear that shitstain on her record," Tommy said. When they all frowned at him, he shrugged. "You know. Figuratively."

"Uh-huh." Johnny gestured toward the front door. "Time's a-tickin', Nelson. You'd better get a move on."

"Yeah, I get it." The man paused to study Lisa briefly and gave her a stiff nod. "Good luck, I guess."

"You too, Tommy."

With a confused frown, the agent hurried toward the front door and poked his head out, looking for the hounds.

"Surprise!" Rex barked and darted after him.

Agent Nelson yelped, hurtled through the door, and skidded across the dirt as he looked back to make sure he wouldn't get a bite out of the other ass cheek this time.

Luther and Rex stopped at the screen door after it banged shut and bayed as the agent scurried into his car. "That's right. You better run!"

"Scatter, motherfucker!"

Amanda smirked and folded her arms. "He deserves that, right?"

Johnny grinned. "Probably."

"So you're taking another case," Lisa said. "Does this mean you're officially out of retirement?"

"It might." He gave her a crooked smile. "I reckon I have a taste for the work. The company ain't half bad, either."

"Oh, is that right?" She laughed and shook her head. "Well, I meant it when I said I'd help you, mark on my record or not. I have one question, though."

"Yeah."

"Who's gonna watch Amanda while we're out lookin' for a gooey Oriceran…whatever it is?"

"Ooh, ooh!" Luther spun away from the front door as a cloud of dust followed Agent Nelson's quickly retreating SUV. "We'll watch her, Johnny."

"Yeah." Rex joined his brother in trotting toward the workshop. "Keep her safe. Keep her warm. I mean, we can't feed her, but she can feed us in trade."

"Unless we take her out as a wolf." Luther sat and let his tongue flop out of his mouth. "Then no one has to feed anyone. I mean, except for ourselves."

"Great plan! Come on, Johnny. You can count on us."

The dwarf looked up and met Amanda's gaze. "You can take care of yourself, kid. Can't you?"

The girl's grin lit up her entire face. "Duh."

"Johnny, I don't think—"

"You heard her, darlin'. It's a duh deal." With a smirk, he stepped around the woman and headed toward the kitchen. "I gotta set up a few things for while we're gone, but that won't take long. The place will be tighter than—"

"Wait, wait. Shh." Amanda lurched forward, her hands outstretched as she stared at the wall and listened. "Do you hear that?"

The low howl of wolves was barely audible over the sound of the coonhounds panting in excitement.

Johnny peered around the corner of the kitchen to see a fiery excitement light up in the girl's eyes.

"Johnny, those are other shifters." She turned toward him and widened her eyes. "There are other shifters out here. In the middle of nowhere!"

Shifters in the swamps. The one thing I didn't consider.

He stepped out of the kitchen and nodded at his hounds. "That may be a problem, boys."

"We got it, Johnny."

"We're on it."

"We'll keep her away from those shifty shifters."

The dwarf snapped his fingers and pointed at them. Both hounds sat. "The only thing I want you to do is keep 'em off the property. That's it."

"Yeah, yeah."

"Keep 'em away."

The dwarf nodded at Amanda, whose mind was somewhere far away from the small, tidy cabin at the edge of the Everglades. *She'll find her way to them eventually but I ain't runnin' a damn motel.*

Lisa frowned at the dogs, then looked slowly at Johnny. "They don't understand what you're telling them, do they?"

He hurried to the kitchen counter again to retrieve his bottle of Johnny Walker Black. He lifted it to the light and shrugged. "I like to think we understand each other fine."

Johnny and the coonhound's story isn't over yet. Far from it. Continue the adventures in *Don't Give a Dwarf*.

Get sneak peeks, exclusive giveaways, behind the scenes content, and more. PLUS you'll be notified of special **one day only fan pricing** on new releases.

Sign up today to get free stories.

Visit: https://marthacarr.com/read-free-stories/

AUTHOR NOTES - MARTHA CARR

SEPTEMBER 29, 2020

This has been the year of staying connected from six feet away... or further and it's happening on a global scale. Is this year over yet? Nope? Okay, then how can I affect my small corner of the world?

That's what it's boiled down to for me. Go very, very local. For my birthday, the Offspring found out that right now it's less than you think to rent out an entire movie theater. A bunch of my neighbors came together, with Louie and Jackie, to help me celebrate and watch Tenet. It was weird to be back in an actual theater, and super weird that all the movie posters were from March.

But after the movie, we all stood outside wearing masks laughing together and pointing out that the women decided to wear eye makeup and dangly earrings to make it special. It was a lot of fun.

And I'm currently awaiting a shipment from Amazon of wax lips and teeth with fangs to go with the other things I've been collecting so I can Boo those same neighbors. I LOVE wax lips and wanted to share that with them. If you're not familiar with being Boo'ed – it's leaving a small bag of treats in a Boo bag at your neighbor's door. Of course, I'm including my five-year-old neighbor, Norah who is still amazed I live in this dream house by myself. She is full of questions that I adore, along with her and I picture her taking over some part of her world some day and killing it.

And I have a couple packs of uplifting postcards that I'm sending out to friends and the Offspring. It's small stuff that won't change someone's life in a big way, but plants seeds in a very real and nourishing way. I've learned that those small things actually add up over time in very powerful ways. Maybe even more than grand gestures or fabulous trips, it's the small things we can still do for each other that add up to a happy life.

I suppose that's what I've really learned this year after having my life stripped down to the studs. What really matters I can still do. I can show up for those people I care about and let them know – and I can include myself on that list.

It leaves me wondering what life will be like once we can all mingle again safely, and I am filled with optimism about all of it. More adventures to follow.

AUTHOR NOTES - MICHAEL
SEPTEMBER 30, 2020

First, thank you for not only reading through our story, but through to the author notes here in the back!

I now live in Henderson, Nevada. I'm close enough to the Las Vegas strip that I can leave my front door and be inside the Aria in 25 minutes.

Might as well say I'm in Las Vegas and save the explanation.

Either way, Henderson is a few hundred feet higher in elevation than the strip and it is noticeably a bit cooler where I live now, compared to my condo (Cave in the Sky™) where I baked in the sun all year long. Mainly because of the mirrored windows reflected all of that heat right into a bowl of heat retaining concrete.

Arguably one of the best heat absorption and retention devices outside of one of those mirror power-generation plants on the border of California and Nevada.

But, I digress.

The 'Covid' (those of us in-the-know just drop the '19', as if any of the previous 18 Covids compare anymore) pushed me in strange directions.

Although 'out of my freaking mind' was certainly one of them.

As Martha mentioned, coming to grips with what I could do was a stressful situation for me. After I got past the feeling I needed to save the world (*You can't Michael, and why would you even think it would be on your shoulders?*) I realized the best I could do was make sure the company was as strong as possible and help locally.

Even helping locally was challenging when the restaurant we supported by purchasing a ton of gift cards to hand out to those on the streets closed. We were stuck with a lot of unusable gift cards.

Lesson learned.

The notes I read on the reviews where the stories help get the reviewer past hard times are especially kind.

I love knowing I provided, in my own little way, a few hours of enjoyment. When I am part of something that accomplishes carrying a person through a difficult time it is special and then a bit more.

I always wondered if, at the end of my life, I would look back and think to myself 'good job, Anderle. You helped a few people out. You can rest knowing you helped others in good ways.'

For those who let us authors know we touched you in reviews, telling us on social media or whatever my sincere appreciation.

Your comments will stay with us until the end of our lives and then, it will bring smiles to our faces as we head into the next story ourselves.

Ad Aeternitatem,

Michael Anderle

Solve a murder, save her mother, and stop the apocalypse?

What would you do when elves ask you to investigate a prince's murder and you didn't even know elves, or magic, was real?

Meet Leira Berens, Austin homicide detective who's good at what she does – track down the bad guys and lock them away.

Which is why the elves want her to solve this murder – fast. It's not just about tracking down the killer and bringing them to justice. It's about saving the world!

If you're looking for a heroine who prefers fighting to flirting, check out The Leira Chronicles today!

<u>AVAILABLE ON AMAZON AND IN KINDLE UNLIMITED!</u>

THE MAGIC COMPASS

If smart phones and GPS rule the world - why am I hunting a magic compass to save the planet?

Austin Detective Maggie Parker has seen some weird things in her day, but finding a surly gnome rooting through her garage beats all.

Her world is about to be turned upside down in a frantic search for 4 Elementals.

Each one has an artifact that can keep the Earth humming along, but they need her to unite them first.

Unless the forces against her get there first.

<u>AVAILABLE ON AMAZON AND IN KINDLE UNLIMITED!</u>

CONNECT WITH THE AUTHORS

Martha Carr Social
Website:
http://www.marthacarr.com
Facebook:
https://www.facebook.com/groups/MarthaCarrFans/

Michael Anderle Social
Website:
http://www.lmbpn.com
Email List:
http://lmbpn.com/email/
Facebook:
https://www.facebook.com/LMBPNPublishing

ALSO BY MARTHA CARR

Other series in the Oriceran Universe:

THE LEIRA CHRONICLES

THE FAIRHAVEN CHRONICLES

MIDWEST MAGIC CHRONICLES

SOUL STONE MAGE

THE KACY CHRONICLES

THE DANIEL CODEX SERIES

I FEAR NO EVIL

SCHOOL OF NECESSARY MAGIC

THE UNBELIEVABLE MR. BROWNSTONE

SCHOOL OF NECESSARY MAGIC: RAINE CAMPBELL

ALISON BROWNSTONE

FEDERAL AGENTS OF MAGIC

SCIONS OF MAGIC

Series in The Terranavis Universe:

The Adventures of Maggie Parker Series

The Witches of Pressler Street

The Adventures of Finnegan Dragonbender

OTHER BOOKS BY JUDITH BERENS

OTHER BOOKS BY MARTHA CARR

JOIN MARTHA CARR'S FAN GROUP ON FACEBOOK!

Made in United States
Troutdale, OR
10/12/2023

13640656R00159